THE WAYWARD WIFE
AND OTHER STORIES

THE WAYWARD
WIFE

AND OTHER STORIES

by

ALBERTO MORAVIA

Pincherle

Selected and Translated by
ANGUS DAVIDSON

FARRAR, STRAUS and CUDAHY • New York

From "I Racconti" copyright 1952 by Valentino Bompiani & Co.

English translation copyright © 1960 by
Martin Secker & Warburg Ltd.
Library of Congress catalog card number: 60-5140

First printing, 1960

Manufactured in the United States of America

CONTENTS

CRIME AT THE TENNIS CLUB

ABOUT the middle of the winter the Committee of one of the best-known tennis clubs in our town decided to give a grand Gala Ball. The Committee, which consisted of Messrs. Lucini, Mastrogiovanni, Costa, Ripandelli and Micheli, set aside a certain sum of money for providing champagne and other drinks and refreshments, and for the hire of a good band, and then went on to draw up a list of those who should be invited. The members of the club belonged for the most part to the class which is commonly called the upper middle class; they were all of them the off-spring of rich and respected families and—since one has to have a job of some kind—they all carried on the appearance, anyhow, of some profession or other: and so it was not diffi-cult to assemble, from amongst relations, friends and acquain-tances, an adequate number of names, many of which were preceded by titles of nobility of secondary importance but none the less decorative that would later give an aristocratic lustre to the event in the society columns of the newspapers. At the last moment, however, when there was nothing left to be done but send out the invitations, there suddenly arose—as generally happens—an unforeseen difficulty.

"How about the 'Princess'—aren't we going to invite her?" asked Ripandelli, a young man of about thirty, handsome in a somewhat Southern style, with glossy black hair, black eyes, and a dark, oval face with perfect features; he was known for his resemblance to one of the most celebrated of American film stars and was quite aware of this and made use of it to make an impression upon women.

Mastrogiovanni, Lucini and Micheli approved the idea of inviting the "Princess"; she would provide an extra bit of fun, they said, possibly the only bit of fun; and with loud bursts of laughter and mutual back-slappings they reminded one another of what had happened last time: how the "Princess" had had so much champagne that she was quite drunk, and someone had hidden her shoes, and she had been forced to wait until the last guests had left so that she could walk out in her stockinged feet. . . .

It was only Costa—bird of ill omen, as they called him—the tall, ungainly Costa, with big tortoiseshell-rimmed spectacles on his long nose and his thin cheeks never properly shaved—it was only Costa who protested.

"No," he said; "let her stay at home this time, the Princess. . . . I had quite enough of her at the last dance. If you want some fun you can go and pay her a visit, but don't do it here. . . ."

His companions rebelled and told him exactly what they thought of him—that he was a spoil-sport and a fool and that, in any case, he didn't own the club.

They had been sitting for two hours in the little committee-room and the air was thick with cigarette-smoke; it was warm and damp in the room on account of the fresh plaster of the walls, and they were all wearing thick sweaters of various colours under their coats. But outside, projecting across the panes of the window, could be seen a single fir branch, so still, so melancholy against the grey background of the sky that there was no need to go over and look out in order to see whether it was raining. Costa rose to his feet.

"I know," he spoke emphatically, "I know your intention is to play some kind of dirty trick on that unfortunate woman. . . . Well, I tell you once and for all—you're mean cads and you ought to be ashamed of yourselves."

"Costa, I thought you were more intelligent," Ripandelli declared, without moving from his place.

8

"And I didn't think you were so evil-minded," replied Costa; he took down his overcoat from its hook and went out without saying good-bye. After five minutes' discussion, the Committee decided unanimously to invite the Princess to the ball.

. . . . .

The ball began a little after ten o'clock in the evening. It had been raining all day and it was a damp, misty night; down at the far end of the suburban avenue in which the club-house stood could be seen, in the dim distance between two dark rows of plane-trees, a glow and a confused movement of lights and vehicles as the guests arrived. In the vestibule a hired man-servant relieved them of their coats and wraps, and then the women in their light evening dresses, the men in tail coats, all moved on, talking and laughing, into the large, brilliantly-lit ballroom.

This room was of considerable size and reached up to the full height of the building: a gallery with a blue-painted wooden balustrade ran round it at first-floor level, and out of this gallery opened a few small rooms which were used as dressing-rooms and for the storage of games equipment. An enormous chandelier in the same style and of the same colour as the balustrade hung from the ceiling, and attached to it, for the occasion, were festoons of Venetian lanterns stretching away to the four corners of the room; the wainscot was also painted blue; and at the far end, fitted in underneath the corner of the little staircase leading to the floor above was the refreshment bar, with its bright-coloured rows of bottles and its shining coffee-machine.

The "Princess", who was not a princess at all but, so it was said, merely a countess (it was also rumoured that once upon a time she had moved in high society and had been banished from it because of some ugly story of adultery, elopement and financial ruin), arrived soon after eleven o'clock. Ripandelli,

9

who was sitting with a group of ladies opposite the wide-open door into the vestibule, saw the well-known figure—short, rather squat, with feet turned outwards like a web-footed bird—as, with her slightly bent back turned towards him, she handed her cloak to the manservant. "There we are", he thought, and, his heart filled with exultation, he went across through the dancing throng to meet her, reaching her just in time to stop her slapping the face of the manservant, with whom, for some futile reason of her own, she had picked a quarrel.

"Welcome, welcome!" he called to her from the doorway.

"Ah, Ripandelli, come and deliver me from this brute!" she said as she turned towards him. The Princess's face was not beautiful. From beneath a forest of curly hair, cut very short, her black eyes, round and beset with wrinkles, shone out livid and wild-looking; the nostrils of her long, sensual nose were full of hairs; her wide mouth, its lips painted and age-roughened, was unceasingly lavish of brilliant, fatuous, conventional smiles. The Princess dressed in a manner that was at the same time showy and shabby: over her out-of-date dress, with its long skirt and a bodice so tight that the two long, meagre swellings of her bosom caught the light, she had thrown a black shawl embroidered with birds, flowers and arabesques of every possible colour—in order, perhaps, to conceal an excessively low neckline; and across her forehead she had tied a band, from beneath which her rebellious hair escaped in all directions. Thus adorned, and laden with artificial jewels, she made her entrance into the ballroom, peering ahead through a silver-rimmed eyeglass.

Luckily, the turmoil of dancing couples prevented her being noticed. Ripandelli steered her into a corner. "Dear Princess," he said, at once assuming an impudent tone of voice, "whatever would have happened to us if you hadn't come?"

The deluded expression in her eyes showed clearly that she took quite seriously any stupid thing that was said to her; but out of coquettishness she replied: "You young men try to hook all the women you can . . . and the more you catch, the better for you. Isn't that so?"

"Shall we dance, Princess?" asked Ripandelli, rising. He led her on to the floor. "You dance like a feather," said the young man, as he felt the full weight of her body pressing heavily on his arm.

"Everyone tells me that," answered the shrill voice. Crushed against Ripandelli's starched shirt-front the Princess, palpitating, seemed in a ravishment of ecstasy. Ripandelli became bolder. "Well, Princess, when are you going to invite me to your house?"

"I have a very small circle of friends," replied the unfortunate woman, who, notoriously, lived in complete solitude; "only the other day I was saying the same thing to the Duke of L., who was asking the same favour of me . . . a very limited circle of carefully selected people. One can't be too careful nowadays, you know."

"Ugly old bitch," thought Ripandelli. "No, no," he went on, aloud, "I don't want to be invited with everybody else. You must let me come and see you in an intimate sort of way . . . in your own boudoir, for instance . . . or perhaps . . . or perhaps in your bedroom."

This was an audacity, but she accepted it without protest. "And if I invite you," she asked, in a voice that was tender and a little breathless owing to the emotion of the dance, "will you promise me to be good?"

"As good as gold."

"Then I'll allow you to take me home this evening. . . . You have a car, haven't you?"

The dance was finished now and, as the crowd passed slowly into the refreshment room, Ripandelli mentioned a little private room on the first floor, where a bottle of champagne awaited them. "This way," he said, indicating the staircase; "up here we shall be able to talk more intimately."

"Oh, you're a rascal, you are," she said, hurrying up the stairs and threatening him with her eyeglass; "you think of everything."

The little private room was a small place with rows of white lockers round the walls, in which racquets and tennis-balls were usually kept. In the middle, on a table, was a bottle of champagne in an ice-bucket. The young man closed the door, invited the Princess to sit down, and immediately poured her out a drink.

"To the health of the most beautiful of princesses"—he stood facing her as he gave the toast—"and the woman I think about night and day!"

"Here's to your health too!" she replied, bewildered and excited. She had dropped her shawl now, and her shoulders and bosom were displayed. The thin back might have been that of a woman still young, but in front, where the edge of her dress slipped downwards with every movement, first on one side and then on the other, the discoloration of the yellowing, wrinkled flesh revealed the ravages of advancing age. Ripandelli, his head resting on his hand, was now gazing at her with two falsely passionate eyes.

"Princess, do you love me?" he asked all of a sudden, in a voice full of emotion.

"What about you?" she replied, with remarkable assurance. Then, as if overcome by a temptation too strong to be resisted, she stretched out her arm and placed her hand on the back of the young man's neck. "What about you?" she repeated.

Ripandelli threw a glance at the closed door; they must have begun dancing again now, he could hear the rhythmic tumult down below.

"My dear," he answered slowly, "I long for you, it's driving me crazy, I'm incapable of thinking or speaking sensibly . . ." There was a knock at the door; and then the door opened and Lucini, Micheli, Mastrogiovanni and a fourth man of the name of Jancovich burst into the room. This unexpected fourth was the oldest member of the club, a man of about fifty and already going grey; in figure he was ungainly, with a long, lean, melancholy face, a thin nose, and two deep, ironical furrows running down his face from his eyes to his neck. An industrialist, he made a lot of money; he spent the greater part of the day at the tennis club, playing cards; and at the club even the younger men called him by his Christian name, Beniamino. Now, as soon as Jancovich saw Ripandelli and the Princess, he gave, as had been arranged beforehand, a cry of pain and raised his arms above his head.

"What? My son here? And with a woman? And, what's more, with the woman I love?"

Ripandelli turned towards the Princess. "Here's my father," he said; "we're lost!"

"Get out of here!" went on Jancovich in his colourless voice; "get out of here, you unnatural boy!"

"Father," answered Ripandelli haughtily, "there is only one voice I shall obey, the voice of passion."

"And you, my love," went on Jancovich, turning with a sad, dignified expression towards the Princess, "don't let yourself be taken in by this rogue of a son of mine; come to me instead, and lean that charming little head on the breast of your Beniamino, who has never ceased to love you."

Biting his lips hard to prevent himself from laughing, Ripandelli flung himself upon his so-called father, crying out: "You call me a rogue, do you?" There followed a fine scene of wrath and confusion. Jancovich on one side, Ripandelli on the other, held back with difficulty by their friends, pretended to make every possible effort to get at one another and come to blows; cries of "Hold them, hold them, or they'll kill each other" rose above the tumult, together with ill-suppressed bursts of laughter; while the Princess, terrified, cowered back into a corner, her hands clasped together. At last it became possible to calm the two raging antagonists.

"There's nothing to be done about it," said Lucini, stepping

13

forward. "Father and son in love with the same woman: the only thing is for the Princess to make her choice."

So the Princess was asked to give judgment. Undecided, flattered, worried, she came out of her corner with her usual swaying walk, one foot pointing this way, the other that. "I can't choose," she said finally, after a close examination of the two competitors, "because . . . because I like you both."

There was laughter and applause. "And me, Princess—do you like me?" asked Lucini suddenly, taking her round the waist. This was the signal for a kind of orgy: father and son were reconciled and embraced each other; the Princess was made to sit down in the middle of them and an abundance of drink was pressed upon her. In a few minutes she was quite tipsy: she was laughing and clapping her hands, and her hair, standing out round her face, made her head look enormous.

The men started asking her sly questions. "Somebody told me," said Micheli at a certain moment, "that you're not a princess, that you're really nothing at all, just the daughter of some little pork-butcher: is that true?"

She was indignant. "That was a slander, and no doubt whoever told you was the son of a pork-butcher himself. . . . I'd have you know that before the War there was actually a Prince of the blood who sent me a marvellous bunch of orchids, with a note; and the note said: 'To my dear little Adelina from her Gogò. . . .'"

These words were received with shouts of laughter. These five men—who allowed their mistresses, in private, to call them by such names as Niní and Lulú, my little cherub or my little piggy-wig—seemed to consider the nickname of Gogò, the pet name of Adelina, as being the height of absurdity and stupidity; they held their sides, they ached with laughing. "Ah Gogò, naughty Gogò," they kept on saying. The Princess, intoxicated and highly flattered, distributed smiles and glances and taps with her eyeglass in every direction. "Oh Princess, how funny you are!" shouted Lucini right in her face, and she

—just as though he had paid her a compliment—laughed. "Oh Princess, my Princess," sang Ripandelli sentimentally; but all of a sudden his face hardened: he put out his hand and mercilessly grasped her breast. Red in the face, she struggled to free herself, but next moment suddenly laughed again and cast such a glance at the young man that he at once released his hold. "Ugh, what a flabby breast," he cried to the others, "it's just like squeezing a rag. . . . What about undressing her?" Now that the programme of jokes was more or less at an end, this proposal met with great success. "Princess," said Lucini, "we've been told that you have an extremely beautiful figure. . . . Well now, be generous and let us see it. Then we'll die content."

"Come on, Princess," said Jancovich, in his serious, bleating voice; and without more ado he put his hands on her and started trying to pull the shoulder-straps of her dress down over her arms. "We can't allow you to keep your lovely body hidden any longer . . . that lovely little pink and white body, all full of dimples like the body of a little girl of six. . . ."

"Oh, you shameless creatures!" said the Princess, laughing. But, after a great deal of insistence, she consented to lower her dress half-way down her bosom: her eyes were shining, and the corners of her mouth were trembling with pleasure.

"It's true I have a nice figure, isn't it?" she said to Ripandelli. But the young man made a grimace, and the others exclaimed that it was not enough, they wanted to see more; and Lucini gave a tug at the top of her dress. Then—whether it was that she became ashamed of displaying her already middle-aged body, or that a flash of consciousness, penetrating the fumes of wine, showed her to herself as she actually was, flushed and dishevelled, her breast half bared, surrounded by brutalized men in that little white room—all of a sudden she began to resist and to struggle: "Leave me alone, I tell you, leave me alone," she commanded, trying to release herself. But the sport had excited the five men. Two held her by the arms, while the

15

other three pulled her dress right down to her waist, exposing a torso yellowish and puckered, with flabby, sallow breasts.

"God, how ugly she is!" exclaimed Micheli; "and what a lot of clothes she's got on! She's all bundled up with clothes. . . . She must have at least four pairs of drawers on. . . ." The others were laughing, exhilarated by the spectacle of this unattractive, angry nakedness, and were trying to free her hips of their encumbering mass of clothes. This was not easy, for the Princess was struggling violently; the crimson face beneath the fleece of hair was pitiable, so clearly did it express terror, desperation and shame. But this resistance on her part, instead of moving Ripandelli to pity, irritated him like the spasms of a wounded beast that refuses to die. "You ugly bitch, are you going to stay still or not?" he shouted at her suddenly, and, to give force to his words, he took a champagne-glass from the table and dashed the iced wine over the unfortunate woman's face and chest. The abrupt aspersion gave rise to a plaintive, bitter cry and a frenzied burst of resistance. Somehow or other she managed to free herself from the hands of her tormentors and, naked to the waist, waving her arms above her head, her hair darting out like flames, a disordered mass of clothes trailing downwards from her hips, she hurled herself towards the door.

Astonishment, for one moment, prevented the five men from acting. But Ripandelli shouted: "Catch her or she'll be out in the gallery!"; and they threw themselves, all five of them, upon the woman, whose escape had been barred by a precautionary locking of the door. Micheli seized her by one arm, Mastrogiovanni round the waist, Ripandelli actually by the hair. They dragged her back again to the table. Her resistance had infuriated them, and they felt a cruel desire to beat her, to stick pins into her, to torment her. "Now we want you naked," shouted Ripandelli into her face; "naked—that's how we want you." She stared at him with terrified eyes, still struggling; then, all at once, she began to scream.

16

First she uttered a hoarse cry, then another like a sob, and finally, unexpectedly, a third of extreme shrillness, a piercing "Ay-eee!" Micheli and Mastrogiovanni, frightened, let go of her. As for Ripandelli, possibly it was only at that moment that he became conscious, for the first time, of the seriousness of the situation in which, with his companions, he had become involved. It was as though an enormous hand had squeezed his heart—with all five fingers, as one squeezes a sponge. A terrible rage came over him, a bloody hatred for this woman who had now flung herself against the door again; shouting, he showered blows upon her with his fists, and he himself, at the same time, was smitten with a black sense of hopelessness, with the kind of anguish that says, "There's nothing to be done, the worst has happened, better accept the inevitable...." He had a moment's hesitation; then, with a hand that did not seem to belong to him, so independent of his will-power did it appear, he seized the empty bottle from the table and brought it down with his full strength, just once, on the nape of her neck.

She sank to the floor across the doorway, in a manner that left no doubt as to the efficacy of the blow, and lay on her right side, her forehead against the closed door, her clothes spread round her like a heap of rags. Standing near her, the bottle still in his hand, Ripandelli concentrated the whole of his attention upon her back. At the level of her armpit there was a mole the size of a lentil; this detail, and perhaps also the fact that her thick mass of hair rendered her face invisible, made him imagine, for a second, that he had struck someone quite different and for a quite different reason—for instance some splendid-looking girl with a perfect figure whom he had loved too dearly and in vain and upon whose inanimate limbs he would throw himself weeping and remorseful, bitterly remorseful, and whom it might perhaps be possible to bring back to life. But then the torso gave a strange jerk and abruptly turned over on its back, showing the woman's bosom with

17

one breast falling in each direction and—horrible sight—her face. Her hair concealed her eyes ("luckily", he thought), but her mouth, half-open in a curiously expressionless way, reminded him all too vividly of certain slaughtered animals that he had seen as a child. "She's dead," he thought calmly, at the same time frightened by his own calmness. Then he turned and put the bottle back on the table.

The other four, who had sat down at the far end of the room by the window, looked at him uncomprehendingly. The table in the middle of the room prevented them from having a clear view of the Princess's body; they had seen only the blow. Then, with a kind of cautious curiosity, Lucini rose and, leaning forward, looked towards the door. The thing was there, across the threshold. His companions saw him turn pale. "This time we've gone a bit too far," he said in a low frightened voice, without looking at them.

Micheli, who was sitting in the farthest corner, rose to his feet. He was a medical student, and his privileged position in this respect gave him, as it were, a feeling of responsibility. "Perhaps she's only fainted," he said in a clear voice; "we must bring her round . . . wait a moment." He took a half-full glass from the table and bent over the woman's body, while the others formed a group round him. They watched him as he passed his arm under her back, then lifted her and shook her, and poured a little wine between her lips. But her head swung from side to side, her arms hung lifelessly from her shoulders. Micheli laid her down on the floor again and put his ear to her chest. After a moment he raised himself again. "I think she's dead," he said, still flushed from the effort he had made.

There was silence. "For God's sake cover her up!" suddenly cried Lucini, unable to take his eyes from the body.

"Cover her up yourself!"

Again there was silence. From down below the sound of the band came distinctly to their ears; but now it was more subdued, it must be a tango they were playing. The five men looked at each other. Of them all, only Ripandelli was now sitting down. He was staring straight ahead of him, his shoulders bent, his head in his hands; he could see the black trousers of his friends forming a circle round him, but they were not close enough together, so that it was impossible not to see, through the spaces between them, the prostrate mass of the body lying against the white-painted door at the other side of the room.

"What a mad thing to do," began Mastrogiovanni as though protesting against some ridiculous idea, turning at the same time to Ripandelli; "with the bottle! . . . What ever came over you at that moment?"

"I had nothing to do with it," said someone in a trembling voice. Ripandelli, without moving, knew it was Lucini who spoke. "You're all witnesses that I was sitting over at the window."

It was Jancovich, the oldest of them all, with his melancholy face and flat voice, who answered him. "Yes, yes," he said; "argue the point, my dear chaps, as to who it was and who it wasn't. . . . Then right in the middle of this interesting discussion someone will come in and we shall all go and finish our argument in some other place."

"Well, we shall go there in any case," said Ripandelli sombrely.

Jancovich made a gesture both violent and comic. "This chap's mad," he said. "Just because he himself wants to go to prison, he wants everyone else to go there too." For a brief instant the whole of his thin face was deeply furrowed by laughter. "Now just listen to what I say."

"???"

"Well now. . . . The Princess lived alone, didn't she? So it will be a week or so before her disappearance is noticed. . . . We'll go down now and dance, and behave as if nothing had happened. When the ball is over, we'll get her into my car and take her right away somewhere, outside the town . . . or perhaps we could throw her into the river. Then it'll be thought that she killed herself. She lived all alone . . . in a moment of depression . . . these things do happen. In any case, if people ask us where she is, we'll say that she left the room at a certain moment and has not been seen since. Are we all agreed?"

The others turned pale with fear. The woman was dead—that they knew; but the idea of having committed a crime, of having killed someone, and of being on that account in a state of guilt, had not yet entered their minds. They felt they were Ripandelli's accomplices merely in the matter of amusement, not of murder. The suggestion that the corpse should be thrown into the river brought them abruptly face to face with reality. Lucini, Micheli and Mastrogiovanni protested, declaring that they had nothing to do with it, that they did not wish to have anything to do with it, that Ripandelli must extricate himself as best he could.

"All right then," answered Jancovich, who had been mentally calculating the legal possibilities of the position, "that means that we shall all meet again in court: Ripandelli will be found guilty of murder, but we none the less shall get a few years each as accessories to the crime." They were silent, in consternation. Lucini, who was the youngest of them all, was white in the face, and his eyes were filled with tears. Suddenly he shook his fist in the air. "I knew it would end like this," he cried; "I knew it. . . . Oh, if only I had never come!"

But it was only too evident that Jancovich was right. They had to come to a decision: at any moment someone might come in. The opinion of the oldest man present was approved and, all of a sudden, as though they wished to stifle thought by action, all five of them started with alacrity to eliminate all traces of the crime. The bottle and glasses were locked up in a cupboard; the corpse was dragged, not without difficulty, into a corner and covered with a large towel; there was a small looking-glass on the wall and each of them went over and examined himself to see if he was clean and tidy. Then, one after the other, they left the room; the light was turned off, the door locked and the key taken by Jancovich.

The ball, at that moment, was at the height of its brilliance. The room was crowded, there were clustering groups of people seated round the walls; others were perching on the window-sills; in the middle the multitude of dancers swirled hither and thither; a thousand "shooting stars" were flying from every direction and people were pelting each other with little multi-coloured balls of cotton-wool; from each corner came shrill and strident sounds of toy whistles and pasteboard pipes; balloons of every colour were swaying amongst the paper streamers hanging from the chandelier, and every now and then one of them would explode with a sharp pop as the dancing couples competed for them, struggling to snatch them from one another and crowding round anyone who had preserved his own balloon intact. Laughter, voices, sounds, colours, shapes, the blue clouds of tobacco smoke—all these, to the bemused senses of the five men who leant over the balcony and gazed down from above into the luminous cavern, became fused into the golden haze of an unattainable Arabian Nights festivity, creating the effect of a paradise of irresponsibility and frivolity which to them was lost, for ever lost. Whatever efforts they might make their thoughts drew them back, forced them again into the little room full of lockers, with the wine-glasses on the table, the chairs in dis-order, the window shut, and, on the floor in one corner, the corpse. But at last they pulled themselves together and went down the stairs.

"Now I do beg of you," said Jancovich, as a final injunction, "be animated, dance, enjoy yourselves as though nothing had happened." Then, led by Mastrogiovanni, they all five went in and mingled with the crowd, indistinguishable now from the other male dancers who, dressed like them in black and holding their partners in their arms, filed past the platform on which the band played, in the slow rhythm of the dance.

END OF A RELATIONSHIP

ONE November afternoon Lorenzo, a rich, idle young man, was driving home in his car; he knew that his mistress had already been waiting for him there for over half an hour. A sudden, unpleasant turn in the weather, with wild, intermittent squalls of rain and a disagreeable wind that never failed to blow in your face whichever way you were walking, a form of insomnia which woke him up suddenly every night after a few short hours of sleep and kept him awake until dawn, a feeling of panic, of being pursued, and of mental dullness which for several months he had been unable to get rid of—all these contributed towards putting Lorenzo into a quivering, raging frame of mind. "Oh, to finish with all this!" he kept repeating to himself even as he drove his car through the streets of the city, and he felt that every trifle caused him so acute, so miserable a pain that he wanted to cry out—the screen-wiper that stopped for a moment as it went backwards and forwards over the streaming glass, the lever which, in the midst of the traffic, refused, beneath his frenzied hand, to go into gear, the useless clamour of horns from the cars held up behind him. But to finish with what? This was a question which Lorenzo would really have been unable to answer. Every time he looked forth from his unjustified wretchedness and examined his own life, he realized that he wanted for nothing, that he had nothing he wished to change, that he had obtained all he had desired and even something more. Was he not rich? Did he not make the most judicious and civilized use of his wealth?

22

A home, a car, travel, clothes, amusements, sport, holidays in the country, society, a mistress—sometimes it happened that he counted up, with a kind of vain, boastful weariness, all the things that he had in life, only to conclude, in the end, that the source of his trouble should be looked for in some physical disorder. But the doctors to whom he had gone with a mind full of hope had quickly disappointed him: he was extremely healthy, they said, there was not a vestige of any sort of illness in him. And so, for no reason at all, life for Lorenzo had become a dull and sterile torment. Every night, as he went to bed after a day of emptiness and gloom, he swore to himself, "To-morrow must be the day of liberation"; but next morning, awakening from an exhausting sleep, he had merely to open, not both, but just one eye to realize immediately that the new day would not be very different from all the others that had gone before it. He had merely to cast a glance at his bedroom, in which every object seemed to be covered for ever with the dull patina of his distress, to be certain that again on this new day reality would appear to him no clearer, no more encouraging and no more comprehensible than a week or a month earlier. Nevertheless, he would get up and put on a dressing-gown, would open the window and cast a disgusted glance at the street already filled with the mature light of mid-morning; then, as if in the hope that hot and cold water might wash away the deadly spell that had been cast upon him, as it washed away the sweats and impurities of the night, he would shut himself up in the bathroom and devote himself to a toilet that seemed to become more and more refined and exhaustive the more profoundly did his strange wretchedness take possession of him. Two hours thus went by in profitless assiduities—two hours during which Lorenzo, again and again, would take a looking-glass and lingeringly scrutinize his own face as though he hoped to catch some special look there, or to trace out some new wrinkle which might enable him to guess at the reasons of the change in himself. "It's the same face," he would angrily reflect, "that I had when I was happy, the same face that pleased the women I made love to, that smiled or was sad, that hated, envied, desired, that had in fact a life of its own; and yet now, for some unknown reason, all that seems to be finished." But, notwithstanding the emptiness and bitterness of all this care devoted to his physical person, these two hours —possibly because the use he made of them was precise and limited and demanded no deep thought—were the only ones of the day during which he managed to forget himself and his own miserable state. Moreover he knew this ("yet another proof", he used sometimes to think, "that I've ceased to be anything but a body without a soul, an animal that spends its time licking its coat") and deliberately prolonged them. But the time came when he had to leave the bathroom. Then the day began in earnest, and with it his arid torment.

Lorenzo's apartment was on the ground floor of a small new building at the far end of a still unfinished by-road which, turning off the main suburban avenue, faded away, after a few more houses, into the country. Apart from his own, all the buildings in this little street were either uninhabited or still in course of construction; the road was unpaved and consisted of thick mud criss-crossed by deep, hard ruts made by lorries coming and going from the builders' yards with loads of earth or stone; there were only two lamp-posts, and those at the point where the road turned off, so that on that day, as soon as he had got past the enormous, ancient puddle that blocked the turning, Lorenzo, seeing a light burning at the far end of the dark, wet, gleaming road, more or less at the point where his bedroom would be, knew that, as he had expected, his mistress had already arrived and was waiting for him. At this thought he was assailed by a violent and unreasonable ill-humour against the woman—who had nothing to be blamed for and had come to an appointment which he himself had made with her—and at the same time by a kind of presentiment that something decisive was about to happen. So cruel was the feeling that darkened his mind that he clenched his teeth tightly; then he stopped the car in front of the entrance, angrily slammed the door and went into the house.

Lying on the yellow marble top of the sham Louis XV table in the hall, side by side with a short umbrella and a handbag, he saw a curiously shaped parcel full of sharp points. Inquisitively, he undid the paper wrapping and found a small tin railway-engine; evidently his mistress, who had been married for eight years and had two children, before coming to her appointment with him had gone, like the good mother she was, to buy a toy to give them that evening when she returned home, tired and languid, shortly before supper. Lorenzo wrapped up the object in the paper again, hung up his waterproof and hat and went on into the bedroom.

Immediately, from the first glance, he realized that, to while away the time as she waited for him, she had prepared both herself and the room in such a way that he, coming in from the cold, rainy night, should at once receive the impression of an affectionate and comforting intimacy. Only the bedside lamp was burning, and she had wrapped a pink silk shirt round it so that its light should be warm and discreet; on a little table stood the teapot and cups, all ready; his silk dressing-gown, spread out over an armchair, and his plush slippers on the floor below the dressing-gown, seemed all ready to jump on to him and cover him up, so great was the care and precision with which they had been arranged. But the ill-humour inspired in him by these quasi-conjugal attentions was redoubled when he saw that his mistress, in order to receive him worthily, had had the idea of putting on a pair of his pyjamas. She was lying on her side on the sumptuous yellow bedspread, and the pyjamas with their broad blue stripes, too tight for her ample, rounded hips and full, projecting bosom, were pulled askew and not properly buttoned up, forcing her into an awkward and indecorous attitude and forming a disagreeable contrast with her hair, which was black and long, and with the placid, indolent expression of her face. All this Lorenzo observed in the first, sharp glance that he threw round the room. Then, without saying a word, he sat down on the bedspread, at the foot of the bed.

For a time there was silence. Then at last, "Is it still raining?" asked the woman, looking at him with a characteristically serene, inert curiosity and at the same time coiling herself up tightly, as though she had unconsciously felt the cruelty in Lorenzo's unmoving, preoccupied look. "Yes, it's raining," he replied. There was silence again. She asked him three or four further questions, receiving each time the same brief, harassed answers, and then, "What's the matter with you?" she asked; and as she said it she slipped down to the foot of the bed and crouched beside him. "What's the matter?" she repeated rather breathlessly, a first sign of apprehension becoming visible in her fine, inexpressive black eyes.

Seeing her so close to him, so alive and anxious and at the same time kept at so great a distance by his own troubled state of mind, Lorenzo felt himself to be throttled by a dry, painful dumbness. "Perhaps the whole cause of the trouble," he said to himself, "is those damned pyjamas that she took it into her head to put on"; and, even as he answered that there was nothing the matter, he started, with indifferent but impatient hands, to pull off the broad-striped jacket.

Thinking that the young man wanted to undress her so that he could caress her the more freely, and very well satisfied at being able to attribute his disquieting silence to the agitation of desire, she hastened to rid herself of the pyjamas and then lay down again, naked and placid, in the same attitude of passive expectation in which Lorenzo had found her when he came into the room. Still without speaking a word, he sat down beside her and began caressing her in a vague, preoccupied manner, almost without looking at her and as though thinking of something else. His fingers twined themselves idly in her black hair, disarranging and re-arranging it, his hand lay open and irresolute first on her bare breast, as though he wished to feel the quiet breathing that quickened it at regular intervals, then on her belly as if curious to detect the pulse of desire beneath its ample, quiescent whiteness; but in reality it was for him like touching a lifeless, shapeless trunk. Quite lucidly, as he went on caressing it, he became aware that he neither felt any love for this handsome body nor was he even sensible of the life in it, whether of its breathing or its desire; and this feeling of irremediable detachment was painfully sharpened for him by the distressed and questioning looks with which, like a sick person lying on the little iron bed in a doctor's surgery, his mistress unceasingly regarded him. Lorenzo all of a sudden remembered the calm, indifferent disgust with which his cat, when its hunger was satisfied, turned away its face from the food offered to it. "The creature's had enough," he exclaimed in an ironical, exultant tone of voice; "it doesn't want anything more to eat." "Whatever creature d'you mean, Renzo?" asked his companion uneasily; "what's the matter with you?" Lorenzo made no answer to these questions, but, as he looked at her, his eye, made sharper and more precise by the hard, parched suffering that pressed upon him within, came to a halt upon the hand which, in a languid, touching gesture of unconscious self-defence, lay covering her breast. It was a rather beautiful hand, rather large, neither too plump nor too sinewy, white, smooth, and its ring-finger bore a plain, heavy gold wedding-ring.

For a few moments Lorenzo looked at this ring, looked at the naked body, young and splendid, curled up in embarrassment on the flat yellow bedspread; then, all of a sudden, it was as though the whole of the hatred accumulated during the last, sad months in the lower depths of his consciousness burst irresistibly out, breaking the weakened barriers of his will, and flooded his soul. "What ring is that?" he asked, pointing to her hand.

Surprised, she lowered her eyes to her breast. "Why, Renzo," she asked with a smile, "what are you thinking of? Can't you see it's my wedding-ring?"

There was a brief silence again, with Lorenzo trying in vain to get the better of the queer, cruel feeling that had taken possession of him. Then suddenly, "Aren't you ashamed," he asked, lowering his voice, "tell me, aren't you ashamed of lying naked like that on my bed, you, a married woman and the mother of two children?"

If he had told her that it was dawn and that the sun was on the point of rising she could not have been more astonished. Showing every sign of apprehension and wonder and distress, she sat up on the bed and stared at him. "What on earth do you mean?" she said.

Lorenzo, by now quite incapable of restraining himself, shook his head violently and made no answer. Then he repeated again: "Aren't you ashamed? Don't you wonder what your husband and children would think if they saw you here, on my bed, without any clothes on, or if they could catch sight of you when we embrace and could notice how you get all excited and red in the face and how you wriggle your body and what attitudes you get into? Or again if they could hear the things you sometimes say to me?" It appeared now to be not so much the shame of which Lorenzo spoke as sheer fright that she felt. Bending her legs back beneath her hips, she knelt on the bed, and with this movement her long black hair fell over her breast and shoulders; then, with an imploring, embarrassed gesture, she placed her hand on the young man's cheek. "What's the matter with you?" she asked once again; "why d'you ask me these questions? What's the point of them?"

"There *is* a point," replied Lorenzo, and with a brusque movement of his head he rudely shook off the affectionate hand. Uncomprehending, bewildered, she considered him for some time without speaking. "But I love you," she protested, revealing at last the true nature of her anxiety; "are you thinking, perhaps, that I *don't* love you?"

Her sincerity was obvious; but it made Lorenzo keenly aware of his own inability to speak this vague, inexact love-language without telling lies, and thus it widened the distance that already separated them. Mute and deeply troubled, he gazed at her for a long time without moving. "The difficulty is that *I* don't love *you*", he would have liked to answer. But, instead, he rose and started walking up and down the big, shadow-filled room. Every now and then he cast a quick glance at the woman squatting there on the bed, and he saw that, each time his eye rested upon her, she timidly changed her attitude, now covering up her lap with her hands, now shaking her hair, now placing a hand on her feet which were crushed beneath the weight of her hips, and all the time following his silent comings and goings with frightened eyes. "She loves me," he was thinking meanwhile. "How can she manage to say she loves me when she doesn't know, even from a distance, who I am or what I'm like?"

The aridity of his feeling seemed even to have dried up his throat. He stopped suddenly in front of a cabinet, gilt and sham like all the rest of the furniture in the room, opened it, took out a bottle and poured himself out a large glass of soda-water. Then, just at the moment when he was straightening up in order to drink, "Renzo," exclaimed the woman in her warm, good-natured, slightly vulgar voice, "Renzo, tell me the truth: somebody's been saying nasty things about me to you and you believed them. Tell me honestly, isn't that so?"

At these words he paused in the act of raising the glass to his lips and hesitated for a moment, observing her: and it seemed to him that, with her disconcerted, imploring expression, her hair spilling dolefully over her breast and arms, her white, plump body all bent and huddled together, his mistress could not possibly have displayed more clearly her own blindness in face of what was happening. Without answering her, he drank and replaced the empty glass on the cabinet. "Get dressed," he said curtly; "the best thing is for you to get dressed and go away."

"You're very unkind," she said, in an indolent, judicious tone of voice that was characteristic of her, as though she were sure that this behaviour on Lorenzo's part derived from some passing ill-humour; "you're unkind and unjust and I quite agree that it's best for me to go away." Then she threw back her hair from her shoulders with a gesture full of indifference and assurance, got down from the bed and started towards the armchair on which she had placed her clothes. Both in her words and in her demeanour there was nothing more than the indolent, rather bovine serenity with which she did every-thing. But to Lorenzo, already irritated, it seemed that they contained an insolent and contemptuous irony; and his reaction was a sudden, cruel desire to humiliate and punish her. Rapidly he stepped across to her clothes, snatched them up and, walking round the room, quite slowly and taking care to choose the most difficult and out-of-the-way places, threw them down, garment by garment, on the floor. "Now she'll have to stoop down and pick them up," he said to himself; and it seemed to him that for her, naked as she was, nothing could be more humiliating and shameful than this ridiculous, painful quest. "Now pick them up," he said, turning back towards the bed.

Utterly astonished but by this time entirely sure of herself and of her grounds for resentment, she looked at him for a moment without opening her mouth. Then, touching her forehead with an expressive gesture, "You've gone mad," she said.

"No, I'm not mad," answered Lorenzo; he went to the lamp, pulled off it the pink shirt that she had wrapped round it and threw it under the bed.

They stared at each other. Then she shrugged her shoulders indifferently and, with no sign of shame, went all round the room, stooping here and there to pick up the clothes which Lorenzo had thrown on the floor. Sunk in his armchair, Lorenzo followed her attentively with his eyes. He watched her pale body as she went lightly about the dark room, bending her head low down with her buttocks in the air, crouching down briskly with her face against the floor and her hair scattered round her, stooping sideways with her breasts hanging down and one foot raised; and it seemed to him that it was himself he was punishing rather than his mistress; for, whereas she did not appear to be feeling either shame or humiliation but merely annoyance, he himself, as he cruelly watched her, felt that her awkward attitudes, like those of some disabled animal, were destroying in him not only sexual desire but all feeling of human sympathy. All was lost, he reflected, filled with wretchedness; it would never again be possible for him to escape from this state of disgust and disillusionment; incapable of loving, he would be like a man sinking in a quicksand, for every effort he might make to reawaken his dead feelings would thrust him yet farther down into the slough of cruelty and cold-bloodedness. Absorbed in these thoughts, he seemed to see his mistress at a great distance and surrounded now with a baleful, hopeless air of detachment as she composedly put on one garment after another, on the far side of the bed. "Good-bye, but I do beg you to take care of yourself," she said to him finally, in good-natured but determined resentment, from the doorway. A minute later the front door closed with a bang, and only then did Lorenzo, shaking himself out of his bitter abstraction, realize that he was alone.

For a long time he sat quite still, gazing at the yellow bedspread upon which the light fell and in the middle of which could still be seen the hollow made by his mistress's body as she lay there. Finally he rose, went over to the window and opened it. As he looked out from the warm, confined room into the cool winter night he saw that it had stopped raining, and he felt his mind, which had been like a cage full of malignant harpies, suddenly discharge itself, remaining empty and unclean. And as he stood there, his eyes were able to contemplate the dark, untidy area of building operations that lay below the house, with its piles of refuse, its growth of weeds and some slow-moving, stealthy shapes that he presumed to be hungry cats; his ears could hear sounds from the avenue not far off, motor-horns, the creaking of trams; yet his thoughts remained inert and he did not seem to exist except through these isolated, fortuitous rifts in his senses. "Just like me, better than me, in fact," he said to himself as he watched the shifting, wary, shadowy cats on the whitish piles of refuse; "those cats hear the same sounds, see the same things as I: what difference is there between me, a man, and those cats?" This question seemed to him absurd, yet at the same time he felt that, at the point which he had reached, absurdity and reality were so inextricably confused that one could not be distinguished from the other. "How unhappy I am," he started murmuring to himself in a low voice, still standing at the window-sill; "how have I managed to reduce myself to this degree of unhappiness?" There suddenly flashed across his mind the idea of cutting short a life which had become so utterly empty and incomprehensible, and suicide appeared to him like a ripe, easily-gathered fruit to be plucked merely by putting out his hand; but he seemed to be held back not only by a sort of contempt for an act which he had always considered an acknowledgment of weakness, not only by a sense almost of duty, but by a strange, and in his present state an unexpected, hope. "I am not living," he suddenly thought, "I am dreaming; this nightmare cannot possibly go on long enough to convince me that it is not a nightmare but reality; one day I shall wake up and recognize the world again, with the sun and the stars, the trees and the sky and women and all the other lovely things.

32

Therefore I must have patience: the awakening is bound to come." But the cold of the night was slowly penetrating into him, and at last he shook himself and, closing the window, went back and sat down in the armchair, opposite the empty bed upon which the light of the lamp fell.

THE WAYWARD WIFE

IN a town in Central Italy there lived some years ago an elderly widow and her daughter; their names were Giacinta and Gemma Foresi. The town, dark and with many towers, is piled up on the top of a high hill and traversed from one end to the other by the street called the Corso in which are the Cathedral and the town's finest buildings; and from the Corso, on each side, you go down by narrow lanes or steep flights of stairs to a road along the ramparts that run all round the hillside.

In one of these lanes, which takes its name from the Passion—possibly on account of an ancient piece of sculpture built into the wall at a corner and representing Calvary—the Foresis occupied the top floor of a decayed and crumbling mansion. The town, being the capital of a province, received a certain influx of life from a large number of clerks, professional men and officers of the garrison. And like a great many other people, the Foresis, who were extremely poor, sought to derive advantage from these outsiders. They let two or three rooms in their apartment, the best rooms they had, rooms which did not look out into the lane but over neglected, sunny kitchen-gardens stretching away behind the house.

Of the two women, the mother might have been about fifty: she was short, fat, shabby in her clothes and humble in her manners; but her soft, small, white hands, her still black hair arranged carefully in a form that was not without a kind of old-fashioned coquettishness, her face which even in its slight plumpness retained a certain delicacy of feature, and, especially, her eyes of a mild and faded blue in which there sometimes appeared a strange look that was half impudent and half laughing—all these made you think that twenty or so years earlier she must have been beautiful and very different in bearing and character. She dressed in the shapeless manner of the provincial matron and housewife, in long skirts of black or grey material that reached down to her feet, high-necked bodices, shawls crossed over on the chest, and she never put the faintest veil of powder on her cheeks; yet it was obvious that a little make-up and some less shabby clothes would very easily transform her. She was very domesticated, and whenever she was not busy in the house cooking or working with her needle, she would put a little mangy fur round her neck, a little black hat on her head, and go off to church. There, retiring into a dark corner behind a pillar, eyes raised to heaven, without fervour but also without distraction, she would move her lips endlessly in complicated prayers. But she was neither the complete housewife nor the complete bigot; it seemed rather as if she had resigned herself to a kind of life that was not her own; and the impudent, laughing gleam still showed itself, at intervals, in her eyes. As a result her whole person exhaled an air of faint, sly hyprocrisy.

Moreover, even if the mother had not had this fineness of feature and this appearance of artificiality, the daughter would still have provided confirmation enough of a contrast between their present humble life and an unknown past that must have been very different. Gemma was not pretty, in fact she was very nearly ugly, but she had the noble and pronounced features which reveal an origin far from vulgar, and which at moments appear to compose themselves into a kind of haughty beauty. She was tall, slender, bony, with long, thin, elegant thighs; her bosom was flat but broad, as were her shoulders. Her face was lean and pale except on the cheek-bones, which were always slightly red; her eyes large and slow of movement, with projecting lids which veiled the pupil of the eye and gave her glance an air of dull, contemptuous dignity. She had an aquiline nose, a big, disdainful mouth, and, beneath her curly hair, a delicate but unhealthy complexion, sometimes transparent, sometimes disfigured with red blemishes. The soft, fine hairs shadowing her arms and the back of her neck suggested a body downy and glowing with warmth in spite of its ungraceful thinness. She had little of her mother about her, except for her nose which, in Signora Foresi too, was aquiline; of her father nothing at all—judging, at least, by the photographs hanging in the house, which made him appear short, squarely built, good-natured: he had been a business man, but had failed and immediately afterwards had died, leaving his wife in poverty with a daughter still very young. Anyhow, with her bony, pallid, elegant appearance, Gemma had nothing either provincial or domesticated about her. On the contrary, as you looked at her you could not help being reminded of those anaemic society women, city-dwellers by vocation, who spend their days lying languidly on a sofa and do not go out until the evening, always in evening dress, true creatures of the night, ephemeral, unhealthy. But of all appearances this was without doubt the most misleading, for Gemma never wore anything but simple dark dresses which she tried to squeeze in tightly at the waist in order to counterblance the thinness of her bust. And as for her life, it was the most monotonous and virtuous that could have been led even in that quiet provincial town.

Notwithstanding their poverty and the fact that they let rooms, the two women enjoyed a certain insecure, indefinable consideration in the town. They were admitted everywhere and known to everyone, and it was universally recognized, to their credit, that they were not importunate and "knew their place". The reasons for this esteem, which was denied to richer and more influential people than they, were many and not all of them clear. Perhaps it was their modesty, perhaps it was a certain air of quality and distinction which made them look as though they had come down in the world, whereas in reality they had never occupied a social position more exalted than the one they now occupied. By the envious, moreover—such are never lacking, even to the least enviable of people—various allegations were made. All of which were founded on one single fact—the daughter's relations with a rich and noble family in the neighbourhood.

Every summer, Gemma went to spend a couple of months on an estate not far off, where this family had a villa. The family consisted of a father, a son, and two daughters of about the same age as Gemma. As a child, she had been taken to this place by her mother, a couple of times, for short periods of a few days, but these were distant and faded memories of which she herself was uncertain; all the more so, because her mother never mentioned these visits nor let it be seen that she knew the villa. Later, they had sent a governess to fetch her, and, when she grew bigger, she had gone there by herself and had always stayed a couple of months. To the two daughters she was bound by an unequal and subordinate friendship which, with the years, as they all three grew older, had become transformed more and more into a relationship of inferiority. The two young ladies made her presents of clothes and other cast-off objects, and entrusted her with all the delicate and difficult jobs that could not be left to a maid. Gemma was, in reality, not so much a friend as something between a lady companion and a housekeeper. But in exchange she had the much appreciated advantage of meeting on equal terms (in appearance at least) all the people who came to the villa, for the most part landowners of the neighbourhood and their wives and daughters. It was a provincial, old-fashioned world, at the same time both simple and haughty, shabby and completely arid, but to Gemma, accustomed to a straitened existence, the titles, lustreless now and without importance, the clothes brought up to date by suggestions from the Paris fashion magazines, the conversations which alluded to gossip and situations of which she was ignorant, all seemed things that were wholly splendid, desirable, full of mystery. As for the master of the house, he

treated her somewhat distantly, with evasive and convention-
ally paternal affection. Exactly, in fact, as he would have
treated a foster-sister of one of his daughters. Nor did it ever
happen—not even one single time in all those years—that he
asked her for news of her mother.

To Gemma, though she hid her feelings beneath a veil of
condescending indifference and familiarity, the two months
that she spent each year at the villa of this family were the chief
event and the one and only amusement of her life. "I shall be
going as usual to Il Querceto", she would reply to the friends
who asked her where she intended to spend the summer. "Oh,
one leads a very simple life, it's even rather boring", she would
add when they asked her what she would be doing there. And
she did not realize that her malicious feminine friends could
scarcely restrain their laughter and asked her all these questions
deliberately in order to see her put on her artificial air of self-
sufficient, *blasé* indifference. She had, in truth, a natural and
irresistible inclination towards luxury, vanity and social life.
And no less strong and natural was her shame for her own condition and her own poverty. And so it came about that, by dint
of building up fancies about the paradise from which she knew
she was excluded and which she longed to enter, she confused
reality with dreams, aspirations with actualities, the present
with the future, and, swept along on this course by an ardent
and fantastic imagination, invented and told—without blinking
an eyelid and as if she believed in them herself—the grossest,
the most improbable, the most foolish lies. According to her,
the clothes that she had received as presents from her two
friends she herself had had made by a very good dressmaker in
Florence; her mother came of a noble house and was related
to the late wife of the owner of the villa; she had refused an
offer of marriage from a certain very well-known, rich young
man; she had spent the winter before in Rome as the guest of a
certain Marchesa: and other, similar pieces of vainglorious
nonsense. Her intrepidity in telling lies increased in proportion

to the absurdity of the lies themselves; timid by nature, she defied ridicule and shame by rattling off her lies in the presence of people who could easily have contradicted her; and such was the astonishment aroused by her pathetic, defenceless effrontery, that these people always ended by keeping silent, as though doubting their own memories. How she had arrived at so complete a surrender to this kind of vice, she herself could not have said. But whether it was that her first lie had been nearer the truth than the others that followed later and, as such, had given her the illusion that she was not lying at all, or whether it was that she had thought she could deceive others as she was already deceiving herself, the fact remains that she was very soon known to her friends and to the whole town as an inveterate and ridiculous liar, of unusual and altogether extraordinary impudence. Deliberately they asked her leading questions, egged her on, laid traps for her and were enormously amused when at last they saw her assume the false air of in-difference and worldly superiority that they knew so well, and, like an automatic machine set in motion by a coin, start rattling off, without a pause and with her usual astonishing self-assurance, the most thumping lies. To watch her telling lies, they said, was a joy, a recreation, a spectacle. And there was indeed a theatrical perfection in this unfortunate passion and in the mechanical and always identical manner in which it manifested itself. Without being aware of it, completely wrapped up as she was in her dreams and her unrealities, she had thus ended by creating round herself an atmosphere of cruelty, ridicule and amused contempt.

Furthermore, she was encouraged in her course of falseness and vainglory by the very person who should have restrained and corrected her, her mother. Beneath her mask of humility and shabbiness there was, in the widow Foresi, the same kind of senselessness as in her daughter. The only difference was that certain far-distant experiences had forced her to repress and lay aside—without however renouncing them—the aspirations which her daughter, still inexperienced, displayed openly. Those same malicious feminine friends who laughed at Gemma would not have been able to make the widow fall into the same traps; she was too prudent and too frightened, and the memory of past discomfitures was still too vivid. Like a politician, defeated but unbowed, who sees in his son the defender and vindicator of his own work and reputation, the widow regarded the follies of her daughter with a more than benevolent, with a positively approving and encouraging, eye. Gemma would come back from her usual stay at the villa where, as usual, she had adapted herself to act as housekeeper. For a month and more her mother would make her recount all the events that had taken place, relate every conversation, however insignificant, describe minutely the appearance and situation of all the people she had had the luck to meet. Then, while she was receiving these reports, the laughing glance of youth could be seen shining in her old blue eyes; she would seem changed, and with muttered words and nods of the head would continually approve her daughter's remarks, commenting favourably upon them. Gemma would relate a piece of gossip about an adultery or some other intrigue on the part of persons she had met or heard spoken about; and her mother, who would not have hesitated to condemn such faults if they had been committed by humble people in the town, would listen with complacency and let it be understood by expressions of approval or curiosity that for people so illustrious such errors were not merely lawful but even, in a way, a matter of duty. Like having a car or wearing jewellery. There existed in the mother's mind, far more precisely and irremediably than in the still open and ingenuous mind of the daughter, an unreal picture of a world in which beautiful, noble, rich men and women intermingled clamorous passions, lived in abodes of the utmost luxury, capriciously dissipated their inheritances, permitted themselves, in fact, every kind of indulgence, beyond all moral limits and all social obligations.

The kind of indulgences, she seemed to imply, that were denied to vulgar persons or to those like herself and her daughter who were persecuted by misfortune; these had to live according to established and quite conventional rules. Such notions went back to the widow's early youth, to a period when they were so universally widespread that they gave rise to a whole literature and a social tradition. The widow knew nothing of books or culture, but none the less she remained faithful to the spirit of that period just as she did to the old-fashioned hat which she put on when she went to Mass. From these nostalgic desires on the part of her mother, Gemma derived assurance and inspiration for her own ambitions and falsehoods. And indeed, on these subjects, the understanding between mother and daughter was perfect, intoxicating, even physical. Both, during such conversations, forgot the room with its sloping roof, the countrified furniture, the dark lane upon which the window opened, the two or three lodgers who slept in the adjoining rooms, and every other sign of poverty, and felt themselves transported, as though by magic, into the fantastic world of their desires. Every now and then the mother would sigh with an air of regret, seeming to say "I too, when I was young . . .", but always she would control herself and end by saying nothing. Gemma, on the other hand, as she sat on the cotton bedspread of the iron bed, talked fluently, with the warmth and vivacity and abandonment that are the natural properties of ingenuous and uncontrolled passion. A drunken man would pass under the window, propping himself against the wall and singing a coarse, rude song, and still Gemma talked. Cats mewed and chased each other up and down the steps in the lane, and still Gemma talked. The ponderous, lonely strokes of midnight would echo from the bell-tower of the cathedral near by, and still Gemma went on talking. And it was almost always the mother who would rise silently and quietly and then, standing in front of the sloping looking-glass on the dark, evil-smelling walnut chest-of-drawers, would

begin—though still responding to what Gemma was saying—
to undo the complicated structure of her hair, putting down the
hairpins, one by one, on the grey marble slab. When, at last,
she stood only in her chemise, she would give her daughter a
kiss, interrupting her in the full flow of her rapturous discourse,
and send her to bed. Gemma, half enthusiastic, half bitterly
disappointed, would obey and leave the room. But in her own
bedroom, when she had put out the light and wrapped the bed-
covers round her thin, glowing body, she would almost always
recover herself and, after indulging for a long time in further
idle fancies, would fall asleep happy.

.   .   .   .   .

It came about, during one of these summers, that the son of
the owner of the villa became suddenly aware of Gemma's
existence—just as it sometimes happens, after you have in-
habited it for a long time, that you discover the colour of the
walls of your room or the pattern on the floor. Up till that
day he had treated his sisters' friend in the same innocent, un-
suspecting manner in which, once upon a time, when they
were both children, they had played together. Long habit and
the familiarity of their relationship had brought it about that,
in his eyes, the figure of Gemma had remained enveloped in
the same chaste, neutral atmosphere as surrounded his sisters. It
can in fact be said that, though they lived in the same house,
he had never observed her attentively. As a result, if he had
been asked what she looked like, he would have been uncertain
and would scarcely have remembered that she was tall and not,
perhaps, ugly. Still, for him as for the people who came to
the villa, Gemma was a kind of housekeeper, somebody whose
place was more with the staff than with the guests, one of those
beings, in fact, whom you look at without seeing. But all of
a sudden this indifference vanished and everything was changed.
    This happened one day in the middle of August, in the
hottest period of the year. One afternoon, immediately after

lunch, the young man, who was called Paolo, after having tried
in vain to go to sleep in his dark, stuffy bedroom, left the house
with the intention of finding a shady spot where he might lie
down and take his repose. The villa, which was ancient and
very large, with loggias, terraces, glass doors and other addi-
tions belonging to various periods, stood, with its garden, in the
midst of fields. The front of the house overlooked an immense
cultivated plain; immediately at its back rose the ridges of some
wooded hills. Paolo, then, came out of the closed and sleeping
villa and made his way towards the hills. He knew that, in a
kind of ravine a short distance away, there was a grove of oak-
trees from which, indeed, the villa took its name. Hot from
walking, thinking of nothing in particular, his head bent in
the sunshine, he started off along a path that wound round the
hillside. From this height he could see the villa with all its
glass glittering in the sunlight, and beyond it the great plain
dotted with olive-trees, far, far away to a horizon white with
heat-mist. From the bushes on each side of the path came an
intense murmur of insects, dominated by the painfully dry,
dusty voice of the cricket; lizards, small shadows beneath their
paunches, darted between his feet over the red-hot rocks; the
sun blazed down and seemed to be one with the silence. When
he came to the wood, he went in under the low branches
seeking a place to lie down: the ground was soft, black and
bare, except for dry leaves, acorns and withered branches; it
was not much cooler here than elsewhere, in fact the air, close
and full of midges, seemed even stuffier, but he could escape
the blinding glitter of the burning sky, the flaming, silent
presence of the sun. He wandered round for a little, then saw a
mossy rock embedded between two tree-trunks, and, thinking
that behind this rock there might be a convenient space, put
his two hands on it and, leaning a little forward, looked over.
There, lying on the ground asleep, he saw Gemma.

She was sleeping on her side, her arms raised above her head
in such a way that they concealed her face. Her light, red silk

dress allowed the straight lines of her thin body to show clearly
through it. He noticed, particularly, the elegance and slimness
of her thigh which was distinctly defined right from the hip
down to the knee; and was so long as to appear dispropor-
tionate. He noticed also how her arms, which were bare, had
a cold-looking, pale skin contrasting oddly with the thick, soft,
glowing hair that darkened her armpits. These details struck
him as though Gemma were not a woman he already knew but
a different woman, unknown to him and desirable. He wanted
to see her face as well, almost doubting, under this new and
disconcerting impression, that he would find in it the features
and expression to which he was accustomed; and so, taking a
little branch, he started tickling her very gently on her arms.
Gemma, still asleep, first shook her shoulders slightly, then
lowered her arm along her side, uncovering her hot, flushed
face with strands of black, curly hair falling over the cheeks.
Her face, like her body, seemed new to Paolo and not without
a certain beauty of its own, a disdainful, harsh beauty that he
had never noticed before. Gemma was frowning in her sleep,
she was curling the nostrils of her aquiline nose and making,
with her mouth, a slight grimace, as of disgust. He noticed
that her half-opened lips were fresh and full, with a rather dark
redness like the redness of a fruit, and that they were freshened,
as it were, by the calm breathing of sleep. These half-closed
lips inspired in him all at once a feeling of sharp desire, and, if
the rock had not been in his way, he would have bent down and
kissed them. Instead, he decided to waken her and called her
by name several times in a troubled voice, at first quietly, then
louder. Finally she woke up and, as she woke, made a movement which completed her conquest of him—the languid
movement with which she turned her head and shoulders
towards the place from which the voice came. "Ah, it's you,"
she said in the normal voice of their usual relationship. But at
the same moment their eyes met and she became confused and
sat up. "I was asleep," she said, bending her head; but even as

44

she rearranged her dress, patting it sharply with her ugly, angular hands, she reflected upon the look she had caught in the young man's eyes and flung herself, with all the violence of her naïve and fantastic imagination, into the path, hitherto unsuspected, which seemed to have suddenly opened up before her. "I was asleep," she repeated, raising towards him a face that surprised him, a face that was different from her usual face, a face full of ill-assured, jocular coquettishness. "But since you've woken me up, you can at least come and keep me company." The young man accepted and with one bound was at her side.

After that, they stayed together the whole afternoon, walking among the hills and picking wild flowers, of which Gemma wished to gather a big bunch. Their conversation that day was in no way different from the kind of conversation they had previously exchanged; the novelty lay in its intonation and manner. It was as if they had tacitly agreed that, from the moment when their eyes had met, a new phase in their relationship had begun, bringing with it an assured future independent of their own will-power, and that for this reason it was better not to force events but to allow the fate that had brought them together to take its own course. Of the two, Gemma was by far the more vivacious, the more insinuating, the more compromising. For Paolo had the frank, simple intelligence that sensible people have, which does not encumber itself with subtleties and enables its owner to have a direct and integral vision of all the consequences of the acts he may commit. As he walked at her side, he sought to repress his feeling of agitation whenever he was conscious of it rising to the surface. He told himself that Gemma was his sisters' friend, and, from the nature of the relations that had hitherto existed between them, almost in the position of a relative. Further, he could not help recalling how poor and unprotected she was; and how, being entertained almost out of charity, she found herself, at the villa, in a situation of dependence and inferiority: all of them things, he concluded, which imposed upon him the greatest discretion, and which, if by chance he allowed himself to commit any imprudence, would place him and, even more, Gemma, in a false and unpleasant position. And so, swayed by these preoccupations, he responded to the girl's obvious coquetries in all the ways that seemed to him permissible, without concealing his own sentiments but also without ever expressing them in the irremediable actions for which, at moments, he felt all the greater desire. It was a dangerous game; all the more so because Gemma had become aware of his reserve and, by simple mischievous ways of her own, was continually goading him on. In this manner, laughing and joking all the time, they spent the rest of the day and came back together to the villa, tired and happy, towards evening.

The days that followed brought no change in these relations. They spent many hours together, walking in the hills at the back of the villa. But however desirous he might feel and however much Gemma might tempt him with her coquetries, the young man could not make up his mind to declare his feelings. The idea that Gemma was being entertained out of charity and that she found herself, at the villa, in a subordinate position—the position, almost, of a housekeeper—prevented him from behaving with the freedom and frankness with which he would have paid court to any other friend of his sisters. It seemed to him that Gemma, owing to the situation in which she was placed, must be either married or left alone; and that any other course of action would lead not to a light love affair between people of the same age, but rather to a furtive adventure, unpleasing and violent and of decidedly debased flavour. Now, however fond he was of her, the idea of making Gemma his wife was still far from his mind. And he realized, on the other hand, with shame and contempt, that he was slipping every day nearer and nearer to the hateful relationship of master and servant-girl: he always felt a little ashamed of speaking to her with less indifference than usual in front of his sisters and other people; he was always conscious, in going out with her, of a feeling of condescension and generosity, as it were; he always felt inclined to meet her almost furtively, during siesta-time or at night, in passages or other deserted places, exactly as he would have done if he had really been carrying on a love affair with his own housekeeper. He was exceeding angry with himself for having these feelings, considering them to be unjust and unworthy of himself; nor did he realize that they were to a great extent both provoked and justified by Gemma's calculating, servile behaviour. He would have liked to consider her as an equal and to have had with her one of those light-hearted love affairs that compromise no one and are often a prelude to marriage. But instead, whatever efforts he might make, he felt himself carried along towards a gross, furtive passion, of the type that seems from the very beginning to exclude all possibility of a conjugal solution and to nourish itself, not only upon a number of dark desires, but upon feelings as unconnected with love as disgust, cruelty and contempt.

He continued for several days to be torn between these contradictory impulses, trying as hard as he could to keep command of himself. Until at last one night, two days before Gemma's depature was due, he was unable to resist any longer and left his own room having made up his mind to go and knock at the girl's door. He himself did not know what he would do; he preferred to think that he would limit himself to a declaration of his love. His bedroom and Gemma's both opened off a big, well-furnished room in which, by day, the house-party was wont to assemble. Black darkness filled this room; he felt his way forward knocking now into a chair, now into a table, and even as he advanced he could not help remarking upon the strangeness and unseemliness of this nocturnal incursion into the place where, in the daytime, his sisters and friends conversed and joked. When he was in the middle of the room he saw a strip of light beneath Gemma's door, and, although he was much agitated by the idea that she was awake as though waiting for him, he was guided by the light and so went forward more easily. When he reached her door he stopped for a moment, hesitating, then made up his mind and knocked. But, to his astonishment, it was not Gemma's voice but that of one of his sisters which called to him to come in.

Gemma was already in bed, sitting up on her pillow with her back against the wall and her thin arms lying on the coverlet. She was wearing a blue muslin nightdress adorned with little red roses: she looked languid and amorous as women often do when they are in bed. At her feet, still dressed in her day clothes, was Anna, Paolo's younger sister, a pretty, foolish girl a little over eighteen years old. She appeared to be in a state of pleasant distress, like one who is seized by doubts over a problem both joyful and flattering. "You've come just at the right moment," she exclaimed when she saw her brother.

Still agitated by surprise and by his own thoughts, the young man stammered an excuse and then enquired what had happened. "Gemma dear, you tell him," exclaimed Anna, not without a touch of affectation, throwing herself down on the bed and seizing her friend's hand; "you tell him . . . really I wouldn't know how to explain it. . . ."

Paolo turned towards Gemma. And she, with a characteristic, almost maternal, air, related how that day a young man, a guest at that moment in the villa, had asked the girl to be his wife. To this piece of news Gemma, as an expert with an inside knowledge of such matters, added a few of her own criticisms of the young man—who, according to her, had many good qualities; principally those of being rich and of very good family. But her friend shrugged her shoulders, for she felt that such qualities might interest Gemma who was poor and humble, but not herself. She answered nevertheless that the proposal was too sudden, and that, feeling herself unprepared for it, she could not make up her mind. Then Gemma started trying to persuade her with all the false and fulsome fervour that is typical of dependent persons when their superiors take them into their confidence over some controversial question that does not even remotely concern them. Filled with zeal and with a curious kind of sincerity, she warmed to her work, describing the joys of such a marriage, praising the young man and his family although she had scant knowledge of either the one or the other, and imploring Anna to think it over before she gave a definite refusal. So fervent and insistent was she that her friend interrupted her all of a sudden with a treacherousness which was not altogether unconscious. "Please don't get excited," she said; "of course these are matters that concern you up to a point . . . but to listen to you, anyone would think it was you who were going to get married, not me." It was a cruel remark, all the more so because a few minutes earlier she herself had implored Gemma to give her her opinion. Gemma, who was not prepared for it and who had thrust herself forward too much with her unguarded, servile enthusiasm, showed, by the manner in which she blushed and fell silent for a moment and by her bitter, disconcerted expression, that she was wounded. "That has nothing to do with it," she at last replied, trying to hide her disappointment under a self-possessed vivacity; "I was just talking. . . . But you asked me what I thought . . . and I'm telling you what I should do in your place."

This remark, the most sincere of the whole conversation, suddenly opened the young man's eyes. It was clear, he thought, that all this enthusiasm came from the fact that Gemma, in giving advice to her friend, really did see herself, as she had asserted, in the other girl's place. However, whether she was conscious of it or not, a yet further substitution was in process; in the place of Anna's suitor she was putting *him*, Paolo. In what she had so far said she had been alluding to *him* and to herself; it was of *their* marriage that she had been pointing out the advantages and the charms, not of the marriage of Anna and the other young man. And so he knew now what she thought and it was up to him to decide.

49

These thoughts completely restored to him the feeling of reality which confused passion had caused him to lose. Suddenly he was deeply ashamed of the desires and intentions which had driven him to enter Gemma's bedroom. Now he saw again, with perfect clearness, as he had always seen her, the defenceless, unfortunate girl at the mercy of himself or of anybody else who wanted to take advantage of her weakness, and he swore to himself that from that very day he would stop paying even the innocent court to her that he had paid hitherto. He was strengthened in this decision by the thought that, in two days' time, Gemma would have left the villa. The following year he would spend the summer elsewhere, or at any rate would remain on the cool, evasive terms of their former relationship.

In the meantime the conversation ᴠ ent on, with Anna doubtful and Gemma enthusiastic and ₁ersuasive. From time to time during the discussion Gemma threw him bold glances, or asked him his opinion, seeking to draw him into it. But he avoided speaking and turned away his eyes from any encounter with hers. Finally he rose, said good night to the two girls and left the room.

.   .   .   .   .

Paolo had not been mistaken in his suppositions. Like a piece of very dry tinder which needs only a spark to set it alight, Gemma's imagination had required no more than a small amount of innocent courtship on the part of the young man to fire it with fantastic hopes. It can in truth be said that, from the day of their first meeting in the wood, she had lived only for him. It is no less true to say that it was a matter of ambition and vanity rather than of love; but Gemma happened to be at the age when feelings are never distinct but become confused, good and bad together, in a single, vigorous desire for life. And so the thought of Paolo could never be separated in her mind from the hope of soon escaping, by means of marriage, from her present state of poverty and inferiority. And she waited anxiously each day for the young man to declare his feelings and to make her the proposal she longed for so much and had so carefully pondered. This, in her, was a passionate desire, far, far stronger than that of her senses which were still timid and unawakened, and sometimes it took the form of a sort of obsession. Thus it came about that, in the evening, she would kneel before the holy pictures and pray for the success of her plans, or again, after lunch, at the most stifling moment of the day, would lie hour after hour on her bed indulging in wild fancies and planning in detail the life she would live after this inevitable, infallible marriage had taken place. She saw herself in a fine house, in a big city, surrounded by friends, invited everywhere, rich, well known, high above the level of ordinary people. They were simple and foolish dreams, but, nourished by a whole life of hardship, humiliation and envy, they presented themselves to her imagination with extraordinary violence, hallucinating and minutely detailed like visions of an ideal world. Meanwhile, without realizing it, spurred on by impatience and ambition, she was gradually becoming corrupted in a perfectly natural and naïve manner. As she waited each day for the declaration which did not come, and as moreover the end of her visit was drawing near, she began to wonder whether it would not be opportune to over-step the limits of honest coquettishness and provoke the young man with some more compromising form of flattery. There could be no doubt that Paolo was in love with her. Ought she to encourage his feeling by giving herself to him, or ought she to refuse? Here lay the whole problem: whether, by giving herself to him, she would succeed in making him marry her. Thus, unconsciously, drawn on by passion, she became cal-culating and self-seeking and began to look upon her own attractions as a useful instrument, to be used cold-bloodedly whenever she felt the need to do so.

In the midst of these doubts came the surprise of Paolo's

nocturnal visit, a transparent fact of whose significance there could be no possible doubt. The young man, she reflected, was seriously in love, and if his sister had not been there, she could, that night, with a little cleverness and a touch of the pathetic and without conceding much, have extorted all the promises from him that she wanted. This thought filled her with joy and at the same time with annoyance. All because of that silly Anna she had lost, perhaps for ever, a most precious opportunity. For a long time after her friend had left her she lay meditating upon what was to be done. Now she cursed her bad luck, now she wondered whether the best thing would be for her, in turn, to go and knock at Paolo's door, now she hoped that the young man would come back of his own accord and listened carefully in the expectation of hearing him moving across the drawing-room. Of one thing, however, she was sure: she held him now in the hollow of her hand, and nothing need be done but leave it to time. This thought in the end persuaded her to make no move but to be content, for that night, with the victory she had partly won. And so, almost comforted, she fell asleep.

But next day, after rising with her head full of intentions and hopes, she discovered, to her disappointment, that the young man had left for Rome—because of his university examinations, said his two sisters. She waited anxiously during the two days still left to her at the villa, and then for another two, for which, under some pretext, she managed to remain. On the third day she received a postcard with greetings. On the fourth day she realized that he would not come back that year at all, and resigned herself to leaving.

Summer was now over, everyone was leaving the villa, and she was taken home in a car by two young men who were passing on their way to Rome. It was a gay journey and Gemma and her two companions did nothing but laugh and joke the whole time. But the latter did so with greater sincerity than Gemma, who was going home with extreme unwillingness and whose laughter did not express true gaiety so much as an attempt to stupefy herself and forget her own troubles. The hills that Gemma knew so well became at last visible on the horizon at the edge of the vast plain, and then, on the top of the farthest distant of these same hills, the town with its towers and roofs and walls, dark and gleaming like steel armour in the ravaged brilliance of the autumn sky. At this sight she felt her heart sink, and, though she went on laughing and talking, she was conscious of a kind of gloomy presentiment. It was as if those towers, those steely façades, those distant windows which caught fire every now and then from the slanting rays of the setting sun had assumed, for her, a face of terror, threatening her with the saddest winter of her life.

"Oh, why don't we go on, why don't we go right on to Rome?" she asked pathetically, all of a sudden. To which the young man who was driving the car answered, not very respectfully, that if she would put up with living in his house he would take her there at once. Gemma blushed, threatened jokingly to take him at his word, and he, hurting her pride, tried to make her understand that he was speaking seriously and was ready, if she would accept his suggestion, to put it into effect. Between banter and provocation of this kind, they reached the town when it was already dark. They parted in the cathedral square, Gemma to go home and the other two to continue on their way to Rome.

· · · · ·

These homecomings had always been extremely melancholy. After the spaciousness and comfort of the villa, the little house in the lane, with its narrow, steep stairs and its small, countrified rooms, gave Gemma so acute a sense of decay and wretchedness that almost always, after coldly embracing her mother, she would go and shut herself up in the bathroom (the only room where the door could be locked), and there, in that evil-smelling corner, gazing dreamily out of the little window at the sun-filled gardens, would weep at her ease for a few minutes. This outburst relieved her, and she would then wash her tear-reddened eyes with cold water and go back to her mother. But the latter, through having the same passions as her daughter, seemed to guess intuitively at the bitterness of these returns. And although she loved her much and had much desired to see her again, she never gave Gemma the festive welcome that might have irritated her. On the contrary, she was even colder and more evasive than her daughter. She asked a few questions about Gemma's journey and her visit; then, without more ado, went back to the kitchen or to her sewing.

But this year the usual bitterness was mitigated by a tender hope. It was indeed true that she was returning to a poverty-stricken home after the comforts of the summer. But this time it was not for long. So full was her mind of this certainty and so long had she delayed speaking of it, that she forgot to assume the contemptuous, ritual ill-humour with which in years past, as soon as she crossed the threshold of her home, she had brought her summer season to an end. It was with a most unusual expansiveness that she ran to embrace her mother. The latter, encouraged by these caresses, remarked timidly that her cheeks were rosier and her eyes brighter than when she went away. "There's a reason for that," replied Gemma. At these words the eyes of the two women met; they understood each other and started embracing all over again.

Later, when Gemma had unpacked her suitcases, they went into the dining-room, sat down at the table in the middle, and the mother put the expected questions to her daughter: who was it? how had it happened? Without at first mentioning Paolo's name, Gemma gave an account, in full detail, of her good fortune. And she concluded it by declaring herself absolutely certain of the marriage which, according to her, would have been arranged already if, on the night when the young man came and knocked at her door, her friend had not happened to be in her room. Her mother did not look altogether convinced but, seeing Gemma so infatuated, did not wish to disappoint her and said nothing except to ask, again, the name of the young man. "Guess," answered Gemma joyfully. Her mother began asking questions and making suggestions, and Gemma—as in the game when someone is searching for a hidden object and you say "hot" or "cold" according to whether the searcher is coming nearer or going further away from the object—kept on telling her whether she was wrong or getting near the truth. However, in spite of the information given her and in spite of the names she suggested, she could not bring herself to make the correct guess; in fact, she appeared to be making an oddly determined effort to exclude Paolo from the field of research. "But is it really possible you can't understand?" Gemma at last exclaimed impatiently; "it's really so simple. . . . He's the first person you ought to have named . . . there's no need to go looking so far afield." "Who is it, then?" "Why Paolo, of course; why on earth didn't you think of him at once?"

She was expecting words of congratulation or at any rate further questions, but instead, she saw that her mother was struck dumb and was looking at her with a bemused expression and eyes in which the laughing, youthful glance of her happier moments had yielded place to a kind of senile uneasiness. "Why d'you look at me like that?" enquired Gemma, surprised at this extraordinary behaviour. "Aren't you pleased?" "No, no," replied her mother slowly, in a low voice, "if what you say is true I'm happy." But her tone was not the tone of happiness, thought Gemma, indeed it was quite the opposite. Her mother blinked her eyelids, shook her head, bit her lips, and twisted her handkerchief round and round by its four corners with fingers that trembled slightly. Finally, with a timid, furtive, frightened curiosity, as though she were afraid of the answer, she asked what sort of relations she had had with the young man. "Ah, that's why she looks so doubtful," thought Gemma; and she hastened to reassure her mother: between herself and Paolo there had been nothing more than conversation, she needn't worry, she had not compromised herself. These assurances did not appear to have much effect upon the widow, who sighed and gazed once more, lingeringly, at her daughter: she kept her hands in her lap and never for one moment stopped turning her handkerchief round and round, and her plump white face was quite overshadowed by an unhappy expression for which Gemma, in her bewilderment, could not succeed in finding a name: sadness, distress, fear, shame, pity—none of these seemed exactly to fit the feeling that oppressed her mother. It brought to mind, more than anything, the kind of deathly sadness a man might feel who, finding himself faced with an incurable invalid who was unconscious of his own state, has not the heart to tell him of his true situation. But this impression did not last long, for her mother, almost at once, roused herself and declared, in a somewhat forced tone of voice, that, if Gemma was pleased, she asked nothing more. Much surprised, her daughter asked her why she talked like that. The mother answered that she was not altogether sure that the young man's intentions were serious: he seemed to her to be a frivolous character, and Gemma must keep a careful eye on the way he behaved. Gemma retorted with some heat that Paolo's honesty could not possibly be called in question. But her mother would not be persuaded; there seemed to be in her a clear and deliberate intention to discredit this marriage and to prepare Gemma for a disillusionment. And during the whole of that day and those that followed it, each time Gemma started trying to speak about Paolo, she never missed the opportunity of insinuating some sort of doubt into her mind or murmuring some suspicion. Gemma, however, paid no attention to her and clung more tightly than ever to her hopes: her mother, she thought, was full of maternal love, and perhaps she had had some disappointment or other in her youth and feared that the same thing might happen to her.

. . . . .

That winter was a hard one for the two women. Apart from the uneasiness in their relationship caused by discussion of Gemma's marriage, they had to endure a poverty greater than before. Of the three rooms which they had, they were successful, that year, in letting only one: Gemma had to give up the idea of buying some clothes that she needed and her mother restricted herself in every possible way in the household expenses. To these occasions for gloom was added yet another one, more tiresome, perhaps, than gloomy: the one and only lodger they had, a young professor of physics called Vagnuzzi, fell in love with Gemma. This Vagnuzzi was a small, precise man, thin, timid, full of ill-repressed nervousness, meticulous, correct, pedantic. He knew nothing and took no interest in anything outside his work, about which he talked continually, to the accompaniment of little giggles, professional witticisms, contortions and other obvious marks of self-satisfaction and delight. Although young, he was already bald and yellow and dried up like an old man. But behind his thick lenses there sparkled and winked two little eyes of fanatical fixity and intensity. Amongst his colleagues at the university, and elsewhere amongst people who understood these things, he was considered not merely promising but already a master; but Gemma, who did not know this—nor, if she had known it, would she have given it any importance—regarded him as a poor creature, innocuous, unbalanced and rather silly. She had, for things of the intellect, a complete and natural contempt which derived, not only from ignorance, but from a particular concept of human values in which she believed passionately and blindly. According to this concept Vagnuzzi, as a professor and a man of modest origins, was on the lowest rung of the social ladder. At the top of it she placed the aristocratic, wealthy, idle young men whom she met during the summer at the villa.

Vagnuzzi, then, fell in love with Gemma, and, like the in-experienced, solitary man that he was, began paying court to her in the clumsiest and most ridiculous way possible, with cunning little tricks and gallantries and other attentions of a truly pedantic and professorial kind. Usually this happened during meals, or, more rarely, in the evenings, if Gemma, in order not to retire to bed too early, resigned herself, for want of anything better, to the company of her awkward suitor. The dining-room was small, long and narrow, with a ceiling which sloped down from roughly whitewashed beams and an enor-mous table which encumbered the whole place. Formerly, as many as five lodgers had sat at this table, two of whom did not sleep in the house; but that winter nobody took their meals there except Gemma and Vagnuzzi. Gemma's mother did not count, for she was continually getting up to serve the food or clear away the dishes. Gemma ate little, and with reluctance; she scarcely opened her mouth and for the most part fixed her eyes dreamily upon the lamp which hung down from the ceiling over the table—a cord upon which the flies perched, a lampshade of enamelled iron that looked like a wash-basin, a big brass counter-weight. Vagnuzzi, on the contrary, poured himself out in a flood of eager, crackling conversation: he related little bits of gossip from the university, speaking with great satisfaction, with winks and hand-rubbings, of his labora-tory researches, and even going so far as to risk a few extremely foolish witticisms, of the kind that become rooted in university lecture-rooms together with the desks and the inkpots and the blackboards; and the professors repeat them every year in order to enliven the teaching of the more serious and difficult subjects. Anyone but Gemma would have divined the qualities of Vagnuzzi, who was a good man and had an intelligence of the acutest kind; and, understanding that this silly conversation was a result of his timidity and inexperience, would have brought him round to subjects that were more familiar. But Gemma, all taken up as she was with dreams of grandeur and vanity, saw in him nothing but a tiresome, indiscreet lodger whom she was compelled to put up with in order to make money out of him. And very angry and exasperated she was at having to talk and listen to him—to such an extent that this general dislike of him was often transformed into a positive hatred. Thus these meals in the little room with the big table, with her mother moving slowly and silently carrying dishes from the dining-room to the kitchen and from the kitchen to the dining-room and the presumptuous Vagnuzzi pursuing her with his attentions, became, for Gemma, a torment. They were in the midst of an extremely bad winter: whenever it was not raining, whenever you did not hear the greedy, hurried gurglings of the drainpipes and the infinite rustling of the rain, the black wind from the rain-soaked mountains would sweep down into the lane, twisting high up in whirling, excruciating spirals, or hurling itself downwards suddenly in heavy gusts like wet sheets which made the window-bars clank and the doors creak even inside the house. Gemma listened to these stormy sounds, to the furtive rattling made by her mother washing up in the kitchen, to the hesitant, nervous voice of Vagnuzzi, constantly interrupted by hiccoughs and giggles; and it seemed to her that all these noises were remote and unreal, like those of a far-off world from which she was separated by a zone of solemn, impenetrable silence. She herself was sitting in the midst of this silence like an image upon an altar, an image that is unmindful of prayers and footsteps and whisperings and that gazes far away into the sky. The sky, for her, was the summer villa, with its comforts and its gay parties. Let Vagnuzzi go on talking, let the wind blow and the rain murmur, let the plates and dishes slip from her mother's hand into the sink, her soul could still take refuge in the world of her dreams, leaving here below nothing but a semblance of herself, her physical presence, motionless, empty, dumb.

And so, in this dismal way, the winter passed. But some time during March a letter arrived for Gemma from Paolo. It had so happened that the young man, pursuing his course of studies in Rome, had remembered Gemma and how much he had been attracted by her. And, just as passion had driven him to knock, that night, at the girl's door, so now, bitten by the memory of it, he had not resisted the temptation to re-establish their old relationship. It was perhaps with the unconfessed hope of preparing her for their meeting in the summer that he did this. The letter began with a number of apologies, it went on to recall their walks together, and towards the end there were unmistakable phrases of longing and desire. Great was the satisfaction of Gemma, who at once answered with a letter twice as long. The young man wrote again, and so there began a correspondence in which—possibly because of the distance between them—they both laid aside the discretion they had observed on their walks and spoke with greater freedom and confidence. So great was Gemma's delight that she imagined herself to be in love; she kept the letters among her most intimate garments, at the bottom of a drawer; when they arrived, she kissed them. Paolo's letters were full of feeling; what with boredom, and loneliness, and his university studies, he was beginning really to love Gemma. But Gemma, in her letters, spoke of nothing but herself and her own life. She described the narrowness, the dreariness, the tedium of the provincial town; she expressed her longing for a change in her life and surroundings; she opened her heart and confided in him with a confused, agonized abandonment that was full of artful candour and involuntary astuteness. Into these letters she put a little of everything—phrases she had heard at the cinema or read in novels, scraps of party conversation, reflections that she had culled even from lesson-books, the only ones she had ever read seriously, and a hundred other second-hand things which were not her own and which she had neither thought nor felt but which intoxicated her to the point of tears.

Her letters were insincere from the first to the last word, but they were written in a flowing style and with the wicked perfection that comes naturally to a certain kind of long-cherished falseness; to Paolo, more ignorant than she, they appeared extremely beautiful; he might have found fault with them for being, if anything, too refined, sometimes, too literary. As for Gemma, after filling eight or ten pages with imaginary, conventional confidences, she would feel as much relieved as if she had cast off a load of secret and intolerable suffering. This illusion had an effect even upon her external appearance. She looked less contemptuous and arrogant; a calm self-confidence took the place of her former frenzied apathy; it was observed by many in the town that she had grown handsomer. And, particularly, by Vagnuzzi, who ended by losing his head completely. One evening at table he seemed even stranger and more nervous than usual. He laughed for no reason at all, he rubbed his hands together and muttered just as if he had been alone, and every now and then he boldly fixed his sharp, sparkling eyes upon Gemma. As soon as dinner was over, he bent forward towards the widow and, seizing her violently by the arm, whispered in a fierce kind of way that he must speak to her alone. But not so quietly that Gemma did not hear. She guessed immediately what was about to happen, and, extremely angry, with an expression of haughtiness and scorn on her face, pushed back her chair, rose, and left the room. Vagnuzzi, however, not understanding, attributed her departure to the shyness of a reserved girl, and, instead of feeling offended, was flattered by it. "What is it, then?" began Gemma's mother, as soon as her daughter had disappeared.

"Signora, Signora," Vagnuzzi started repeating as he twisted about on his chair, his two hands between his legs, "there are certain things it's very difficult to talk about . . ."

"Yes, indeed!" said the widow, who had already grasped the situation. "Perhaps you're not satisfied with your treatment here?" she added calmly, giving her ball of wool a jerk and starting, without more ado, to ply her knitting-needles.

"Please, please," protested Vagnuzzi, as though seized with horror, "I'm extremely comfortable here. . . . I've never had such excellent food. . . . Please, please . . ."

"Or is it that you don't like the room? . . . You want to change your room?"

"No, no, no. . . ." Vagnuzzi, frenzied, exhausted, horrified, put his hands up to his head. "No . . . no. . . ."

"Well, then," went on the widow, enjoying herself, "you must be going to tell me that you're on the point of leaving. . . . Gemma and I would be very sorry . . . we'd got used to you. . . ."

"No, no, no," interrupted Vagnuzzi, imploring and almost prostrate; "no, Signora. . . . This is a joyful, a joyful thing . . . for me, anyhow. . . ."

"I'm glad to hear that," said the widow without raising her eyes from her work; "so much the better, then. . . . And now you must pull yourself together and tell me . . ."

Vagnuzzi gave a nervous laugh. "Ah, if it was just a question of pulling myself together!" he exclaimed; and in his irresolution, incapable of sitting still, he looked as if he were trembling with fever. Then, all at once, he made up his mind and, seizing the widow's arm with his hard, bony fingers, "What would you say?" he whispered, "what would you say if I asked you for your daughter's hand? Would you refuse, eh? Would you laugh in my face?"

The widow put down her work and, pulling back her head a little, looked at the anxious, bowed head of the young man. "I shouldn't say anything," she replied calmly. "You will have to hear what my daughter says."

The passage from the conditional of "I shouldn't say" to the future of "you will have" filled Vagnuzzi with joy. "And so," he insisted, "you have nothing against it, and are ready to speak to your daughter about it. . . ?"

"Yes, why not?"

"Now, at once?"

"Yes, now at once."

Agitated but pleased, Vagnuzzi rose to his feet and went right round the table, hopping and rubbing his hands together. "Signora, Signora," he said then, "perhaps you won't believe me but I am in a state of anxiety which makes me feel feverish ... taking a wife is not a thing that happens every day, is it?"— and as he said this he gave a foolish little nervous laugh—"I am conscious that I am taking a very serious step. . . . I had never thought of starting a family . . . this has all happened so very suddenly. . . . Can you see me as a husband, as the father of a family?" He laughed again and stood still, looking at the widow. "Can you see me? The mere thought of it makes me laugh. . . . And your girl, what will she say, what will she say?"

"Don't worry," said the widow, gazing at him and appearing to be deep in thought; "my girl will say either yes or no. . . ."

The young man made a kind of leap into the air, accompanied by a burst of strange, convulsive laughter. "Yes, of course—yes or no . . . two little words: yes or no . . . for her it's quite simple: yes or no. . . . But what if she were to say: 'yo'?"

This witticism on the part of the poor wretch failed to bring a smile to the face of Signora Foresi, who remained serious and perplexed. "But in the meantime, Professor," she replied, "I don't know anything about you, about your family, about your situation. . . . Now come and sit down beside me here and tell me a few things. . . ."

Vagnuzzi rushed forward. "Forgive me, forgive me, dearest Signora Foresi, please forgive me"; and, sitting down opposite the widow, he proceeded to supply the information for which he had been asked. And thus the widow came to know that Vagnuzzi, an orphan and an only son, was in comfortable circumstances if not exactly rich, since he owned some houses in Rome which produced a good income. With regard to his profession, Vagnuzzi launched out into an extremely long and complicated story about hostile university intrigues over which he would triumph shortly, thanks to the publication, soon to take place with resounding effect, of a book upon which he had been working for years. In fact he carried his pedantry so far as to run off to his bedroom and bring back a bundle of printer's proofs full of numbers and theorems and scientific figures. His was a book, he asserted, without a sign of modesty but also without vanity, and with the certainty and simplicity of a self-evident truth, which was destined to cause a revolution in the already uneasy and highly competitive field of modern physics. And which would ensure his obtaining, not only a number of honours, but also the professorial chair at the University of Rome. All these remarks were made to the accompaniment of the nervous, clumsy mannerisms that Vagnuzzi was never able to shed, even when, as now, a calm, serious tone, of the kind to inspire confidence, was clearly required. But even though she was quite incapable of understanding the young physicist's university embarrassments, and, even less, of appreciating the value of the proofs he was waving in front of her, Signora Foresi nevertheless divined that beneath all these oddities and nervous tricks were real, solid facts, far more important, probably, than anything the young man's extravagant self-consciousness would allow to appear. So that, while Vagnuzzi struggled and sweated, as though he despaired of convincing her of his own worth, the widow was already fully convinced that in that respect there was much more than she had dared to hope.

There remained, however, the fact that Vagnuzzi, apart from being of mediocre and not very youthful appearance, did not form part of the noble and illustrious world towards which she herself and her daughter had all their lives aspired. This was inconvenient, indeed extremely serious, and, in face of it, all her good sense as an elderly, experienced woman vanished. It seemed to her little less than insuperable.

Yet, notwithstanding this rooted, ambitious folly, the widow was wise enough to realize that, in their situation, Vagnuzzi's proposal was not at all to be despised. Hitherto, the only candidates for Gemma's hand had been a few coarse, middle-aged merchants and shopkeepers in the town who had thought it would be a good plan to install a poor but well-brought-up girl in the house who, at little cost and with few pretences, would raise them in the scant, malevolent esteem of their fellow-citizens. Even a blind man could see that, in comparison with them, Vagnuzzi, with all his oddities and the mediocrity of his personal appearance, was a far better match. Signora Foresi therefore answered with words which were evasive and careful and which, without promising anything, at the same time did not reject anything. She concluded by advising Vagnuzzi to go to bed: in the meantime she would speak to her daughter, and next day an answer of some kind would certainly be given him.

After many prayers and exhortations Vagnuzzi departed, and the widow remained sitting for some time at the head of the deserted table, deep in reflection, her hands in her lap and her eyes fixed upon the light of the lamp. She thought of her own life, now finished, of her daughter's life scarcely begun; but she was not repenting of her own errors which were now displayed in an entirely new and significant light, nor yet was she preparing to prevent her daughter from committing other, similar errors; it was rather that she was deploring, disconsolately, the failure of her foolish, vainglorious hopes. She had never repented of her errors, in fact she had always clung to them as the one and only reason she had for living. And just as once her greatest regret had been that she had lost the possibility of committing errors, so now her greatest bitterness lay in the discovery that perhaps her daughter too would have to renounce them. This discovery filled her with a profound, stupefied, positively painful sense of desolation and impotence. It was as though she were faced by some flagrant, incomprehensible piece of injustice, such as gives the lie to the most hard-tried virtues and makes a man think he has lived and struggled in vain. In the same way as others might pray for their offspring to attain military or political honours, so had the widow always lived and adapted herself and made sacrifices in the determined hope of seeing her daughter turn into a society lady, venal and vain, immensely corrupt and selfish. The idea that this hope was not going to be realized, and that in the end Gemma would have to resign herself to marrying Vagnuzzi or someone of that kind, filled her with consternation. She almost felt the need to ask forgiveness of her daughter, whom she had brought up with quite different promises and patterns. And for the first time in her life she thought of death with particular bitterness. She thought of it as blind, lost spirits think of it, seeing in it the last and darkest of their well-deserved misfortunes.

Finally she rose, put out the light and went to see Gemma in her room. The girl was already in bed, and her mother sat down at the foot of the bed and told her of Vagnuzzi's proposal. Motionless, examining her finger-nails with a cold, disgusted expression on her face, Gemma listened to her mother without saying a word. "He's mad," she then said with assurance; "rather than marry him I'd become a nun." Her mother looked at her for some time without opening her mouth. She was troubled; she could not help sharing Gemma's contempt, but at the same time it seemed to her that the proposal should not be entirely turned down. Then she tried to point out to her daughter that Vagnuzzi was a rich man. Gemma shrugged her shoulders in scorn. "A silly, ungainly creature like that," she said, "I wouldn't marry him even if he was *covered* with gold." Her tone was calm, with no spitefulness in it, and it was clear that for Gemma the problem admitted of no possible doubt, that she had made up her mind even without talking about it. This calm was far more disconcerting to her mother than violent rebellion. Cautiously she tried to suggest that Gemma ought to show some regard for Vagnuzzi: after all, at that moment, this was the only match that offered. But Gemma smiled scornfully. "As far as matches go, I've a better one," she replied, "a far better one"; and with a simple, disdainful gesture she took four or five of Paolo's letters from the drawer of the night-table and threw them down on the bed in front of her mother. The latter, who knew nothing of the correspondence between the two young people, was turned to stone. She did not dare touch the letters; she could hardly bear even to look at them. At last, with an energy which, in her, was strange and new, since generally she was almost completely submissive to her daughter's will, she again started insisting that Vagnuzzi must not be given a negative answer. What did it cost Gemma to say that she wanted to think it over? Nothing; and in the meantime she would still have Vagnuzzi within reach, like a dish being kept hot. "Do just as you like," was all Gemma would answer; she was anxious to display the most complete indifference to her unfortunate suitor. Now she had taken up the letters again and was re-reading them here and there with fatuous, ostentatious concentration. The widow stayed a little longer, staring at her daughter as she read her letters; then, with a sigh, she rose and, saying good night to Gemma who scarcely answered her, left the room.

Next day Vagnuzzi came tremblingly to ask for the reply that had been promised him. According to her agreement with Gemma, the widow kept to general terms: her daughter wished to think it over, she explained, and though she thanked him she begged him, for the moment, to wait. Vagnuzzi, who had been fearing a refusal, agreed fervently. Let them think it over at their leisure, let them think it over as much as they wished, he understood perfectly well that in such a delicate matter prudence and reflection could never be excessive. Then the widow, in order to avoid effusions which might have aroused a dangerous frankness in Gemma, advised him not to speak to her daughter about the proposal, not even to hint at it: let him leave it to time; things must not be forced; one of these days, as soon as Gemma had grown accustomed to the idea of becoming his wife, he would have the answer he desired.

Vagnuzzi praised and approved this advice, too, with his usual fussy enthusiasm. In fact, he carried his zeal to such a point that he adopted with Gemma a respectful reserve which bordered on coldness. But later, as soon as the girl had gone out, he spared no pains to recommend himself and to implore the widow's assistance. As for her, she flattered him a little, and deceived him a little, in such a way as to keep him—exactly as she had said to her daughter—always in readiness and always within reach, on the slow fire of ill-disguised impatience and repressed hopes. And so, with manœuvre and subterfuge, the winter passed at the house in the lane.

.   .   .   .   .

After March, still wintry on those heights, had departed, after a rainy April, at last came May with fine weather. The wind, which never ceased, at any season, to blow round the walls of the town, grew warmer, lost its icy, cutting sharpness, became abundant and capricious, chasing great white, buoyant clouds across the sky, swelling out the curtains at wide-open windows, no longer howling and lamenting but uttering low, long, sleepy, whistling sounds, as though tired, as though overcome by the languor of the new season. This was one of the best periods in Gemma's life. Every day, in the mornings towards noon, in the evenings at the hour when people go for a stroll, she would go to the extreme end of the town, to a belvedere whence the eye could embrace the whole of the immense plain as far as the blue mountains that rimmed the horizon; there she would gaze at the vast landscape and especially at that part of it in which she knew her friends' villa nestled. Away down here, in a fold of the hilly ground, lay the grove of oak-trees where she had met Paolo; that grey, orderly pullulation of olives on the rounded slopes concealed the lanes through which they had so often walked together. She leant her hands on the balustrade and, so as not to be noticed by the friends who stood beside her, pretended to be examining some detail of the landscape—the white smoke of a train moving along behind rows of elms, the changing shapes of the clouds, a motor-lorry that came clanking up the road that ran round the walls of the town. But, irresistibly, her eyes sought the place where the villa lay. In a month's time, she thought, the course of my life will be decided; in fact, after languishing so long, I shall at last begin to live. It seemed to her that good fortune, like the sky and the sunshine and the lovely cultivated plain, was smiling upon her and caressing her; and she had a feeling as of an injustice committed in her favour, a feeling at the same time delicious and incredulous. During that time she enjoyed, for the first time, many things which her vain and discontented mind had hitherto prevented her not merely from appreciating, but even from seeing: the beauties of nature, certain sensual or gluttonous pleasures of everyday existence which previously had been unknown to her. Softened by the hope of happier days, the graceless, foolish austerity which is a necessary part of ambition yielded place to an attitude of mind more open to joyful and pleasing impressions. In reality she was living, for the first time, naturally, with no helpless longings, no calculating subtleties, no lies.

But one day towards the end of the month, when she returned home after her accustomed evening walk, she found her mother wandering from one room to another in a state of agitation and perplexity. A sheet of paper and a torn envelope were sticking out of her apron pocket, and as soon as she saw her daughter she beckoned to her to follow her. They went into Gemma's bedroom, where the widow, after making her daughter sit down on the bed, took her hands in hers and gazed at her for a long moment in silence with a kind of sorrowful compassion. "Gemma, my dear," she said at last, "you must prepare yourself to hear some bad news."

At these words, the girl's heart started beating faster; she thought of Paolo and, white in the face, felt herself almost fainting. "What is it?" she asked instantly.

Her mother mentioned the name of the owner of the villa. "He has written to me," she began, "and he says he is very sorry but he is unable to invite you there this summer. . . . Of course," she added hastily, "you and Anna and Luisa will go on seeing each other . . . but not at the villa."

"What?" Gemma could not help exclaiming. "It's not only just for this year but for future years as well?"

"Yes, he says it will be better for everybody for you not to go there any more. . . ."

The widow expected to see her daughter weaken and burst into tears beneath the weight of this blow. A mournful, resigned grief was what she would have preferred, as better suiting her plans. But Gemma's character was not a weak one; the very intensity of her passion precluded tears and inclined her rather towards scorn and fury. She did not for long remain frozen in astonishment. All at once she tore herself from her mother's pitying hands and jumped to her feet. "I know what the reason for all this is," she cried angrily; "it's Paolo. . . . Tell me truthfully, it's because of Paolo that they don't want to see me at the villa again. . . ?"

"Yes, Gemma," her mother tried to speak soothingly, "it must be because of him. . . . But now, what's the good of getting angry? It doesn't help . . ."

But her daughter, enraged, would not let her finish. "He doesn't consider me worthy to become part of his family . . . to be his daughter-in-law. . . . Well, well, I've the misfortune to be called Foresi . . . and I'm not well-off either, into the bargain. . . . Because, if I were the daughter of some big business man from Milan, all these difficulties about birth would vanish as if by enchantment. . . . Neither rich nor aristocratic— that's my trouble, that's my crime. . . ." She gave free rein, as she spoke, to disappointed vanity and wounded pride, and as she spoke she walked up and down the room with excited steps on her long, slim legs. Every now and then she stopped, clenching her fists and tapping with her heels. Her mother, with a strange look of combined relief and pity, gazed at her silently from the bed where she sat. She hoped that anger would boil away in vain cries and impotent reproaches; but without any other consequences. "What can you do, Gemma?" she tried to say; "surely now . . ."

"Nothing at all," answered her daughter, stopping in front of her. "As for their villa, and their guests, and them too—I don't care the very least bit about them . . . but about Paolo I *do* care. . . . Let them do just what they like, but don't let them touch Paolo. . . . We're both of age, we can get married in spite of them and of everyone else who hates us. . . . Oh yes, indeed, that I swear to you. . . ."

"But, my poor darling Gemma," asked her mother, "what can you *do*?"

"What can I *do*?" Gemma was shouting now. "I can do the simplest thing in the world—write to Paolo to come here at once, tell him how things are . . . and he will see that I'm right. And after a fortnight at most we shall be married. . . ."

Her mother, suddenly, was frightened. In the letter, amongst other things, the young man's father made clear mention of his son's wish to make Gemma his wife. In fact he let it be understood that he had learned of the relationship between Paolo and Gemma only when it was already too late, when his son had come to inform him of his love for her and of his decision to get married. Being in love with Gemma, and seeing no other honest way of making her his except by marriage, the young man had resolved to marry her. Now Gemma's mother did not know that Gemma was still ignorant of this decision on his part and that she was speaking more from bravado than from knowledge of the facts; and she was desperately frightened at the thought that her daughter was really in a position to carry out her purpose. "Promise me," she said all of a sudden, "that you won't do anything and that you'll give up the idea of writing to him."

"No," said Gemma frankly, "I shouldn't dream of such a

thing. . . . What, to let *them* win? So as not to tarnish their highly illustrious name? To let myself be treated like a servant-girl? Why, I should be mad. . . . No, indeed, I shall write to him this very evening."

"What will you say?"

"I shall tell him to come at once because I want to speak to him."

For a moment they looked at each other in silence. Gemma's mother was shaking her head slightly, with a movement that was both sad and deprecating. Then she sighed: "Gemma dear," she begged, drawing the girl to her side, "come here and listen to me. . . . There are very serious reasons, quite different from the ones you are supposing, which make this marriage absolutely impossible . . . but, if you love me, you must refrain from asking me for them and must do as I tell you."

Her mother's grave tone of voice could not escape Gemma. But she was obstinate and, suspecting some kind of trap, had no intention of yielding in any way. "Personally," she replied, "I can't see any other reasons against it except the ones I've already mentioned. . . . And so I shall write to him. . . ."

Her mother went on to attempt—without much confidence —an appeal to filial feeling. "Gemma," she began, "you will make me very unhappy indeed . . ."

But her daughter interrupted her briskly. "I would rather," she answered, "make you, as you say, very unhappy indeed than act without knowing why."

"But there is a 'why'."

"Well, then, tell me."

Her mother was unable to make any objection to this demand; she hung her head and was silent. "Now you see, my dear Mother," resumed the girl, almost with pity, "you've allowed yourself to be intimidated. . . . But surely this is a case in which we must dig our heels in . . . and show we're just as good as they are."

Her mother, far from understanding what she was saying, did not seem even to be listening. She looked up at her and appeared to be hesitating. But Gemma's last words seemed to bring her to a decision. She lifted her head, and in her eyes was the impudent, laughing look of her most sincere moments. "Of course you're just as good as they are," she said brusquely, "because you have the same blood in you."

"What on earth d'you mean?" asked Gemma in astonishment.

"When I was a girl," replied her mother, who now—as though the forcing of her secret from her actually justified an immodesty that was anything but maternal—had upon her face an expression of confidential hilarity and vanity, "he"—and she mentioned the name of the owner of the villa—"and I had a love affair . . . and you, who were born before I got married, are his daughter . . . no more and no less than Anna and Luisa. . . . I never expected that Paolo would take it into his head to fall in love with you . . . otherwise I should have told you before. . . . So now you understand," concluded the widow without emotion, "why it is that this marriage is impossible."

Gemma's scornful air had vanished, but her astonishment remained. And so great was it that she doubted whether she had heard aright. "And so Paolo and I," she asked, "would be brother and sister?"

"Yes, that's it. . . ."

Like her mother who gave her this news without shame and without sadness, in fact with a sort of retrospective complacency, Gemma was entirely incapable of perceiving how much tragedy there was in this mistake which had led her to look upon a brother as a lover. Horror she might perhaps have felt if she had been truly in love, but, cold and ambitious, she had never cherished any feeling towards Paolo except that of vanity. She had always thought of him merely as an instrument; her empty social dreams now saved her from shuddering at a passion as deadly as it was impossible. Thus she did not notice the unseemliness of her mother's confidential, nostalgic tone,

nor did it enter her mind that this calamity was not a mere
matter of chance and that it had been she herself who had
provoked it with her calculating, ambitious coquetries. On the
contrary, once her first astonishment had vanished, she was
assailed by a strong sense of injustice, a stubborn, bitter regret.
She did not admit it to herself, but she almost regretted that
she had not learned the news of this unexpected relationship
after marriage; they would have parted, of course, but in the
eyes of the world she would have remained his wife, and that
was what mattered most. And so, where another would have
felt relief combined with terror at a danger incurred and nar-
rowly avoided, she saw nothing but social disaster: lost were
the villa, the friendships, the invitations, the parties, the comforts. Her eyes filled with tears; she made a sign to her mother,
who was seeking to console her, to be quiet, and, with bowed
head, her handkerchief over her face, wept for a long time.
Every now and then she heaved a deep sigh and felt as if the
diaphragm were being torn asunder in her breast, while fresh,
abundant tears rushed to her eyes. Anxieties, vanities, ambitions, desires, the whole tangled knot of things repressed and
things longed for during recent times, all were unloosed in
those tears, as an unhealthy sultriness is dissolved by a thunderstorm. At last she raised her head, showing eyes already dry
in her thin, flushed face. "Oh yes, I know, these are not pleasant things," said her mother, who had been waiting almost
impatiently for her weeping to stop, "but what is there to be
done about them, my dear Gemma . . . ? I too . . ." And she
would have gone on mingling expressions of comfort, of cold,
unfeeling common sense, with confidences about her long-
dead love affair if Gemma, more from a feeling of annoyance
than of dignity, had not interrupted her. "Don't let's talk about
it any more, Mother," she said; "never again." To her mother
this injunction was far from agreeable: for thirty years she had
awaited the blessed moment when at last she might recall,
aloud, after so long a silence, this favourite of her errors; and

74

now that this moment had come, she had to restrain herself and again keep silence. To whom, now, would she ever be able to speak of it, if even her own daughter refused to listen to her? And when? Truly, life was now no longer worth living. But, resigning herself afresh, she fell silent, in some confusion, and pretended to be rearranging something or other on the chest-of-drawers. "Well, well. . . . He loved me very much at that time . . . and he wanted to marry me but his family objected . . .", she could not help starting again after a moment. Gemma remained motionless and made no answer. "At any rate," continued her mother, emboldened by this silence, "you have absolutely nothing to be ashamed of. . . . You are of the same blood. . . . You would have a right to the name. . . ." Again there was no answer. "But you'll see, next year they'll invite you again," she insisted. This was too much for Gemma, who resented all these silly, indiscreet comments just as though they had been made in mockery. "Stop it!" she cried all of a sudden, jumping to her feet in a rage, "I told you not to talk about it. . . . Please be good enough to leave me alone." Confused, mortified, truly resigned, this time, to shutting herself up in a silence that must now be final, the widow embraced her daughter as she stood there stiff and impatient, and then hurriedly left the room.

.   .   .   .   .

Contrary to the popular saying, night brought extremely bad counsel to Gemma. For some time she could not get to sleep. She lay in the darkness with her eyes open and thought about the future. And from the future her thoughts now withdrew themselves with intense horror, like fingers from a cold, lifeless corpse. The ambitious spirit which hitherto had lent some of its own smiling and festive colour to those future days was now truly dead, for good and all; and, in face of the empty perspective of time Gemma—like one of those sick beings who feel their legs give way beneath them and fall in a faint at the

sight of an empty square or some other vast, deserted space—
felt no curiosity, no desire to rush forward, but rather a violent
shudder of disgust, a hysterical urge to turn and flee. To go
back; not to the more recent years, already unhappy in her
eyes, but to the remote years of childhood. To the years in
which there had not yet dawned upon her any consciousness of
herself or of the world. She knew herself to be beaten and,
understanding nothing of the disaster that had befallen her nor
of the forces that had brought it about, she also understood
nothing of her own life and would willingly have sacrified all
prospect of its continuance.

In this despairing state of mind she fell asleep, and in the same
state of mind she still found herself on the following day. Her
mother came in, as usual, in the morning, to awaken her.
"Come on, you must get up," she said softly, walking round
the darkened room; "there's Vagnuzzi waiting for you to go
out with him. . . ." Without moving, scarcely unclosing her
eyes on the pillow, Gemma recalled that it was Sunday and
that she had promised Vagnuzzi and a friend of his to go for an
excursion with them in the neighbourhood. The name of
Vagnuzzi reminded her confusedly of many other things, and,
there and then, like an invalid who wakes up and, feeling again
the pain of the evening before, quickly stretches out a hand for
the soothing potion that will plunge him back into sleep, she took,
without hesitation, an extreme decision. "Tell him," she pronounced in a slow, bitter voice, "that I am tired and that I won't
go on the excursion. And tell him also that I accept his proposal
and that I am ready to become his wife as soon as possible. . . ."

"What, what?" demanded her mother, almost frightened.

"Tell him that I am prepared to marry him," repeated
Gemma, closing her eyes again.

"But are you speaking seriously?"

"Yes, I'm speaking seriously," she answered with a sigh.
And then in a louder voice that was beginning to be angry:
"D'you understand?"

"Yes, yes, I'll go and tell him at once."

"That's right ... and now go away and let me sleep." Having uttered these words, she turned her face to the wall and very soon, weary as she was from having slept only a couple of hours, was fast asleep again.

It was midday when she awoke, and, remembering the command she had given to her mother, she was pleased at having taken such a decision almost without thinking, in a moment when she was half asleep: now she had no hope left, she no longer desired anything, Vagnuzzi was as good as another. With this idea firmly fixed in her mind, she was able to carry off very easily the first meeting with her betrothed. She found Vagnuzzi in the dining-room: as soon as he had heard the news from the widow, he had not merely given up the excursion but, sitting down at the table, had remained motionless for three hours with his eyes fixed upon Gemma's bedroom door. When he saw her appear, he rose to his feet and, taking off his glasses, asked her stammeringly whether it was true that she agreed to become his wife. For a moment, as though she were now noticing him for the first time, Gemma was terrified at seeing him standing there in front of her, so meagre and yellow and bald. So this, she could not help thinking, this was the man to whom she was going to tie herself for the whole of her life. But she at once overcame this aberration, and, assuming an expression of serenity which she was far from feeling, answered his question affirmatively. Vagnuzzi then started explaining in a confused fashion all the feelings that were inspired in him by so great a stroke of fortune: he was happy, he did not believe in his happiness, he knew he did not deserve it, it seemed to him unbelievable that the two of them would soon be united by the bond of marriage. Emotion, thrusting aside the usual superficial covering of nervousness and oddity, revealed in him a curiously old-fashioned, romantic world of feeling. It was as though he had never had anything at all to do with women, and had inherited, from some

77

extremely out-of-the-way family background, the ideas of another age, now grown stale and fallen into disuse. In spite of his education, Vagnuzzi had remained, as regards feelings, a century behind, if not more. He had the candid, unconscious ability to idealize and transfigure the beloved woman that peasants and simple people sometimes have. But Gemma, who had only the appearance of serenity and who, behind the mask she had assumed, continued to cherish the same contempt as before for the unfortunate man—a contempt now aggravated, into the bargain, by disappointment—Gemma saw nothing, was aware of nothing. For her, as before and more than before, Vagnuzzi remained a silly, absurd, contemptible creature, entirely devoid of all the qualities that would have been desirable. However, she listened to him, forcing her face to an expression of patient benevolence. Then she answered: "I prefer to tell the truth. I don't love you, at present anyhow. . . . But I feel that with time I shall come to be fond of you. And so it all depends on you." These words were nothing but lies: she did not love him, she had already made up her mind never to love him. But they had been uttered in a particular tone, full of frankness and goodwill, which made an extremely good impression upon Vagnuzzi. He thought, as so many other unfortunate lovers have always thought in similar circumstances, that time and kind attentiveness would be able to change tepid affection into ardent love. And he thanked her with excessive warmth, as if for an act of truly unhoped-for generosity. After a moment her mother came in, dressed to go out, with her hat on and the little fur round her neck. Insincere but cordial, she insisted on congratulating Vagnuzzi, who defended himself as best he could by pointing at Gemma. He was like an actor deprecating applause and indicating the author of the play. Finally the two women went off to Mass, leaving Vagnuzzi to enjoy his new happiness by himself.

Thenceforward, in her relations with her betrothed, Gemma maintained uninterruptedly this same serene bearing, devoid, it is true, of its original haughtiness but devoid also of all sign of affection. It was like a single true note which it was better to repeat indefinitely, rather than go out of tune. Vagnuzzi as a fiancé disgusted her even more—if that was possible—than as a lodger. His usual oddities and nervous tricks were now mingled with expressions of tenderness, with swoonings and sentimentalities which had the power to irritate Gemma beyond measure. Furthermore he had entirely given up going to the café in the evenings and stayed at home to act the lover with Gemma. And she, now that they were engaged, could no longer, as formerly, take refuge in her own room, leaving him alone with her mother. So the engaged pair sat upon an old, hard green sofa at the far end of the dining-room, while Gemma's mother, under the pretext of staying close to the lamp, placed herself at the opposite extremity of the table and sewed or read. Vagnuzzi would take Gemma's hand between his and, twisting right round on the sofa in a gallant but uncomfortable attitude, would discourse to her in a low voice. He spoke of their marriage, he described their future life, he gave her information on the subject of his tastes, of his ideas, of his wishes, he sought to get to know her and to make her know him. He made great efforts, in fact, to behave like a fiancé; nor did he realize that he succeeded only too well. Gemma, motionless, absent-minded, scarcely answered him, but when she did, it was without either harshness or impatience. Yet it very often happened that she felt herself inwardly boiling with rage and boredom and restlessness. Every now and then Vagnuzzi would kiss her respectfully on the forehead or the cheek; only once during the whole time of their betrothal was he so bold as to touch her lips. Gemma, resigned, let him do what he wanted: in a way, physical contacts disgusted her less than conversation. She derived the strength for her game of pretence and for her endurance of so much boredom from the hope that, once they were married, they would as soon as possible leave her native town, where she could no longer bear to remain, and go and settle in Rome. Putting aside the villa and its social splendours, she now consoled herself with the mirage of the capital. Like the ant which, when its nest collapses, immediately sets about building another, her industrious, tenacious imagination was already beginning to set up complicated and fantastic fabrications of success and unexpected fortune there.

These evenings were long. So very long were they that she learned the game of chess, for which Vagnuzzi had a passion, and tried alternating conversation with carefully thought-out, hard-fought games. But what happened was that she hated Vagnuzzi while they were playing even more than when talking to him. For she did not like losing, and the innocent delight of her fiancé, when he won, made her quiver with rage. At such moments she could not resist the temptation to fling some ill-natured remark at him, which he, failing to understand it and being also ignorant of all unkindness, mistook for harmless mockery. Another thing which filled her with uncontrollable anger was the incautious sarcasm to which Vagnuzzi, in his pedantic, professorial facetiousness, from time to time gave rein on the subject of smart high society. He had no notion of the firm and unshakeable contempt which Gemma felt for his profession and, in general, for any intellectual occupation; absorbed in his work, he had never experienced any envy or desire to form part of that world: merely he could not understand how people similar in appearance to himself and his colleagues could spend their whole lives dancing and gambling and flirting and, in fact, running after amusements and frivolities. Society people seemed to him affected, full of absurd preoccupations, fatuous, futile in their restlessness and in their crazes, altogether ridiculous. As he spoke of them, he could not help starting to laugh in his own characteristically nervous, awkward way. Or again, he would give vent to witticisms which almost always were not even original but were dug out of the comic papers that he devoured with so much avidity. Now to make a mock of the world she so passionately adored and yearned for was, to Gemma, worse than irritating, it was positively irreverent. Moreover, she had not yet given up the hope of making her way into it some day, even if it had to be under the mean, contemptible name of Vagnuzzi. Besides, by one of the paradoxes of vanity which can derive advantage from anything, even humiliation and defeat, the revelation made to her by her mother of her secret relationship to the family at the villa, instead of humbling her, had increased her pride. Even if she was an illegitimate daughter, she thought, at any rate she was not of plebian blood but of clear, traceable descent. If she had not felt a regard for her mother, she would willingly have proclaimed her origin publicly. And so her exclusion from a world to which it seemed to her that she belonged by right appeared all the more unjust. And all the more offensive appeared the gibes of the tactless Vagnuzzi.

The first time, she gave him to understand that jokes on this subject did not amuse her. The second time she remained silent, though with some difficulty. But the third time she did not try to control herself; she attacked Vagnuzzi with so violent an onslaught that even her mother, who shared her opinion and, on this disputed subject, considered her always to be in the right, was astonished. The principal motif of this onslaught, which recurred like loftily inspired notes in a symphony, was that the finger-nail of one of these persons against whom Vagnuzzi's gibes were directed was worth more than the whole of himself, including his science and his professorship. And that he talked like that out of envy and ill-concealed jealousy, because he knew that the gates of that world would always remain shut in his face and that it would never think him worth so much as a glance. In Vagnuzzi, who had never imagined that one could either desire or do anything in the world more interesting than studying and teaching physics, this scene aroused immense astonishment. But he had no time to attempt a protest or an explanation, for Gemma rose to her feet and left the room, banging the door behind her.

This was their only quarrel. And Gemma's mother brought them together again next day, not without difficulty. At the end of July, after an engagement which had lasted little more than a month, they were married almost furtively in a little country church in the neighbourhood. To her friends at the villa Gemma wrote a letter in which she apologized for not inviting them. But at the end, yielding to her old instinct for telling lies, she could not resist alluding to her husband as a very rich man. He had a big house in Rome, she said, where they would be going to live that winter. Then, after saying farewell to her mother, they left for their honeymoon in Venice.

.   .   .   .   .

With the same passion that she had once infused into her hope of becoming the wife of Paolo, Gemma clung to the idea of leaving her native town and going to settle in Rome. Her husband had promised her this—without, however, the absolute certainty with which she had written of it to the two sisters at the villa. But when they came back from their travels about the middle of September, he told her that, for the moment anyhow, he could not hope to be appointed to Rome. And that, in any case, it would be out of the question for them to move from the town that winter.

This disappointment, added to the many others that had preceded it, plunged Gemma back into the old raging, desperate boredom: was she then fated, even as a bride, just as before she was married, to pass her whole life in this town where everything, every street, every person reminded her only of the pinch of poverty, of humiliations and bitter disappointments? Had, then, her subjection of herself to marriage with Vagnuzzi served no purpose at all? These and other similar thoughts charged with rage and impatience came more and more to dominate her. And, like a badly stowed cargo which, in a high sea, rolls and shifts so much in the hold that finally it smashes up and sinks the ship, so these thoughts, shaking and stirring in an empty, idle mind like hers, ended by sending her astray altogether and preparing the way for evil designs.

They had now left Gemma's mother in her old abode in the lane and had gone to live in a new house outside the ramparts. This house, with its walls of rough grey stone, its red-tiled roof and green shutters, stood on a kind of rocky spur from which could be seen ravines and hills as far as the eye could reach, right to the distant mountainous horizon. It was a dark, wild landscape, with no farm buildings or cultivated fields, bristling endlessly with a low, malignant vegetation of short scrub. In the shooting season the sharp sound of gunfire echoed there; some small section or other of the scrub was always being burnt to make charcoal—a black, smoky patch amongst the yellow of the brushwood; otherwise there was no sign of life. In the direction of the town there were a few other houses exactly like theirs, scattered untidily among the rocks and crags; beyond them the view was blocked by the great, iron-grey walls which rose gloomily to the sky, following the bulges and re-entrants of the rocky hillside with a series of towers and buttresses. Since the town gate happened to be concealed by one of these towers, the walls, seen from the Vagnuzzis' house, looked quite solid and smooth and as if they had no opening in them; so that, on that spur of land, you had the impression of being entirely alone and cut off from the world. The house was brand new; inside, the doors of ill-seasoned wood creaked and still exuded resin; the rooms echoed with a kind of damp sonority like that of a grotto; there were still splashes of whitewash on the window-panes. There was a square piece of garden, but it was bare, with little soil and a great quantity of sharp, white pebbles upon which, in the hours of sunshine, the iron spikes of the surrounding fence gloomily cast their thin shadows. It seemed to Gemma, the first time she went there, that she was in the annexe of a hospital or a prison, and she said so to her husband. Vagnuzzi was astonished, for, being a great lover of nature and an enthusiast for panoramas, he had thought he would be giving his wife pleasure by taking a house like this, from which the eye could roam over half a province. But he had failed to notice the melancholy aspect of the walls and the monotony of the wild, woody landscape, all brown and misty at this season, with the white smoke-plumes of the charcoal-burners rising here and there. He stubbornly refused, however, to recognize these disadvantages, and the only thing he would do—repeating all the time that it was a beautiful house and in a splendid position—was to promise Gemma that, after the winter, if the transfer he hoped for had not come about, they would without fail go and live in the middle of the town. This disagreement about the house was their first divergence of opinion since marriage. And Gemma discovered, with scornful wonder, that beneath his silly, nervous exterior Vagnuzzi concealed a far stronger and more tyrannical character than she had previously imagined.

In that lonely house, while her husband was teaching or carrying out his experiments in the university laboratory, she was immensely bored. Of reading there was no question, for, apart from film magazines and detective stories, she had never had the slightest love for it. Her house did not interest her and she therefore left it entirely to servants, with the result that it remained just as dismal and bleak as the day she had first entered it. All those other occupations such as sewing, embroidery, playing the piano, to which she had been devoted as a child, now disgusted her, perhaps because they recalled that unpleasant period. As for the garden, she did not think it worth even looking at, so that it remained bare and stony, with only a few withered weeds here and there and the black, naked spikes of the railings which were truly reminiscent of a prison. All that was left was the care of her person and the few amusements the town provided. Gemma acquired the habit of rising from her bed about midday and devoting a good half of the afternoon to varnishing and filing her nails, curling her hair, and other such occupations. Then, with extreme slowness, she would dress in her best clothes, as though she were going to a festival, and betake herself with one of her women friends to walk up and down the Corso. There, in the crowd that filled the wide, badly-lit street, she would recognize and greet the usual people that she had been seeing for so many years. Sometimes she would also go and sit in the big room at the confectioner's shop, the meeting-place of local society: as she went in, the smart young men of the town would welcome her with some gallant remark and turn to look at her. Less often—not because she did not like it, but because the show was only changed once a week—she went to the cinema. This was located in the old town theatre—an enormous, gloomy hall with four rows of red and gilt boxes and a dome painted with frescoes. Originally this theatre had given only grand opera, then, at the beginning of the century, the decadence had begun: from opera it had passed to prose plays, then to operetta, then to variety, and finally to an occasional dramatic entertainment for charity. The cinema had saved it from finally closing down and at the same time had, in a way, consolidated and enshrined its decadence. The gilt was peeling off, showing the white plaster; the rosy nymphs painted inside the dome were mottled with large damp stains; the old red velvet seats had been replaced by iron chairs that lifted up and half-closed themselves with a hollow clang. There was always a stale smell of wet shoes, of cold tobacco-smoke, of damp sawdust. During the intervals the lights in the first row of boxes only were turned on, while the rest of the house remained plunged in a grey gloom, like a deserted circus, and the white screen hung on top of dark red velvet curtains was reminiscent, in that dim light, of some mournful funeral trapping. But upon Gemma, who had scarcely been outside her own town and who had the insensitiveness to squalor that is typical of provincials, this dreariness had little effect. Immense, on the contrary, was the effect upon her of the loud, ugly voices that echoed so strangely in the drowsy spaces of the theatre and of the enormous faces, dark and full of pores, whose lustrous lips came together on the screen in long, crackling, sultry kisses. She did not miss a single film, and, when she failed to find a companion, did not hesitate to go there alone.

Friendships are not made by chance but in accordance with our ruling passions; and during the remainder of that autumn Gemma formed a close tie with a Rumanian woman called Elvira Coceanu. In what manner, and after what adventures, this woman had happened to arrive in the little town, nobody could have said. It was stated on good authority that she was a countess and of extremely good family. But if anyone had taken the trouble to find out where this information came from, he would have discovered that it had been Elvira Coceanu herself who had put it about. The only certain thing that was known about her was that, a couple of years before, she had come to settle in the town, where, thanks to her foreign name which gave her a kind of distinction, thanks to the reports which she had so carefully spread, and thanks, above all, to an extraordinary, an insolent enterprise, she had succeeded in a short time in getting herself accepted by all the best society of the place. Certain wealthy young men, especially, who were forced by their families to live in the provinces and who found relief for their thirst for dissipation and adventure in gambling and an occasional jaunt to the capital, had taken a liking to her because of her air of cosmopolitan experience. She said she had lived for several years in Paris and she spoke French very well, far better than Italian, which she mangled in a ridiculous fashion. She asserted also that she had travelled all over Europe, there was no cosmopolitan watering-place where, according to her, she had not stayed; for ever in her mouth were the names of personages belonging to the great world, of those whose photographs appear constantly in fashion magazines and who are better known to some people than the learned men and writers of their own countries. Having very quickly assimilated the slang and the habits of a certain type of Italian society, she did not call the smart young men of the town by their surnames or titles, but, in familiar fashion, Giulio, Gianni, Paolo, Piero or Renzo. Nor did she ever talk about other well-known society figures in other towns of Italy without calling them by their Christian names, or by their pet names if they had one. Thus she gave the impression of having had extremely intimate, even compromising, relations with them. Furthermore, whenever the name of somebody of noble family came up in conversation, she had a habit of interrupting the person who was speaking and asking for information, or giving information, about his ancestry or relations. Thus she was able to display a profound, assured knowledge of all the vicissitudes, past and present, of the Italian nobility. Like a soldier who knows by heart every subtlety of promotion or variation in army rank, so she knew to a nicety—as though society were an army drawn up in battle—all the scandals, the marriages, the births, the deaths, every scrap of gossip and every secret. She was, in fact, a real authority in such matters; nor did she rest on the knowledge she had acquired; on the contrary she amplified it continually, managing somehow or other to keep her news always fresh and to introduce into it any modifications that might be required from time to time.

She was of uncertain age, somewhere between thirty and forty, but she had lost all youthful freshness and had, in fact, an experienced, worn look, the look of one whose health had been seriously impaired by much travelling and many adventures. She was of medium height, plump, with a fat, smooth, cold-looking face like that of a greedy, unctuous nun, in which the most noteworthy thing was the contrast between the little grey eyes, very hard and snake-like, and the sugary, insinuating, sickly smile upon the thin lips. It was a smile of honey in a black and lipless mouth, beneath a curious nose, hooked and rounded at the end like the head of a tortoise. But her face, notwithstanding this honeyed smile and a great many artifices of make-up, had a look of impure over-ripeness because of its hundred minute little fat wrinkles. And it was the same with her body, which was all bound up and tight-laced into a kind of bundle—which did not however prevent her from swaying her hips when she moved, like a gossipy old hen in a farmyard. She was full of giggles and trills, of wriggles and glances and other girlish coquetries. And if anyone asked her her age, she would answer without hesitation that she was just over twenty-eight.

With this woman Gemma formed a very close friendship, or rather, it would be more correct to say that Elvira Coceanu, in her own insolent way, took possession of Gemma and of her life. The two women took to seeing a great deal of one another, sharing as they did the same prejudices and the same preferences. Elvira had found two or three sure ways of ingratiating herself with Gemma. She gave her descriptions of the brilliant world in which, according to herself, she had always lived during her European peregrinations; she disparaged and made fun of the little provincial town; and finally, in an astute, oblique, discreet manner in which she was highly skilled, insinuating a remark one day and another the day after, she set about demonstrating to Gemma what a boorish, silly, unworthy husband she had. This was a demonstration of which Gemma really had no need, being herself already fully persuaded of its truth; all the same it gave her a great deal of pleasure because it gave authoritative encouragement to her feelings of impatience and disgust. At first with caution, as though venturing on dangerous ground, then, when her remarks were given, as she had expected, a favourable reception, more openly, and finally with obvious and complacent cruelty, Elvira took to making a mock of Vagnuzzi every time his name cropped up in conversation. She had a considerable gift for mimicry, and was able to imitate not only the rather strident voice but also the grimaces and gestures of Gemma's husband. As for Gemma, she took a gloomy delight in these gibes and laughed heartily at them. Further, in order to make herself useful, Elvira advised her about her clothes and her hats and often made them for her. For, being very poor, she not only cadged lunches and dinners here or there but worked hard at cutting out dresses and making hats—never, of course, advertising herself as a dressmaker or a milliner, but with the manner of a great lady, of a dilettante, condescending to allow a few friends to share the secrets of her own elegance. Her stale and remote Parisian experiences and her knowledge of the French language served Elvira Coceanu in good stead. And she always found some good provincial lady to pay for her far from disinterested pieces of advice. Other specialities of hers were creams and perfumes which she boldly concocted from recipes of her own creation. Also Rumanian lampshades, of plain or shot silk and laden with little pearls and fringes, in the worst possible "Oriental" taste, which she sold at very high prices.

In a short time the intimacy of the two women reached such a point that Gemma, who, out of vanity, was longing to tell somebody, gave the Rumanian woman a full account of what she now considered the secret of her life—the story of her birth and of the marriage that had been broken off. On this occasion, too, Elvira contrived to flatter poor Gemma. She listened to her in horrified, astonished silence, interrupted her constantly with exclamations of indignation, curiosity and sympathy, and at the end added her own comments, which—so at least it appeared to Gemma—were full of penetration and friendliness. It was a bitter injustice, declared Elvira, an infamous thing, and all the blacker in that the owner of the villa, seeing the havoc that the revelation of her origins had wrought in Gemma's life, ought to have made reparation by giving her a dowry and finding a husband worthy of her. Instead, he had allowed her to marry Vagnuzzi—a further proof, if one were needed, of his insensibility and selfishness. Elvira went on to assure her that there had been a similar case in Bucharest high society. The only difference lay in the fact that there the truth had become known too late, when the brother and sister had already been married for some time and were surrounded by a brood of lovely children. Such is life, concluded Elvira very thoughtfully, in French; one can never be sure of anything, it's just like the game of roulette in which the changing of a single number is enough to ruin a person or make him rich; and that is why one must try to enjoy oneself while one can, and not give thought to the future.

It seemed to Gemma, that day, that she had never in her life had a better friend than this Rumanian woman. They happened to be, at that moment, in Gemma's house. Having talked a great deal about this strange and unusual case, the two women went out and, threading their way through the maze of little lanes and flights of steps, reached the Corso. It was the hour of sunset, and the wide street between the two rows of massive buildings was filled with a slow-moving crowd of strolling people. "There's provincial life for you!" said Elvira contemptuously, indicating the black, well-behaved multitude. "Just strolling along without stopping even for a drink of water, then home to dinner, and in the evening, unless there's a raffle or some other amusement of the kind, to bed at nine." Gemma agreed: she knew very well what that life was like and what it led to. While they were conversing in this way, moving very slowly towards the square, a voice out of the multitude called Gemma by name: "My dear Gemma, fancy seeing you . . . !" She turned and saw in front of her a certain Vittoni, who was, in fact, the young man who had driven her in his car, the previous autumn, from the villa back to the town and who, in a half serious, half facetious way, had suggested that she should go on to Rome with him and come and live in his house. "Oh, my dear Gemma," he said, taking her familiarly by the arm, "it's really a great pleasure to see you . . .

really a great pleasure . . . I heard you were married . . . to
Professor Lagnuzzi or Bagnuzzi. . . . My congratulations . . .
my warmest congratulations. . . . But why didn't you come to
the villa and show us this Ragnuzzi of yours?" To these half-
serious questionings Emma replied, with an air of mysterious
self-importance, that she would never again go to the villa.
But Vittoni showed no curiosity and abruptly asked her
whether she was alone and would come and have a drink with
him. Slightly disappointed at such indifference towards the
mystery of her life, Gemma turned and introduced him to
Elvira Coceanu. The latter immediately asked if he was
Luciano Vittoni of Rome. Vittoni answered gaily that he was.
Elvira then started, in her usual insolent way, to rattle off a
whole string of names of friends they had in common.
Vittoni, a good-looking, thoughtless, rather rude young man
who led a social life more from love of women than from
ambition, took very little notice of the faded, insincere Elvira
and her snobbish cravings and while answering her absent-
mindedly, never took his eyes off Gemma. She appeared to
him to be much changed and almost beautiful, in a passionate,
discontented sort of way. And, remembering how attractive he
had found her the year before, he found her twice as attractive
now. He noticed also how she avoided speaking of her husband, how she failed to react to his jokes, and how, when she
did speak of him, she limited herself to cold conventional
remarks which certainly did not bear witness to an over-
powering love. In the meantime they had all three started
walking along the Corso in the direction of the Cathedral.

They strolled along in this way for a little, chatting and
making jokes. Vittoni gave Gemma the latest news of what had
been happening that year at the villa and told her how much
they had missed her, Gemma replied scornfully that that was
not possible when there were so many girls younger and
prettier than herself: a close interchange of compliments and
coquetries, in fact, had already established itself between them.

As for Elvira, she had seized hold of Vittoni's arm, who in turn was firmly holding Gemma's, and so great a cordiality now existed between the former pair that anyone might have thought they were very old friends. Both of them, besides, as people of worldly experience, were laughing at Gemma, winking at each other and teasing her with jocular remarks. Naturally the victim of these jests was poor Vagnuzzi, of whom, without having ever met or even seen him, Vittoni had managed to form a pretty accurate idea—as of one specimen amongst thousands of the everlasting, immutable figure of the husband. Elvira, with many false protests and scoldings, pretended that she was allowing a few mocking criticisms of Gemma's husband to be torn from her by Vittoni, and the young man, bursting with laughter, turned towards Gemma asking if it was true. At first she pretended to be offended. Then, yielding to the temptation afforded her by any ridicule of the manners and appearance of her husband, she bore all the overbold jokes of her friend and Vittoni with smiles and in an almost gratified silence. Vittoni was now squeezing her arm tightly in a manner that excited her and seemed to her full of meaning. But she did not dare confess to herself what that meaning might be.

All these jokes and blandishments made time pass quickly, and now it grew late; and, the Corso having by this time completely emptied itself of people, the three found themselves standing irresolute but cheerful in the middle of the cathedral square. At that point the Corso ended, and from there you could see the whole length of its wide, deserted perspective, with the dark buildings tall and erect on each side; from there also started the winding lane that led to Gemma's house. But Vittoni would not hear of her going home; he said it would be cruel to leave him all alone like that after so much friendliness and gaiety, and finally he suggested that the two women should dine with him at his hotel. Elvira agreed fervently to this proposal. It was a brilliant idea, she said; and

Vagnuzzi, who did nothing but think about his physics problems, would never even notice his wife's absence. Gemma was reluctant, feeling in some obscure way that she was in danger; but in the end the other two prevailed. She telephoned to her husband to say she was dining in town. Then they all three went to the Albergo di Spagna, where Vittoni was staying. They dined in the far corner of the dining-room at the old hotel. The worn, yellowed floor tiles, the lamplight filtering through opaque globes, the dome with its panes of green glass, all made the room look like an empty swimming-pool, a swimming-pool at the bottom of which had been placed little tables and sideboards. The silence was stale and dense like a musty smell, and the only sound that disturbed it came from the voices and laughter of Vittoni and the two women. The other guests—a couple of commercial travellers and three officers of the garrison—being accustomed to eating their *table d'hôte* meals alone and in an enforced, meditative silence, looked at them half enviously and half shocked. Even the waiters, old and bent in their worn white coats, seemed, with their slow service and their ill-humoured expressions, to be disapproving of such a very unusual din. It was Vittoni, especially, who became noisy and excited. The two women, on the other hand, tried to assume attitudes suitable to great ladies of extreme fastidiousness who had dropped by chance into an old-fashioned, provincial environment. Vittoni who, without being really intelligent, was yet not lacking in a certain coarse, sarcastic power of perception, had understood the weaknesses of his two guests marvellously well. He sought accordingly to give the meal an extravagant, dissipated, rackety air, like some riotous revel in a low tavern. That was what was needed, he thought, to make a conquest not only of Elvira but of Gemma too. In the case of the former, because she had always lived for such things, and in the case of the latter because she aspired to do so. He ordered French wine, which Gemma had never drunk and which the Rumanian woman examined with the dubious eye of a connoisseur and finally approved with an air of authority. And then he started to tell daring little stories, of which Elvira showed that she appreciated the full flavour, as with the wine, but which left Gemma embarrassed and un-comprehending. "Here's to the health of Piagnuzzi," he cried from time to time, deliberately distorting that unfortunate name, "here's to the health of the great Absent One"; and he would force the reluctant, bewildered Gemma to drink with him. At the same time, with an old-fashioned sort of gallantry which seemed to him to be suggested by the place in which they were, he pressed Gemma's foot under the table. She, excited and frightened, dared neither to respond nor yet to withdraw. Furthermore, to her excitement was added the effect of the considerable quantity of wine which the young man, by his repeated toasts, had made her drink. She felt by now as though she were swimming in a marvellous, unreal atmosphere, an atmosphere in which, as in dreams, no kind of action, however grave or perilous, appeared to lead to any kind of consequences. Life there was sweet, and it was sweet to abandon restraint.

It was in this atmosphere of a reality dreamed and passively accepted that she heard Elvira propose that they should go and drink a bottle with her; and Gemma surprised herself by agree-ing to the suggestion with noisy enthusiasm. There were by now two people in her, as a result of the baleful double person-ality that comes into being through drunkenness; the first acted as if without any brain at all, in a mechanical, vacant manner, the second observed the first quite lucidly but seemed entirely powerless to take action. In this double and divided state, she saw herself leave the hotel on the arm of Elvira and also on that of Vittoni who, with the excuse of supporting her, had his arm round her waist. So deserted did the Corso look to her, between its receding double rank of lightless façades, that for a moment she did not recognize it. On the pavement in the far distance she saw a tiny black man stop, make a half turn, thrust a key into a lock and then vanish, and he looked to her like a marionette in a cardboard street, between houses of painted wood. They were the only three people in the wide, gloomy thoroughfare, and each time they passed under a lamp their shadows made strange dark shapes on the asphalt. As they came under the cathedral walls, the first stroke from the *campanile* fell right on top of them with such weight and solemnity that it brought them to a momentary halt, and they stood in astonishment listening to the bronze waves spreading in circles all round them till they reached the encircling town walls; at the second stroke they walked on again. Elvira, their guide, led them through many damp lanes, up and down many slippery flights of steps, through many black tunnels; until at last she stopped in front of a small green door, saying, "Here we are." From her bag she took an iron key of extraordinary size, opened the door with some difficulty, and, asking the other two not to make a noise, preceded them into the darkness. The staircase was steep, almost vertical, and so narrow that there was room for only one person at a time: Gemma did not so much walk up it as allow herself to be pushed by Vittoni. The latter took advantage of the darkness to touch the back of her neck lightly with his lips. Finally, on tiptoe, they came into a series of dull, scantily furnished little rooms which Elvira exhibited, with ironical swagger, as her "palace". In one of these rooms Vittoni, with a sigh of satisfaction, threw himself down on a divan and drew Gemma down beside him. "How nice you look together!" cried Elvira; "you look as if you were made for each other!": and she disappeared in search of a corkscrew to open the bottle which they had brought from the hotel. As soon as she had left the room Vittoni took Gemma in his arms and tried to kiss her. She at once thrust him away from her and rose to her feet, declaring in a sharp, offended tone of voice that she wished to go home. But Vittoni, and then Elvira who had come back with the opened bottle, both implored her and laughed at her so much that she gave up the idea of leaving. They began drinking again, and Gemma, as she drank, and in spite of her increasing drunkenness, could not help drawing a comparison between the robust, youthful Vittoni with his healthy complexion, and her thin, yellow-faced husband. It was not only Vittoni's appearance that she liked but also his manners, which were a little rough but had nothing mean or pedantic about them, as seemed to her to be the case with her husband's. It was obvious that Vittoni had always lived among well-bred, self-possessed people; this was shown, too, in his contempt for formalities, in the tone of authority in which he spoke. These reflections were coupled in Gemma's befogged brain with an entirely new desire never again to resist any temptation and never again to deny herself any new experience, and also with a desperate curiosity to throw herself headlong into the dangers of which she could now catch a glimpse. What in the world was the use, she said to herself, of fighting, what was the use of restraining oneself? For whom? For what? As so often happens with impatient and superficial characters, she was unable to distinguish the idea of virtue from that of immediate advantage, of safe recompense. To such an extent, indeed, that profitable vice sometimes seemed to her almost a virtue. She herself had been virtuous, but what advantages had she derived from it? A wretched, miserable marriage, a life sacrificed, little or no hope for the future. Better, then, as Elvira never tired of repeating, better to enjoy life without thought or scruple. As she reflected thus, she was talking and clinking her glass against Vittoni's. Soon Elvira left the room again to look for some biscuits, and this time she did not push the young man away from her but allowed herself to be embraced. They stayed a little longer in the bare, gloomy little room, sitting on stools or cushions, until at last Elvira herself began to say, in a motherly, protective sort of way, that she was very sleepy and that it was time for Vittoni to take Gemma home. To the young man such an attractive invitation seemed almost too good to be true, and

Gemma, with a little stab of jealousy, found herself fearing that Elvira would want to go with them and then come back into the town with Vittoni. After long and confused good nights and tipsy promises for another party of the same kind next day, they allowed themselves to be pushed out of the apartment by their hostess, and found themselves back in the street again, alone.

They went back by the road that runs all round the town under the high, battlemented walls. It was the period in early November which, because of the mildness of the weather, is known as St. Martin's summer, and in the cloudless sky the full moon was brilliantly clear. From the parapet at the edge of the road the whole vast expanse of hills was visible, clothed in this brilliance; the woods in the shadowy ravines seemed to be breathing it in as though it were sunlight; the few lights in the cottages scattered on the slopes seemed, in that serene brightness, to be superfluous. High in the sky the full moon blazed, and on its right the white, glittering planet of Jupiter. Excited by this unusually brilliant moonlight there had arisen, from inside the city walls, a confused barking of numerous dogs which echoed loud in the stillness; and which was answered, from one of the far-away cottages scattered in the hills, by a single dog whose distant voice seemed to grow weary and become lost in the immense space. The lonely, helpless barking of this animal anxious for company made an impression upon Gemma, who felt it as an invitation to stop and listen and to contemplate the night. She sat down on the parapet, and Vittoni, with one bound, placed himself at her side. Carried away by the silence and serenity of the night, she now felt far removed from all desire of the senses and was conscious of a sentimental need to have the young man's arm round her waist and to sit, quiet and still, with her head on his shoulder, gazing at the nocturnal landscape. Was not this perhaps love, she wondered? Did not love perhaps mean holding hands, being close together, admiring beautiful things together, being silent together? And thus, beneath her vain, artificial longings, there grew up in her again an old-fashioned, provincial sentimentality. "I like listening to that dog far away over there," she whispered to Vittoni, "and what a magnificent moon! . . . I could sit and look at it for hours. . . ." This remark brought a smile to the face of her companion, who thought nothing at all of the moon except as one of many means by which he intended to achieve certain ends of his own. But, being the experienced man that he was, he kept silence, realizing that it was best to let the stream follow its own course and, in fact, to give as much encouragement as he could to these impulses on Gemma's part. From them it would be easy to pass on to others of quite a different kind. They sat thus for some time on the parapet, facing the silent nocturnal landscape. From time to time Gemma turned her head towards the young man and, with her cheek against his, whispered some remark—words of admiration for the beauty of the night, confidences, reflections, memories. The sight of the full moon over the dark hills, she murmured to him, gave her the same feeling as she had in church, on winter evenings, when the aisles and columns and arches are in darkness and you kneel in a hidden place behind a pillar and can see nothing but the altar with all the little candle-flames burning amongst the flowers round the dark, gilded picture of the Madonna. It was, she tried to explain, a feeling of great sweetness, a feeling of forgetfulness, of trustful abandonment, of communion. To all of which Vittoni replied firmly that he too had a feeling like that. At the same time he tried to kiss her, and, as he had calculated, met no resistance. By now Gemma was convinced that she had found the delicate soul she had been looking for. Didn't Vittoni listen to her with a serious expression and eyes full of affectionate understanding? Her husband would have either laughed, or have said something stupid, one of those things that strip away all enchantment and make you ashamed of having been too confiding. She decided that Vittoni was perfect and was convinced that she

loved him. That evening, on the parapet, in the brilliant moonlight, there were many whispered confidences which found,
every time, a wise and compassionate hearing. Confidences
were followed by kisses: by now it was child's play; and if
Vittoni had been observant he would have admired the almost
mechanical regularity with which certain causes were followed,
always and infallibly, by the same effects. At last they left the
parapet and, still continuing along the same road under the
walls, from tower to tower and from gate to gate, arrived at
Gemma's house. Here Vittoni gave her a last kiss and then, by
the same road, went back to his hotel at a brisk pace, whistling
merrily.

. . . . .

Next day, thinking over what had happened, Gemma felt
undecided rather than frightened or repentant. She was conscious of no remorse, nor of any fear either; the charm of that
walk home, she thought, was enough to justify the whole
adventure. More than anything, she felt herself to be in the
state of mind of one who sets out upon an unknown path and
finds it easy going but does not know whether later it may not
turn out to be dangerous; he looks back, therefore, seeking
reassurance and encouragement. She was hopelessly confused;
all she wanted was the support of some kind of authority to
continue upon the road she had taken. This support, needless
to say, was given her by Elvira Coceanu, in whom she hurried
to confide next morning; and it was of the warmest kind.
Immediately sweeping aside, with dictatorial energy, all moral
issues, as being both inopportune and unfounded, the Rumanian
woman took her stand, without more ado, upon a practical,
strategic plan, a plan of action, as she called it, rather than one
of barren and listless doubt. So that, in the quarter where
Gemma had hoped to find, at most, an impartial judgment,
she discovered, instead, an attitude of enthusiasm and encouragement and co-operation. For Elvira, once she had established,

in a peremptory manner, the supremely important fact that Vittoni was a man of the world with all the qualities necessary in such affairs and that he and Gemma loved each other, the great question was not so much to discover whether this love was likely to have any result—for on this aspect of the problem no doubts could possibly exist—as to bring it about that the relationship already started might develop to the satisfaction of both of them and without the knowledge of her husband. And here, in elaboration of this theme, an experience both abundant and verbose made itself felt. Elvira had already been concerned in complications of this kind, more than one married lady in trouble had turned to her for help; and always, every time her advice had prevailed, all had gone well. Upon Gemma such self-possession had the effect of a conjuring trick: instead of declaring her guilty, Elvira showed her an undertaking which had already been approved and decided upon and which now had merely to be put into execution. If she had not been in such a state of confusion, she would have discerned, lurking in the background of her consciousness, a feeling of mingled disgust and remorse. But Elvira left her no time to analyse her impressions; she carried her off into a new, intoxicating atmosphere in which even the most risky acts of daring appeared not merely lawful, but indeed perfectly obvious. In Elvira's eyes, evidently, there was not a shadow of doubt that wives ought to betray their husbands, especially if the latter were men like Vagnuzzi. It was a law of nature, a normal and necessary fact like the rising or setting of the sun. And she came very near congratulating Gemma for not having tried to create a churlish exception to a rule so universal and so agreeable. Then she returned to her eulogy of Vittoni who, according to her, was exactly the man required to make her friend happy. She ended by proposing to Gemma that she and Vittoni, in order to avoid all suspicion, should meet at her house. This proposal was left unanswered, because, tantalized and confused as she was, Gemma had not the courage to accept it there and then. In any

100

case Elvira did not press the matter; in fact she was so ready to change the conversation, and with such firmness did she avoid any return to the subject, that for a moment Gemma was frightened, thinking, with sudden regret, that she had offended her and thus, by false modesty, deprived herself of a valuable helper. This thought tormented her all day; but when she went back in the afternoon with the unconfessed intention of reminding her friend of her proposal and giving her to understand that she would accept it, she found no one there but Vittoni, already installed in one of the dark little rooms in front of two empty coffee-cups: Elvira, he explained, had had to go out in order to take a lampshade to one of her clients and would not be back till the evening. At first Gemma wanted to leave the house at once; she said it was a trap, and she had, more or less, a confirmation of this in the ironical way in which the young man chuckled. But in the end, after a great deal of supplication from Vittoni, and after he had sworn that he would behave respectfully towards her, she consented to stay. Vittoni moved about the apartment as though he owned it; he insisted on Gemma removing her hat; he even discovered a quite new bottle of liqueur in the kitchen, which appeared to have been just bought. Then he sat down beside her, and, forgetting his oath, started kissing her. At last Gemma understood what was about to happen. And, suddenly losing all restraint, she thought of nothing but of being frank at all costs. As on the previous evening, on the parapet in the moonlight, it seemed to her that she could give Vittoni no greater proof of her feeling than this: the giving of her body, she felt, was a very small and quite ordinary thing in comparison with the surrender that shone out in some of her remarks and attitudes. Only, by a mean pre-ordination, every single thing that she was able to say to her lover was secondhand, and, just when she believed herself to be most frank, she was most false. It was a soul borrowed from the cinema and from popular magazines and cheap novels that talked about love to Vittoni, not hers.

Thus did despised intelligence avenge itself. And true frankness, the tumult in the blood, the original, profound impulse of experience—all these were resolved into a few worn-out words like the scanty coins jingling together at the bottom of a poor beggar's pocket.

During the days that followed both Vittoni and Elvira had reason to be proud of their perspicacity. The former was at last satisfying the desire he had always felt for Gemma; the latter had the pleasure of seeing her advice followed and her dubious services accepted. The only one who was not content either with herself or with the others was Gemma. She had never been particularly subject to the fury of the senses; she was, if anything, inclined to a sort of tenderness and sentimentality which were entirely unknown to Vittoni. The result was that, after a week, the whole coldness and superficiality of her relations with the young man became irreparably obvious to her. Moreover Vittoni, who was not very gallant by nature, as soon as he was sure of his conquest quickly grew tired of acting the part of attentive, devoted lover which he had assumed at the beginning. Nor did he have any scruples about showing quite clearly that, in his own rough, hardhearted way, he was disappointed: he had believed that he was pursuing an exuberant, sensual woman, instead of which he found himself saddled with a cold, sentimental, melancholy provincial. Furthermore, since it seemed to him that Gemma talked far too much about love, in a tone partly disappointed, partly imploring, he was afraid that she might attach herself to him and become jealous. He was, in fact, entangled in the exact opposite of the brief, intense adventure he had hoped for. Nor were his fears altogether unjustified. For, in spite of the fact that she was aware of the coldness of their relations, it might well be that Gemma, in the end—partly from cowardice, partly because of the loneliness of her life—would develop a real affection for him and deceive herself into thinking that she really loved him. She was indeed so hopelessly at sea and so desperate that she would never find strength enough to break off their empty relationship.

In the meantime the character of Elvira Coceanu became no less clearly apparent to her than that of Vittoni. And if it was still possible for her to deceive herself and to mistake the young man's roughness and brutality for simplicity and frankness, such good will, in the case of the Rumanian woman, proved ineffective. Now that the first enthusiasm was past and nothing remained between them but a relationship founded on questionable collusion, she became aware of all her defects with a clarity that was actually exaggerated, as though she saw her through a magnifying, distorting lens, and, marvelling that she had never noticed these defects before, she now experienced, all the time she was with her, an increasing and intolerable feeling of shame. Vittoni, in his way, had been sincere, even too much so, and it was her own fault if she had yielded to him; but Elvira, with her honeyed manner, her insolence and her cool self-possession, now appeared to Gemma as the living, hateful incarnation of deceitfulness. She felt her to be cold-hearted, false, treacherous, capable of every wickedness, a veritable shrew; and she was afraid of her, too. This aversion on her part was confirmed by the equal antipathy felt for the Rumanian woman by Vittoni. It had taken him a very short time to understand her character, but, for his own advantage, he had said nothing of it to Gemma. Now, however, Elvira appeared to him as one of the greatest disadvantages of his unfortunate adventure, and to Gemma he openly complained of her.

The thing that disgusted Gemma most of all was the specially earnest and zealously indiscreet manner displayed by the Rumanian woman every time the conversation came round to her relationship with Vittoni. In reality she would have preferred not to speak of it at all, but Elvira immodestly questioned her and asked for information and tormented her with enquiries. Then, without being asked, she would pour out suggestions, comments, advice and warnings, always with an unctuous, protective, gossipy affectionateness which was seemingly disinterested and even motherly but in reality vague and dangerous and sometimes very close to blackmail. It so happened that one day Gemma rebelled against this indiscreet behaviour. But it was a rebellion of short duration because Elvira, immediately dropping her usual sugary manner, revealed all of a sudden a face that was pale and icy and pitiless, and truly frightful to see. "Oh, so that's how you answer me," she said calmly; but her plump hand, usually so soft and insinuating, closed hard, as she spoke the words, on Gemma's arm, like the clawed paw of a beast of prey; "I who've been helpful and useful to you in every way. . . . You're the most ungrateful . . . but be careful, because I know a bit too much. . . ." These words contained so obvious a threat, they revealed a preparedness so cold and premeditated, that Gemma felt herself almost fainting with fear. She quickly changed the conversation, saying she was sorry, putting it down to her own nervousness, seeking to reassure Elvira. The latter, however, just as though this clash had confirmed her in certain of her calculations, assumed from that day onwards an increasingly tyrannical, mercenary attitude towards Gemma. She compelled her to buy her ugly, expensive lampshades; she forced her to lend her money; she praised so extravagantly, and with so many hints, certain hats and dresses belonging to her friend that Gemma had to make her a present of them. From Vittoni too—though in a different way—Elvira tried, capriciously and with girlish blandishments, to extort certain benefits. But he, who at first had given her a number of presents, did not intend, now that Gemma had disappointed him, to go on spending money; and he answered her in so rough and sarcastic a manner that now it was Elvira's turn to be frightened. And from that moment she started to hate him, fiercely and bitterly, to be as rude as she could to him, and to speak ill of him to Gemma. She said he was a blackguard, a bully, an ignoramus; she tried to persuade Gemma to finish with him; she shouted that he lived on women and on the unlawful gains of dishonest gambling. Finally, one day, in the presence of Gemma and to her consternation and horror, Vittoni seized Elvira by the wrists and threatened that, if she went on slandering him, he would give her a couple of the soundest slaps she had ever had in her life. He went on to say that he knew quite enough, and was sufficiently influential, to get her sent back, in double-quick time, to her own country. Livid with fury, helpless, Elvira was forced to give way. Between the three of them, closely bound together as they were, there had thus grown up an atmosphere of mistrust, defiance and hatred, by reason of the divisions and dissensions that intrude with fatal inevitability into alliances of this kind. But Gemma, being the most unprotected and the most sensitive, was the one who suffered most.

At last Vittoni, who possessed estates in the neighbourhood and had come to the town in order to sell them, completed his business and announced to Gemma that he had made up his mind to leave. Gemma received this news in silence and without surprise. At this Vittoni, who, in his vanity, had expected a scene of jealousy and rage, was not a little angry. At the same time he felt almost a regret at leaving her, as though he had only that moment become aware of her qualities. This parting took place in one of Elvira Coceanu's little rooms. The latter, however—who, since he had threatened to slap her, had given up speaking to Vittoni—had taken refuge in another room the moment the young man came in, crying out ostentatiously to Gemma to let her know as soon as the interloper went away. Vittoni was distressed by the coldness of the leave-taking. He no longer knew whether he was doing right or wrong to leave Gemma; she appeared to him now in a new, disconcerting, desirable aspect, and he was afraid that he had neither understood her nor enjoyed her sufficiently. Thinking not to break completely the already tenuous thread of their relationship and thus to keep her in reserve for the moment when the whim might come upon him to take up with her again, he finally suggested that they might write to each other —a suggestion that came oddly from the mouth of a man as rough and uncultivated as himself. But Gemma answered him boldly that she could see no point in such a correspondence. They were lovers and already they could never find anything to say to each other: what would they find to write in these letters that he suggested? Vittoni, seeing her so drained of all emotion and so calm, realized that his provincial adventure was indeed finished. "A pity," he said to himself as he went downstairs; "when all's said and done, it was better than a good many others." And that was the last time his thoughts were directed towards Gemma.

When Vittoni had gone, she went to look for the Rumanian woman in her room at the far end of the passage. With her frizzy hair all ruffled and full of curl-papers, her fat, soft bust squeezed into a tight-fitting leather jacket all greasy and split, wearing no skirt but merely a petticoat of yellowish silk, Elvira was sitting on the bed with a litter of rags all round her, intent on threading little pearls on to one of her usual lampshades. Between her lips, thin as a cut, she was holding two of these little pearls; pale, cold-looking beneath the little paper snakes in her hair, her lips pressed tightly together, she had the malignant, untidy look of a Medusa without terror and without beauty, a Medusa grown old and familiar and corrupt. The sight of her face made Gemma shudder. "Vittoni's gone," she could not help saying to herself, "and I'm left with this woman." As though she had divined this thought, Elvira at the same moment raised her eyes and gave Gemma a disagreeable look. "So he's gone at last," she said with clenched teeth, in a dry, guttural voice that sounded like that of a parrot; "that blackguard's gone. . . . Now one can breathe freely." Gemma did not answer. It was true that she had never loved Vittoni, but, in spite of his roughness, she still maintained no rancour against him. However, she was not disposed to talk about him to Elvira. So, without saying a word, she crossed the room and went and stood with her face against the window pane. The weather had turned unpleasant, the air seemed dark and close in the lane outside, the blackened stones of the house opposite glistened with rain, but the rain was so fine that the raindrops were invisible. "I don't like," went on Elvira, still busy with her work, "I don't like the attitude you've taken up, for some time now, towards me. . . . I warn you, dear, that I don't intend to let myself be trampled under the feet of anyone." She spoke in a voice that hissed like a blast of winter wind through a keyhole, and Gemma, feeling a chill run down her spine, turned towards her. "Isn't it enough," she asked, leaning her back against the window-sill and looking at the Rumanian woman with calm, gloomy dignity, "isn't it enough to have made me commit this folly, to have made me betray my husband who is the best man in the world? What more do you want of me?" This was a new tone, and she herself was surprised at it; and the ideas, also, were new, for never before had she expressed herself in this way on the subject of her husband. "Tut, tut, tut," said Elvira, like a parrot, throwing her a brief glance of surprise; and then in a less peremptory tone: "What are you thinking about? . . . You must have a good sleep and you'll forget all about it. . . ." She finished threading a few more pearls, then, putting down her work, came over to Gemma and put her arm round her waist. "Come along. . . . Sit down here beside me and tell me what the matter is. Why are you so sad? Surely it can't be because that horrible man has gone away?"

To Gemma the woman's arm round her waist, her voice, her breath brought a feeling of violent disgust, almost of horror. "I'm depressed . . . that's all," she replied, standing stiffly and looking straight in front of her.

Elvira shook her head. "You're too much alone, allow me to tell you," she began; "it's loneliness that makes you depressed. . . ." And after a moment she went on, as though by chance, "D'you know what I've just thought of?" she said.

"A splendid idea. . . . So that you won't be so much alone and so bored, I'll come and stay at your house. . . . We'll keep each other company and snap our fingers at all the Vittonis in the world."

Gemma was frozen with horror at this suggestion and for a moment she stared terrified at the floor in front of her. "My husband won't agree to that," she said at last in a very small voice. Elvira shrugged her shoulders gaily. "Gemma, what nonsense, you're quite unlike yourself. . . . You know your husband does exactly what you want. . . . You go and tell him you need company—which indeed is perfectly true—and he won't have any objection. . . . You're a child, my dear, you don't know what life is. . . . Husbands must be made to do what they're told. . . ."

Such pithy remarks from Elvira, which formerly had seemed to her to be filled with a gay, persuasive wisdom, now caused Gemma the utmost irritation—almost as much irritation, indeed, as her presence. "But supposing," she insisted, "supposing he doesn't agree?"

"My dear," replied the other woman, "I should know at once what that meant. . . . I repeat—your husband does what you tell him. . . . If he doesn't agree, it means that *you* don't want it. . . ."

"Well," hazarded Gemma, "supposing I don't want it . . . ?"

"I can't believe it," exclaimed Elvira coolly, "we're such good friends! . . . Why should you want to make an enemy of me? I know so many things about you that, if I was forced to it, I could do you quite a lot of harm. . . . But what would be the point of that? It would cause you pain, as you can imagine . . . and it would cause *me* pain too, because I prefer, if possible, to live in peace and on good terms with everyone. The very idea of certain things happening, of your husband getting to know what's been going on in my house, horrifies me, I assure you."

Gemma was now trembling all over. "Ah, so you'd be capable of telling . . . ?"

"Please, please," protested Elvira, "these are just things one says . . . and don't let's speak of them again, I beg of you. . . . Now," she went on, taking Gemma round the waist again, "tell me when it would be convenient for me to come to your house. . . . Today? Tomorrow?"

"Tomorrow," replied Gemma without moving; "I must tell my husband."

"That's excellent," said the other eagerly, "whatever suits you best . . . tomorrow. . . . That will give me time to get my things ready. . . . And you know which room I should like to have? . . . The one on the first floor, looking out towards the walls. . . ."

"As a matter of fact," said Gemma with a deep frown, "that's the room I was intending to keep for a nursery . . ."

At these words the other woman looked at her with feigned, and exaggerated, astonishment. "Gemma . . . you're not really going to tell me you would have the bad taste to want children. . . ? And by Signor Vagnuzzi, into the bargain?"

Now Gemma had known for some days that she was with child, and being sure, from a calculation of the number of months, that this baby was her husband's, was very pleased about it. Elvira's remark, her tone, her expression aroused a violent hatred in her. It was with difficulty that she refrained from rushing at her and tearing her saccharine face with her fingernails. "All right," she said, "but now let me go and speak to my husband about it."

That afternoon, as soon as she reached home, she lay down on the bed and, wrapping herself up in a blanket, did not stir till evening. The room was on the first floor and looked out over the escarpments. Whitewashed and cold, with black, sham-*quattrocento* furniture, it had, in the dim, stormy light of a wet afternoon, a look of mournful gloom. On the window-panes the last dying flies buzzed distastefully; outside, the heavy warm-seeming rain flowed down the glass in streams. She looked at the window as she lay, and, feeling her whole body frozen, trembled violently from time to time. She no longer felt either fear or indignation, merely an acute sense of ignominious oppression. It was as though she found herself condemned to live tied for ever to a dead body. And as though this body were decomposing on top of her. It was not so much a moral suffering as a physical sensation, for it was a physical repulsion that Elvira Coceanu inspired in her. Her raging, horrified imagination showed her her familiar life all changed and corrupted by this foul encumbrance. For the first time she had a feeling of jealousy for this house that she had never loved. And she saw Elvira, in the room she had intended for her children, like a big, soft, whitish insect growing fat and filling it with her impure smell and with countless minute abominations. She knew that Elvira drank, that she dyed her hair, that she took purges. With the utmost repugnance she seemed to see, in that room, all her disgusting little black bottles standing in a row on a shelf. And her damp, sweaty garments on the chairs. And shoes, forced out of shape by her feet, arranged in a line behind the door. Again, she seemed to see Elvira standing in the doorway of her bedroom, her face greasy with night creams and her head full of curl-papers, saying good morning to her. The thing that terrified her most in these imaginings was the idea of the length of time involved. Never, she said to herself, never would she succeed in getting rid of this vampire. And at this thought she could feel a kind of secret frenzy twisting inside her, and she felt she was not far from going mad.

But the fear of losing her husband, whose qualities she was only now discovering, and of having to go back to the house in the lane and to her mother's lodgers, prevented her from telling Vagnuzzi the truth and so obtaining not merely a generous forgiveness but also a complete and final liberation. She was not courageous by nature, and now, intimidated by Elvira, desperate, resigned to misfortune, she felt not only cowardly but hysterical. And so, half-way through dinner that same evening, she announced to her husband that, as she was bored all alone in the house, she had decided to invite her friend to live with them. She expected, she hoped that Vagnuzzi would make objections. But, partly out of love, partly from remorse at not having taken her to live in Rome as he had promised, Vagnuzzi was truly anxious to satisfy her every wish. Besides, knowing Elvira very slightly—he had seen her very seldom, and only in brief glimpses—and having, in any case, little understanding of the human character, he had formed a pleasing, conventional idea of her as an accomplished woman, gay and amusing, the very person, in fact, to make an entertaining companion for his wife. And he had not been able to help noticing, recently, the latter's silence and depression. Much to Gemma's disappointment, therefore, he at once gave his consent. "I've been thinking just the same thing," he added, as if in apology, "and I don't know why I haven't spoken to you about it already. . . ." And he ended by declaring that, apart from anything else, they would, by inviting Elvira Coceanu, be doing a charitable deed, for he knew from what Gemma had told him that she was poor and had difficulty in making a living.

Next day, as had been agreed, Elvira arrived with her belongings. All she had was one ugly fibre suitcase full of rags and a few cardboard boxes tied with string. To welcome her, as Gemma's husband had pointed out, was truly a deed of charity. Elvira assumed a thousand coquettish airs for the benefit of Vagnuzzi, who tried to talk French to her and asked her a great many questions about Rumania and, in particular, about various professors and scientists in that country with whom he was in constant correspondence. To Gemma these cordialities were so much poison; at table she never opened her mouth but left the other two to chatter and make jokes together. After dinner, during a tour of reconnaissance through the rooms, Elvira immediately proclaimed that the house was not as comfortable as it might be: here there should be a sofa, there an armchair, and one of her lampshades would look extremely well in that corner. She also found fault with the employment of the two maids, the cook and the housemaid, and, having summoned them to an interview, gave them orders and advice. She behaved, in fact, as though she were mistress of the house, while Gemma was all the time chafing with rage. She told Vagnuzzi that she had had a big house in Bucharest with menservants, grooms and a carriage and horses; and that she had been one of the best-known and most popular hostesses there. Vagnuzzi did not believe her, but he was amused. Next day he lingered longer than usual after lunch, and, when he went away, gave the Rumanian woman a secret injunction to keep Gemma as cheerful as possible. To which Elvira replied that, wherever she was, all sadness was banished. Vagnuzzi left the house full of confidence.

Having attained her purpose of getting herself invited to the Vagnuzzis' house, Elvira was now anxious to return to the same cordial relations with Gemma as before: she was too clever not to realize that her ends were better served by trust and friendship than by the rigid situation which blackmail would create. But Gemma did not look at things in this light. And, even if she had wished, she could never now have overcome her physical repulsion, nor have looked upon her former friend with any feeling other than the bitterest and most steadfast hatred. And so, as soon as her husband had crossed the threshold, she rose from the table and, without even looking at the cigarette-case which Elvira was holding out towards her, scornfully left the dining-room. Later, Elvira came and knocked at the door of her room and obtained no answer. She tried to turn the handle and found that the door was locked. Gemma, who was lying on her bed, heard her name called several times in a voice which at first was subdued and gentle, then loud and angry; finally she heard the other woman go away. All that afternoon she lay on her bed, shut up in her room, until she was sure that Elvira had gone out. Then she dressed in haste and ran off to her mother's. She wanted to confide in someone, to give vent to her wretchedness, to ask advice. But when she saw the old woman and her eyes that were still young and full of innocent folly, she realized that it would be like confiding in a child of twelve; and all she did was announce the news of her pregnancy. Her mother displayed an immediate and sincere delight and kissed her over and over again, but then, changing the subject, she started talking of the villa: her fixed idea was that, Gemma's marriage having removed all danger of misunderstandings like the one with Paolo, Gemma ought to be invited again every summer, as had always happened in the past. The people at the villa were in her debt, she averred, and later on—why not?—she might perhaps make some important person fall in love with her and so, even if married to Vagnuzzi, enter and play her part in the world of high society. Gemma listened to her with impatience, feeling herself to be now very far removed indeed from such matters—matters in which she had once taken so passionate an interest. As soon as she could, she took leave of her mother.

The days that followed brought about no change in the situation, except that Elvira, by uttering a few little words, full of double meanings, in the presence of Vagnuzzi (who understood nothing of what she was saying), made it quite clear to Gemma that to have taken her into the house was not enough: she must also be treated with every kind of courtesy, as an honoured guest. And so Gemma, at least at meal-times, had to make conversation and smile at the Rumanian woman. During the rest of the day she avoided her as much as possible. But, however much she shut herself away and tried not to see her, she was always present to her. It was like having an ugly festering sore, cold and moist, painless but incurable, under her clothes, a thing she could never manage to forget though at the same time she did not dare uncover it and look at it. In her own bedroom she was perpetually straining her ears to listen to the sounds made by Elvira in the room next door. Into that room, since the woman had been living in it, she had never entered;

she imagined it filthy, the air thick and evil-smelling, with loathsome stains on the walls and floor. "Now she's undressing", she would think with a shudder of repugnance; and she seemed to see her, white and quivering like a glossy lump of bacon strung up on a butcher's hook. "Now she's asleep", she would say to herself at night, and would lie listening with frantic abhorrence to Elvira's snores, alternately shrill and deeptoned, which seemed to her like a blackmailing oration directed against her own sleep. Or again—and this was the most poisonous aspect of her obsession—it was not images and sounds which oppressed her, but the mere feeling that Elvira Coceanu existed. But where were the marks of this existence? About the house, or in her own confused consciousness? For the first time Gemma discovered that it is not only material things that can be banished or suppressed. There is also an ideal world in which the soul likes to see itself reflected as in a piece of smooth water. And it has no peace unless it sees this world always clear and transparent.

She was not conscious of it, but her hatred of Elvira now went beyond the figure of the woman herself and embraced all the errors and aspirations of her own past life. During those sad winter days, without her being aware of it—as a person who suffers from poisoning may, by a violent crisis, be cleansed in a few hours of all the poisons absorbed during several years—the acute irritability of her state of mind had the effect of liberating her not merely from her former admiration for the Rumanian but also from all the other infatuations that had blinded her ever since the years of adolescence. Through confused suffering she was cured of many fevers, and the complete obscurity that oppressed her was the prelude to a new clarity. This, in proportion to her powers and to the kind of mistakes she had made, would be both feeble and limited. Far preferable, however, to the innocent folly of her mother, or the perversity of Elvira.

In the end it was the Rumanian herself—after each victory

over her friend's timidity she had shown herself more brazen and exacting—who, without either seeking or desiring it, gave Gemma the opportunity to get rid of her. Barely a month had passed of their dismal, false existence *à trois* when, at dinner one evening, Vagnuzzi announced in his usual awkwardly sudden and casual way that he had at last obtained the professorship at the University of Rome which had been his ambition for so long. At these words Gemma made no attempt to conceal her joy; rising from the table, she went and planted a kiss upon her husband's bald forehead: it was not only the prospect of the change that pleased her, but she saw herself at last freed from Elvira's tyranny. It was a great, an unhoped-for, a marvellous stroke of fortune and she seemed to live again; almost it seemed to her that she did not deserve it. But this scene of family emotion took place in front of the Rumanian. She, assuming an air of reserved, discreet sadness, finally declared that she envied Gemma very much indeed because she herself had always longed in vain to go and live in the capital. This was a trial cast of the hook, and the credulous Vagnuzzi immediately swallowed it, hastening to declare that he had no intention of separating two such affectionate friends and that he therefore hoped that Elvira, at any rate during the next few months, would continue to be their guest in Rome. At these words Gemma turned deathly pale and sank back in her chair. But Elvira, catching the ball on the rebound, at once accepted the proposal and thanked Vagnuzzi. He answered that it was for *him* to be grateful to *her* for the companionship she was giving, and would go on giving, to his wife, and that, if anything, it was up to *him* to say thank you to *her*. Elvira, feigning modesty, said it was not even worth mentioning: she did what she was doing because she was so fond of Gemma. And she carried her effrontery so far as to turn towards her friend and ask in a honeyed voice: "Isn't that so, Gemma darling?" This competition in compliments was followed by Gemma with pained and tearful attention. Behind the irony of the conversation between the other two she could visualize her life in Rome in the not so distant future, in a house that was still new yet already contaminated, from top to bottom, by the presence of this woman. And in that gloomy atmosphere, full of violent passions, under those evil auspices, her baby would be born. Suddenly a burst of premature maternal jealousy caused her to imagine, absurdly, that Elvira Coceanu would try, by means of yet further blackmail, to take away from her the child that was going to be born. With fantastic but hallucinating clearness she saw her child in the woman's arms, her fat, treacherous, impure face bending over it, while she herself was thrust aside, forced to embrace her child secretly, or when the Rumanian woman allowed her to. It was a kind of vision and it sent her out of her wits with rage, making her blood boil, all of a sudden, with frenzied violence. It was like a spark on a heap of dry brushwood: there was nothing left inside her but passion, suffering, uncontrolled carnal feeling. Her eyes, wandering crazily over the table, fixed themselves upon the long, sharp knife which her husband used to cut the household bread of which he was so fond. Unhurriedly her hand reached out to this knife and grasped it; for a moment, as she turned it round and felt its weight, it looked as if she wished to examine it. Then, pushing back her chair, she rose to her feet with a strange, mechanical suddenness and threw herself, knife raised in her hand, upon Elvira.

The Rumanian, who was sitting at the end of the table, only just managed to avoid the blow: she rose with a scream from her chair, stumbled, and finally succeeded in taking shelter behind Vagnuzzi's chair, shrieking out words of terror and hatred. Vagnuzzi, helped by the maid, was easily able to take the knife from Gemma's hand. The latter was now extremely pale; she stood leaning back against the table as though she felt giddy and, without answering the anxious questions of her husband, passed her hand, with the fingers open, across her face. Vagnuzzi feared she was going to faint and, taking her

round the waist and supporting her, led her away towards the
stairs; she, dazed, offered no resistance. But Elvira had had too
great a fright to be able to contain herself. Furthermore, there
was now blazing up in her a hatred no less violent than
Gemma's towards herself. And so, as Vagnuzzi urged his wife,
little by little, towards the staircase, Elvira, in a fury, began
shouting out disconnected remarks concerning Vittoni. Immediately Gemma roused herself to a kind of dull, painful energy
and, stopping half-way up the first flight of stairs, answered in
a calm voice, speaking with great difficulty, that she could now
tell the whole story, and *she* would not try to prevent her.
The Rumanian, in a voice strangled and shrill with rage,
replied that she would certainly do so. And she added a string
of coarse insults, amongst which there recurred constantly,
uttered with frantic hatred, the word "murderess". "Murderess!" she screamed in a hoarse voice; and went on to say that
she would have no peace until she saw her flung into prison.
This dialogue between Gemma half-way up the stairs and the
Rumanian writhing on the bottom step continued for some
time longer; and in this way poor Vagnuzzi, standing on the
stairs beside his wife, came to hear of his misfortune. But all
the time Gemma's pallor was increasing; she appeared to be
smitten with giddiness and seized hold of the banisters with
both hands. Her husband realized it was not the moment for
reproofs and explanations, and, without replying to Elvira who
was now railing against him too as though possessed by the
devil, he compelled his wife—using no violence but with a
delicate masterfulness—to go up to her room and lie down on
the bed. He feared that Gemma's disorder might not be a
mere passing attack but might become aggravated because of
her condition. And so, in fact, it happened. After a few minutes
she was taken with a high fever and, soon, with rolling eyes
and strange words and gestures, she became delirious. She
thought she saw a creeping beast, soft and many-footed,
flattening itself in corners or under the furniture or running

rapidly across the floor; and, jumping up in bed to a sitting position, she pointed it out in terror to her husband. Then she constantly repeated the movement of pulling up the bed-covers, as though someone were trying to tear them off her. Or again she would assume curious attitudes of mystery and solemnity and, with an expression of remorse on her face, would murmur words that had no meaning. Vagnuzzi sent for a doctor; and sat, meanwhile, at his wife's bedside.

Gemma's illness lasted more than a week, during which all the complications that Vagnuzzi had feared came into existence. He sat all day long at his wife's bedside and at night slept in the same room. During all this time, while Gemma was delirious or lying prostrate, he had leisure to reflect calmly and at length upon the things that had happened. His first pained astonish-ment had for a moment been succeeded by angry contempt. But then, as her illness continued, his contempt yielded place to a deeper, more serene thoughtfulness. From Elvira's furious remarks and Gemma's replies he had been able to understand very little beyond the main fact. But he realized that it would now be useless—nay worse, ridiculous and actually harmful—to go and seek out Elvira, who had made her escape immedi-ately after the scene had taken place; or, indeed, to question Gemma when she was well again. He pondered for a long time upon what course of action he ought to take. In the end love for his wife was more potent than disappointment or anger, and he made up his mind that the best plan would be, once Gemma was recovered, never even to speak of what had happened. It would be best for him to look upon the Vittoni adventure as a mere youthful error. Later on, in a different town and with a different circle of acquaintances, Gemma and he would in time forget all about it and even think it had never occurred. Perhaps the greatest bitterness was having to give up, for the moment anyhow, all thought of the child he had so longed for. Then, putting aside all further reflection on these disagreeable subjects, he directed every effort towards his wife's recovery. After about a fortnight she was able to get up. And they at once decided to leave.

They left very early one January morning. It was a harsh, rather misty dawn; along the deserted Corso, glistening from the dampness of the night, the arc-lamps were still burning; and as the bus which took them to the station went gaily spluttering and creaking down the road along the ramparts, Gemma was able to see, for the last time, the dark town piled up on its hilltop, with a few reddish lights still winking here and there beneath the cloudy, uncertain sky. "In an hour's time," she could not help thinking, "Elvira Coceanu will wake up and, her face all greasy and her hair full of curl-papers, will go into the kitchen to make herself a cup of coffee. My mother, too, will begin moving about the house. At the confectioner's in the Corso they will pull up the roller-blinds with the usual clatter. And the big and little bells in the churches will start ringing all together for the morning services. But I shall never see Elvira Coceanu again, I shall never again live in the house in the lane, I shall never again hear those bells." Distracted by these thoughts, she ceased to look at the town. The bus had now entered on the straight road and was moving along between fields towards the station, whose low, yellow buildings and fences could already be seen behind rows of trees; also a white plume of smoke from a moving train.

A BAD WINTER

I HAVE never been able to endure the sound of running water in darkness when combined with an enveloping murmur of rain. The splashing of fountains at night within the vast rustling of a thunderstorm, the metallic hiss of surf in a sea whipped by a passing shower, the dreary twittering of an iron drain-pipe in the gloom of a flooded side-street: it irritates me, it makes me indignant, it seems to me an excess of almost incredible magnitude, this clamour of water in darkness while so much water is spilling down from heaven on to the earth. In the city, especially, the cheerful sound of the water of innumerable fountains becomes for me, on rainy nights, a positive torment. I think, then, of the city as an enormous body which has reached the last stage of decomposition and from which, beneath the deluge that rots it, there drips and spirts, in the most unexpected places, the copious fluid by which it is cumbered and distended.

I recall that this horror of the sound of water tormented me most sorely during the particularly rainy winter of 19—. I was depressed at the time, although, to tell the truth, I had no reason for this, for I had become engaged, that very autumn, to the girl I loved—or at any rate thought I loved; I was sad with the uncomfortable, disagreeable kind of sadness that is inspired by the obscure consciousness of an unrecognized error lodged in one's life like a worm in wood; and, as always happens during such states of melancholy, when one's sensibility is sharpened to a morbid degree and becomes aware of many things that had formerly remained unnoticed, this matter of the continuous rumble of water audible amidst that other diffused, never-ending sound of rain aroused, at first, my curiosity as a thing newly observed and then, aided by my hypochondria, very soon became a real obsession. I fled from it, yet at the same time I sought it out. It used to happen that, when I was walking along some unknown street in the rain and the darkness, I would say to myself: "Three more paving-stones and I shall hear a sound of water." And then, indeed, a gurgling or rustling sound—some kind of watery sound, in fact—coming from goodness knows where, would bring me to a sudden halt and make me shudder with alarm and vexation. In truth I had never realized that the city contained so many fountains, large and small, so many drain-pipes, runnels, rivulets and other kinds of watercourses. I avoided one, only to fall into another. And meanwhile, on top of it all, the rain went on falling, darkly, quietly.

Every evening, after dining alone in my mediocre boarding-house, I used to start off on foot for the not far distant villa in which my fiancée lived. The Malinverno family—that was the girl's surname*—had been a large one some years before. Then, the grandparents and the father having died and the elder sister having married and gone to live in the provinces, no one was left in the villa except the mother and the younger daughter, Clara. The villa had originally been built on the edge of open country, but as the years went by the city had enveloped it; and now it stood in the midst of a quarter of more or less working-class dwellings. It was a very solid, but gloomy, building, with walls grey and cracked, shutters faded, and a narrow garden in which the swarming black foliage of a gigantic ivy meandered in every direction. On the ground floor of the villa there were two or three large rooms furnished in a style that was showy but lacking in intimacy, with the great gilded settees full of curly wood-carving and the theatrical curtains and hangings with which the middle classes formerly sought to rival the magnificence of the great historic palaces;

* There is a play upon words here: *Malinverno*=a bad winter.

but, as far as the rest of it went, there was nothing but valueless stuff, decrepit, ill-assorted pieces fit only for a junk-shop. The two women, having shut up the downstairs rooms into which no one ever penetrated, spent the greater part of their time in a few smaller rooms on the first floor. The Malinvernos had never been rich and now they were actually in straitened circumstances.

My way into the house lay through a spacious, dismantled hall and up two flights of a wide, clean, dreary staircase; on the first floor I would push open a glass door that served to announce my arrival, and pass through into a long, completely bare passage. At the far end of the passage a wide-open door came in sight, and then, in the light of an old-fashioned hanging lamp with a counterweight, I could see the old lady sitting bent over her sewing, a piece of cloth or linen draped over her knees and falling to the floor. In this room there was a round table on which the old lady had her workbasket and her scissors, needles and reels of cotton; also a console-table with a looking-glass and an extremely hard settee with an upholstered back. I would greet the old lady, sit down on the settee, and await Clara's arrival. In a short time I would see her appear at the end of the passage, tall and rather ghostly-looking, on account, mainly, of the rigidity of her carriage which was quite inconsistent with the unsteadiness of her gait on her high, thin heels. She would approach in a leisurely manner, bumping against the walls of the passage, faltering and unstable as a shadow that wavers according to the flickerings of a candle-flame; and almost always she would come in without giving me either a greeting or a smile, but with her handkerchief held to her nose, or with a remark of some sort to her mother, just as if I had not been there. This coldness and reserve constituted one of her most notable characteristics; and, combined with the hard, unpleasing beauty of her person and the pallor of her complexion, of a quality so far from sensual that it reminded one of marble slightly veined with blue, went far towards emphasizing

her resemblance to a statue. She would sit down beside me,
bending her knees in order to do so but keeping the upper part
of her body erect and rigid as though it were all in one piece;
and in this way, perched at my side on the bulging upholstery
of the settee, she would spend the evening, conversing at rare
intervals about matters of no significance. Never once did she
allow herself to lean against the back of the settee, nor did she
in any way modify the sedateness of her attitude. If she wished
to cross her legs—a thing she very seldom did—it was, for me,
almost a form of entertainment to watch the slowness, the dis-
creetness with which, very gradually, she placed one of her
thighs upon the other beneath her long skirt, without lowering
her eyes, without ceasing to speak, then putting her large, soft,
white hand down to the hem of her dress and giving it an
extremely discreet tug in such a way as to re-establish it, as
before, half-way down her calf. I say "thigh" and "calf", but
these terms, purely physical as they are, are entirely unsuitable
when referring to *her* thigh, *her* calf; for her excessive modesty
prevented one not only from observing, but even from imagin-
ing, that she was made in the same way as other women. And
sometimes, in idle moments, if I tried to picture her as she
would be when naked, I was irritated at finding myself incapable of doing so and unable to think of her except as I always
saw her, fully dressed, precise, impenetrable. That winter,
owing to the icy cold in the villa which was almost entirely
devoid of heating, she often had a cold; and the handkerchief
which she kept at her wrist, inside her sleeve, provided yet
another pretext for a whole series of extraordinarily slow,
modest, discreet gestures. How almost imperceptible was the
pressure with which she pinched her nostrils inside the little
piece of cambric, how temperately she blew, what circumspection she used in withdrawing her nose from the handkerchief and replacing it in her sleeve! Quivering and full
of passion beside her cold immobility, I often asked myself
what there could be in common between us, whether

indeed we did not belong to two utterly different, hostile races.

Clara's head appeared rather large, owing, chiefly, to her puffed-out black hair which she wore gathered into a chignon at the back of her neck; her attractive face was white and clean and without the faintest trace of powder or rouge; her eyes big but inexpressive. No doubt this lack of expression was partly due to that same deliberately reserved manner, as a result of which, if she had to move her eyeballs, she did so with great slowness and circumspection, as though to assure herself first that the object she was looking at was neither unpleasing nor unworthy and that the movement of her eyes could not be wrongly interpreted. The same could be said of her smiles, which were rare and always so slight that it was hard to understand whether she was really smiling from gaiety or simply in order to please the person she was talking to.

I had met Clara after a particularly disorderly period in my life. Perhaps it was the contrast between her and the women with whom I had associated during that time, rather than a true, deep attraction, which deceived me into thinking I had fallen in love with her. And indeed this often happens: that one regards as a feeling of real affection something which is in fact nothing more than a sense of boredom, a desire for change, an ideal aspiration or some stimulus of the kind which has little to do with love. My state of mind, at the time, was little less than desperate; and Clara, appearing to me at that moment as a kind of dawn after a murky night, had aroused in me a transient enthusiasm, full of good will, which I mistakenly took to be passion. Impetuously, without proper reflection, I asked her to be my wife. My proposal was accepted and the marriage fixed for a few months later, as soon as preparations could be concluded. The table-cloths and the sheets which so frequently enveloped the legs of Clara's mother were in fact the ones off which I should eat and in which I should sleep after I was married. But, just when everything seemed to be going as well as possible, I began to repent my hasty decision.

I had asked Clara to marry me without knowing her; and when I saw her so cold and reserved I had deceived myself into thinking that such behaviour was to be attributed, more than anything, to our lack of intimacy. But now, after we had been engaged for nearly three months, during which I had been with her for several hours each day, I began to take fright at the unchanging chilliness and embarrassment of our relations. "How on earth," I sometimes thought during those evenings, after I had explored all possible openings, I don't say for closer intimacy, but for a normal conversation, "how on earth can I manage to spend my whole life at close quarters with a woman who is so inert, so frozen, so unfeeling?" I repented; and, as happens in such cases, having once taken the road of repentance, my spirit, which knows no middle state but passes with ease from joy to discouragement, very soon reached the lowest depths of the most abject despair. The presence of Clara, to whom I did not know what to say and who said nothing to me, became singularly exasperating to me; and when I found myself alone again in my room at the boarding-house, the violence of my repentance made me want to beat my head against the wall. "I'm finished," I said to myself, pulling at my hair and twisting my hands together, "I've buried myself alive. . . . I'm dead and under the ground. My life is over. Never again shall I love and be loved." A freer and bolder man would, in my place, have solved the problem by seeking a pretext for breaking off the engagement; or else, without any pretext at all, by informing Clara of his true feelings. But I haven't a strong character and irresolution, in me, is an almost morbid infirmity; to take such a decision was more than I was capable of; and although not a day passed without my feeling the growing necessity for a rupture, I never plucked up the courage to speak of it to the two women. To my own anguish, I felt that this courage would never come to me and that inevitably, unless some new circumstance arose, I should end by getting married.

In the meantime, as my regret steadily increased, so did my antipathy towards Clara; or rather, my irritation and my bitter, furious desire to shake her. Often I wondered what she could be made of, whether of flesh and bone or of stone; and at moments during those long evenings I was seized with mad impulses to shout indecent remarks, to break something, to lay hands on her, just in order to see her become human even if only through a feeling of disgust or astonishment or indignation. As I have already said, I was exasperated, above all, at having not the slightest, the most remote, feeling of desire when close beside her; and of being incapable, however much I might force my imagination, of picturing what she was like underneath her stiff, ungraceful clothes. Had she a bosom with two breasts like other women? And what about her belly? And her legs? And was her skin warm and did muscles move beneath it and blood circulate, or was it not, perhaps, petrified like that of a mummy? I ruminated upon these things and upon others of the same kind as, sitting on that hard settee, I strained and struggled in my various efforts to keep alive the dying flame of our listless conversation. And, as if infected by my closeness to her, I sometimes felt that, like her, I too had ceased to be a human being like other human beings, of flesh and blood and bone; I felt indeed like a kind of phantom afflicted by contradictory impulses and incapable of taking bodily shape and form. This feeling of unreality made me suffer acutely; it was like a cocoon of falsity inside which I should find myself, in time, irremediably enclosed.

One night when, full of ill-humour, I turned into the street in which the Malinverno villa stood, just as I reached the corner formed by the villa itself and a cross-road, I heard distinctly, through the rustling sound of the rain, the gurgling of water, quiet but abundant and apparently flowing underground. One step further forward, and the gurgling sound became more precisely defined, and a little further on still it became, so to speak, palpable, as though the water were gushing

out right under my feet. Puzzled, and seeing no source of
water anywhere near, I turned and went back along the same
part of the street and again noted the same phenomenon. Half-
way along the wall of the villa, the gurgling sound became
louder and seemed to reach its highest note; a little further on
the noise decreased and then vanished altogether.

I noticed then for the first time that the side of the villa
facing on to the road had not merely two rows of windows
but also five unglazed crescent-shaped apertures at ground level
which, it appeared, were intended to give light to the cellars.
I switched on my pocket torch and examined these apertures.
I could see now that they were all blocked at the back by a
roughly whitewashed wall; this showed that the cellars must
be very deep and that the light evidently had to pass between
the inner and outer walls and fall vertically, as a mere feeble
glimmer, much as happens with a certain kind of window
sometimes used in prisons. The rumbling sound of the water
came, precisely, from the third opening, which was the middle
one; at each side it diminished, though it remained perceptible
as far as the corners of the house. I put out my electric torch and,
after listening for a short time in the rainy darkness, with growing irritation, to the continuous roar of water that sounded as
though reverberating beneath spacious, ice-cold vaults, I went
on to pay my usual evening visit.

I found the old lady in her accustomed place in the room at
the end of the passage, bending over a large sheet which fell
from her knees in stiff folds down to the ground. She was
embroidering a big monogram of interwoven letters and she
told me, without lifting her head, and with a satisfaction that
made me shudder, that this was the sheet for our wedding
night. I bent down to feel it, and it seemed to me almost
impossible that this piece of linen would soon be covering our
two embracing bodies, my own and Clara's. A short time
afterwards the daughter tottered in on her high heels, handkerchief to nose, eyes lowered. That slow walk, as of someone

who is in no hurry, so sure is he that he is missing nothing, that handkerchief held to the nose—these filled me with irritation. I allowed none of this to appear, however, and sat down beside her on the settee. Her mother, as usual, had her back turned to us, which may have been intended to make me think that she was not watching us; but right in front of her was the big looking-glass above the console-table in which, whenever she had the curiosity to do so, she could follow all our movements.

I felt irritated and angry; my mind was divided between the desire to press forward in my intimacy with Clara and that of breaking off our engagement. After a little trivial conversation, I took hold of her hand, seeking to keep it in mine and at the same time stroke it with my other hand. For a moment she permitted this, though she sat quite numb and rigid; then, in her usual slow manner, she disengaged and withdrew her hand; and all this without looking at me or uttering a sound, giving me to understand, however, by her silence and indifference, how much she disapproved of my gesture. This wayward-ness infuriated me; and I asked her, in a low, resentful voice:

"We're engaged . . . and yet am I not allowed even to hold your hand?"

"It's not that," she answered, "but your hands are so freezing cold."

This was a lie; for, being always in a feverish state, my hands are, in fact, exceptionally warm. But her answer reconfirmed what other similar incidents had already made me suspect—that I should never achieve intercourse with Clara; she would always find a way of thrusting me back into a realm of con-vention where intimacy was impossible.

"But when we're married," I persisted, speaking in a low voice, "shall I be able to hold your hand *then*?"

She raised her handkerchief to her nose. "Let's talk of some-thing else, shall we?" she said.

A short silence ensued. The old lady made an abrupt movement with the sheet, and I, still with the same fixed determination to shake and arouse Clara, murmured: "That sheet—your mother told me it's to be the sheet for our wedding night. . . . Have you ever thought about that?"

She must certainly have told herself that I was crazy; and the low, intense tone of my voice, the expression on my face as I brought it down close to her shoulder could not but confirm her in this idea. I saw her bend forwards, very slowly, and raise one corner of the sheet, at the same time asking her mother: "How far have you got?"

"I've almost finished," said her mother without turning round.

So she didn't even take the trouble to answer me. I thought of all the many occasions upon which, after we were married, she would adopt these same tactics of silence; and with a great rage in my heart I clenched my teeth with such force that I could hear them grate together. Then again I heard the rain murmuring against the shutters, and all of a sudden I remembered the subterranean sound of water which I had noticed shortly before on my way to the villa.

"By the way," I asked, "what is that loud noise of water that one hears as one walks past your house?"

Clara looked at me uncomprehendingly. I repeated my question, describing the exact spot and the quality of the sound.

"Oh," she said simply, "that's the water for the tank where they wash the clothes."

"But a gurgling noise like that," I insisted, "seems to me far louder than the sound of water could be in a tank for washing clothes."

"It's a very big tank," she replied; "it takes up the whole floor of a room. . . . Besides, the inlet is high up."

The idea of breaking off the engagement came back into my mind. But there, in front of her mother, it seemed to me impossible to say anything. I felt that in some other place, in the cellar for instance, I might at last pluck up the courage I lacked.

"Look here," I said, with an air of anxiety, "I don't believe it's just the inlet; the noise was too loud. I can't help thinking there's something wrong. . . . Perhaps a pipe has burst. Perhaps the cellar is flooded."

"Something wrong," she repeated slowly. "Why should there be anything wrong?"

I had now found the excuse I needed. Her mother, in alarm, had interrupted her work, had turned half round and was looking at me with an expression of perplexity. I took up my arguments again, with singular warmth, surprised, almost, at myself for being so eloquent. The truth was that I clung with all my strength to this ridiculous idea—that in the cellar I should be able to speak the words which I was totally incapable of uttering upstairs. Clara did not appear convinced and remained silent. Finally her mother came to my assistance and begged her daughter to do as I asked.

"You see," I said, rising at once to my feet, well satisfied, "I shouldn't like to think that, owing to these torrential rains, something had gone wrong. That gurgling sound was really extremely loud."

She said nothing, but walked off in front of me down the passage. I followed behind her as she advanced through the familiar gloom of her home, tottering a little, slow, erect, down to the end of the passage and then on down the stairs. As soon as we were on the staircase I started urging myself to speak. I said to myself that at last we were alone, and that an opportunity like this would never occur again. But I had only to look at Clara to feel the words die away on my lips.

"Clara," I managed to ejaculate suddenly, as we were going down the second flight.

"What is it?" she answered without turning, her hand on the brass rail.

I was close behind her, so close that my nose was almost touching her white, round, strong neck, and for a moment I felt a strong desire to squeeze that same neck until I rendered her silent once and for all, after all the many deliberate, offensive silences she had inflicted upon me. But I thrust back the temptation.

"Is it a very long time," I asked, "since this villa was built?"

"About fifty years," she replied.

"Yes, I thought so," I said, passing my hand over the wall with the air of a connoisseur.

In the hall downstairs Clara opened a little door hidden behind the leaves of a palm-tree and revealed a small staircase with steep steps which appeared to be hollowed out in the thickness of the wall. She turned on a red lamp and went down the steps in front of me. The staircase twisted very sharply and was so steep that Clara's head was almost against my stomach; but once again I lacked the courage to speak, or—as the temptation again assailed me—to seize and finish with her in that narrow, tomb-like place.

We came out into the cellar. From a landing on the stairs I looked down into a large, low room with a number of grey pillars supporting a vaulted ceiling. The cellar was empty; across the rough cement of the floor lay the slender shadows of the pillars; but from the far side of the arches echoed the continuous splash of water which I had heard from the street. It was quiet and plaintive, a strange thing to hear in that underground vault.

"This is the cellar," she announced, standing still and looking down.

I said nothing, but descended the last few steps, in the direction of the sound. Clara followed me. When we had passed beyond the row of pillars I was able to see the tank, just as Clara had described it to me. It was very long, and occupied three-quarters of the room. Its top was at floor level, and it made me think of the hippopotamus tank at the Zoo. There was the same dark water from which you expect to see the beast's gleaming hide rise to the surface at any moment; there was the same look of perilous depth. A small platform of dark granite on one side suggested to the imagination a figure of a kneeling washerwoman rinsing and wringing out clothes in the murky pool. As for the jet of water, it came from a large iron spout which stuck out from the wall. The flow of water, to tell the truth, was not very abundant; the noise was to be explained by the height from which the water fell and by the echo in the chilly vaulted cellar.

"And that's the tank. . . . Are you satisfied now?" said Clara. I made no answer, but instinctively put my arm about her waist. I was astonished to feel, not a soft girdle such as a young girl generally wears, but something harsh, something hard and tight, a corset or a stiff waistband. She turned her head and shoulders slightly in my direction, saying: "What's come over you now?"; and at the same time, with her usual slowness and composure, she tried to free herself, as though confident that the mere touch of her hands would make me loosen my hold. But I clasped her to me even more strongly and, without uttering a word, seized her by the hair with my other hand and sought to bend back her head in such a way that our mouths should meet. And meet indeed they did—except that she, with her arrogant obstinacy, pressed her lips tightly together and drew them inwards; so that all I felt against my mouth were two ridges of hard, cold flesh. Such stubbornness filled me with a terrible rage. "Our engagement is off; this is our last meeting," I wanted to cry out; instead of which, all I could do was to thrust her unyielding body violently away from me. She fell back, tripping over the rim of the tank, with a scream that further aggravated my hatred, a scream that even in her terror was imbued with moderation and self-sufficiency; next moment I heard the dull, heavy sound of her head striking against the stone platform. I saw her body plunge sideways into the black, foamless water and then turn so that one arm and one cheek, both of them white in the surrounding gloom, rose to the surface again. I leapt into the tank and, slipping on the soapy bottom, dragged her, not without difficulty, out of the water and started to carry her towards the stairs. She appeared to have fainted; and I, panting as I hauled her along under the low arches in the half-darkness, was smitten with a sense of guilt so acute that I was tempted to consummate that first instinctive gesture and throw her back into the tank from which I had dragged her. It was a temptation at the same time violent and exquisitely sweet, similar to the irresistible temptation of sexual possession. And perhaps it may have been inspired by love; by the kind of love, at least, to which she had forced me by her demeanour; a love changed into hatred, which preferred to kill rather than remain unsatisfied.

She recovered consciousness that same night in her bed, and at once calmed my ignoble fears by saying, with her usual simplicity, that she had slipped accidentally. Now that she was conscious again, her mother was relieved from her first apprehensions and even found time to reprove me for my disastrous curiosity. But I myself, after my first feeling of relief, became more and more frightened at the prospect of a wedding after what amounted to little less than an attempted murder. I held Clara's hand in mine—she, as though to endorse my terrors, no longer refused it me—and I told myself that my life was finished.

I was once again so desperate at the idea of my now inevitable marriage that next day, when I learned that, contrary to earlier hopes, Clara's condition had worsened and that she was approaching her last moments, I felt a renewed and greater relief. She lived for two more days, and during that time I watched beside her together with her mother and her sister who had hastened up from the country. Often, as I sat gazing at her motionless face, I wondered what she was thinking about, and more than once, as though seized with my former frenzy, I was tempted to grasp her by the arm and shake her and command her to speak; but, as before, I was frozen into stillness by her demeanour, which seemed to be in no way altered by approaching death. I had only to observe the look with which she asked her mother to give her something to drink, in order to realize that she was entirely unchanged. Probably, if I had asked her forgiveness—as several times I was tempted to do—in spite of the fact that she was dying she would have pretended not to hear me, or would have given me an evasive answer. These reflections, I suppose, made me continue to hate her till the very last moment.

She died as she had lived: decently, composedly. Death did not seem to produce any change in her appearance, which had been always so cold and expressionless.

On the day of the funeral—for the first time—it did not rain; and, next day, tolerable weather set in, moist and mild under an exhausted grey sky. I went out for a walk along an avenue near the house where I lived, and realized to my surprise that at the thought of Clara my only feeling was one of enormous relief: I had not, after all, got married.

It occurred to me all of a sudden that the mere fact of living was a piece of true good fortune; and for the first time for many months I felt again a secret zest for life, made up of mild boredom, of hope and of freedom to dispose of myself.

Clara's mother endeavoured to see me again, no doubt in order to weep with me over her daughter's death. But I contrived to excuse myself, under the pretext that my sorrow forbade such evocations of the past. Clara, in any case, has a place in my heart; how could it not be so? As for that noise of water, I am now cured of my obsession; and I no longer take any notice, on rainy days, of any source of running water whose voice may reach my ears. And so, by virtue of living, I forget my past life.

HOME IS A SACRED PLACE

ABOUT the beginning of the summer Giacomo suddenly found himself entirely alone. He thought he had many friends, that he knew a large number of women; but no more than a few departures had sufficed to create a desert around him. The truth of the matter was that, like everyone else, he moved in a restricted circle of people; and it occurred to him that when he was old such departures would be without return and his solitude would be complete and final.

He got into the habit of rising late and staying in his room at the boarding-house until lunch-time, reading a little or smoking as he lay on his bed. After lunch he would go out for a short time; he would drink a cup of coffee in a bar, buy a newspaper and then go back and read it in his bedroom. Sometimes, if he was tired and if it was hotter than usual, he liked to let the newspaper drop from his hand and doze off for half an hour. About the middle of the afternoon he would get up, wash, comb his hair and dress; and then leave the boarding-house.

He used to go and sit in a café in the smartest street in town. In this café they served a German beer in small bottles which Giacomo liked very much indeed. He would slowly drink the good iced beer as he watched the people walking past and others sitting at the little tables. All the idle people of the town, the best dressed young men, the most attractive girls, made use of this stretch of pavement, of these little tables, as a meeting-place. There would be many people standing in front of the café windows, pretending to be in conversation but in reality posturing in an indolent fashion beneath the gaze of anyone who happened to be looking, and themselves watching, out of the tail of an eye, the passers-by and the others seated at the tables. Animated women, cigarettes held between their fingers, would rise from their tables and go to other tables, laughing and talking in loud voices. Waiters carrying trays moved with difficulty through the crowd. People joked and called to each other and chattered unreservedly, and there was an incessant hubbub of an entirely self-sufficient and exclusive kind as though it were not a public street but a private drawing-room. And indeed, if some poor man with ragged clothes, or even somebody like Giacomo, solitary and without friends, ventured amongst this crowd, it seemed exactly as if he had happened to arrive in some house where he was neither invited nor wanted. It was in truth a private affair between those who sat at the tables and those who strolled up and down in front of them. And all this went on under the great plane-trees whose mature foliage cast playful lights and shadows over tables, glasses, faces and clothes. It was hot, but there was no sultriness in the air and the sky was clear and brilliant. At twilight all these people dispersed and went off to their own homes. The waiters pulled up the awnings and cleared the last of the tables.

Having drunk his first bottle of beer, Giacomo usually drank a second one, and this took him until sunset. Then he would get up and stroll home in a leisurely manner. In the evening he came back again to the café, where the same scenes, the same flauntings, the same social parade as in the afternoon was again repeated; except that it was on a smaller scale and illuminated, now, by the street lights. The evenings were particularly pleasant in that wide, airy street that wound upwards in ample curves between tall buildings and gardens. The breeze stirred gently beneath the plane-trees; in the mild, tired air voices sounded clear and gay; women's faces were mysterious in the shadows. There were fewer passers-by than in the daytime, so it was possible to observe them more closely and at greater length.

Giacomo would order an ice in a glass and enjoy it slowly, diligently, as if he had been paid for doing precisely that, eating an ice and watching the people.

He had a feeling of calm and emptiness; and at moments he was even able to deceive himself into thinking that he was in perfect control of the lonely, forsaken state in which he found himself. But there was always a kind of anguish lurking in the background, and, when he least expected it, it would suddenly clutch at his heart. Sometimes it was his feeling of gluttony for beer and ices that brought him to despair, as being a mean characteristic worthy only of someone who expects nothing further from life than such facile pleasures; or again it was a glance, a gesture, a word caught unexpectedly from some unknown passer-by that made him imagine how much richer were other people's lives in comparison with his own. Then he would become aware of a vague distress and would realize that before the end of the summer he would have to do something that would restore to him the sense of his own freedom. For at these moments it seemed to him that after all he was not free, as anyone might have supposed; on the contrary he was bound and impotent, a slave to the loneliness which he had not sought and which did not depend upon himself.

One night, as he was returning home after spending his usual hour at the café, his attention was attracted by the glimmer of light from the basement windows of a night-club in the same street. He recalled that in the winter this cellar resort was used as a place of rendezvous by women in search of adventure—so at least he had been told; and he wanted to see whether, in summer as well, it might be possible for him to pick up a companion there for the night. He went down a few steps, pushed open a glass door and found himself in the bar. It was dark inside, on account of the heavily shaded lights; and the stuffy heat of summer mingled in a disagreeable way with an old musty smell of smoke left over from the winter. In the dim light, against a background of rows of bottles on shelves, the barman's face appeared black with heat as though all the blood had coagulated in his head as the result of an apoplectic stroke. Against his brilliant white jacket his hands, too, looked black as he moved them about behind the zinc counter between the nickel-plated coffee-machine, the water-jet, the jars of olives and the other knick-knacks. Giacomo, at first, could think of nothing better to do than climb up on one of the stools and ask the barman to serve him a liqueur.

No sooner was he comfortably established and beginning to sweat under the low, vaulted ceiling than he realized that what he was looking for was not in the bar but in the small room adjoining it. From the bar his view extended right to the farthest end of the place, which consisted of a succession of extremely small rooms. Each room had only a few tables and a few settees fitted into the recesses formed by the windows. At the moment the rooms were empty—except for two women sitting on one of these sofas in a window-recess.

For a little time, as he examined them, he remained uncertain as to what kind of people they could be. They were respectably, even elegantly, dressed, but without pretentiousness. They were both fair, and one of them looked seven or eight years younger than the other. The younger one wore her hair loose on her shoulders. Her face was fresh and without make-up, her large eyes somewhere between blue and green, her nose pointed and her mouth big and full and red. She was hatless and dressed in country clothes; she had taken off her jacket and thrown it over a chair, and was wearing a blouse which left her neck and arms bare. The elder woman's hair was carefully curled and waved, and upon it, tilted forward over her forehead and precariously balanced, was perched a minute little hat. She, too, had light-coloured eyes, but her eyelids were narrowed and slightly puffy, and this gave her a vicious, hypocritical expression. Her eyes were painted, as were her cheeks and mouth, the latter being sinuous and almost lipless. She was better dressed than her companion, with a commonplace, elaborate, urban smartness; and at first glance she might even have seemed the prettier of the two. But a second look convinced Giacomo that the younger one was to be preferred—very much so, in fact—if only because she had not, like the other one, the conventional appearance of a respectable lady.

The two women were sitting quite still without saying a word to each other. Giacomo saw one of them full face, the one with the hat; the other in profile. What convinced him, all of a sudden, that they were a couple of prostitutes was the excessive, ostentatious dignity, quite inappropriate in that place, of the elder one. Also her hands, which she had placed on the table, and which were dark in colour and not beautiful, with nails painted a purplish red. The younger one also had painted nails but her hands were pale and long.

"Here you are, Sir," said the barman suddenly and put down a small glass in front of Giacomo. Giacomo, in the ordinary way, would not have had the courage to question the barman about the two women; but he already felt himself to be in an atmosphere of unreality in which shyness is replaced by off-handedness even though, beneath the surface, it still remains unchanged and no less troublesome than before.

"Who are those two?" he asked abruptly.

The barman was wiping the counter with a damp rag. Without raising his head or interrupting his wiping operations, he answered: "I don't know, Sir. They were here the other evening, too. . . . I'd never seen them before." But all this was uttered in a particular tone of voice, as though giving Giacomo to understand that they were undoubtedly women of the kind that his question seemed intended to suggest.

"Will you be so kind as to take my glass to that table?" Giacomo replied.

He got down off the stool, and without more ado went over and sat down at the table beside the two women.

He found himself still in the same position with regard to

them, with the younger one in profile and the other full face. But the latter, who could not avoid seeing him, lowered her eyes. The younger one, on the other hand, who could well have ignored his presence, looked at him obliquely, in a bold manner, with an enigmatical gleam of gaiety in her green eyes. It seemed to Giacomo that the woman with the hat was aware of her companion's glance and disapproved of it. But possibly, he thought, he might be wrong.

The barman came over, put down his glass on the table and went back to the counter. There was no one in the little room except the three at the table. The younger woman said suddenly, in a loud voice: "Your friend doesn't seem to be coming. . . . I think it's disgustingly rude of him."

"Sh—sh—sh," whispered the elder one in annoyance.

"Why," asked the younger one, "can't I speak, now? If he doesn't come, it's very rude of him, as I said before."

"All right," said the elder woman without moving, sitting very erect and straight as if she feared her hat might slip down on to her nose; "but why shout?"

"Who's shouting?"

"You are."

"That's enough, then; I'm not even going to answer you." But all this was said apparently without anger, almost gaily, and possibly—so it seemed to Giacomo—in order to attract his attention. "Well then, give me a cigarette."

Giacomo had placed his cigarette-case on the table beside his glass and was ready to bend forward and hold it out open. The girl was no less ready to accept his offer. She thanked him, coolly took the case and held it out to the other woman, enquiring whether she wanted to smoke. Her companion seemed to be torn between the desire to accept and the scorn which the girl's gesture inspired in her.

"Really one oughtn't to accept cigarettes quite so quickly!" she remarked regretfully. But she took one and, before putting it in her mouth, looked at the name of the brand. Then, with all the little gestures of a refined lady allowing her cigarette to be lit by an accomplished cavalier, she leant forward across the table towards Giacomo's lighter. The other woman had lit her cigarette herself and was already blowing smoke from her nostrils.

"How hot it is, isn't it?" said Giacomo, turning instinctively to the elder of the two as being the one whom he felt to be still hostile.

The conventional question appeared to please her as a token of almost undeserved respect. "Terrible," she said, in a detached, high-society tone, sucking in the smoke in little mouthfuls, puffing it out again without inhaling it and gazing at the glowing end of the cigarette; "I don't remember such heat for a very long time."

"I'm all in a sweat," said the younger one, laughing; and, raising her arm, she showed how the sweat had soaked through her blouse under the armpit. This movement caused the silk of her blouse to be stretched tightly over her breasts in strong relief, seeming to reveal their weight rather than their shape. "It's impossible to breathe in this hole. . . ."

The elder woman appeared to disapprove of this demonstration; she cast a disgusted glance at her companion. Then, turning to Giacomo: "This place is more suitable for the winter, isn't it? In summer open-air cafés are really preferable."

So she wants to carry on an ordinary middle-class conversation, does she? said Giacomo to himself; and this in spite of having accepted his sitting down at their table, in spite of her brazen companion. . . .

"Yes," he replied, "open-air cafés are certainly preferable—especially those that are situated in gardens."

"That's where we always go," said the woman.

"When?" asked the other.

"Always"; and she shook the ash off her cigarette, bending her head to one side; "this evening is a mere chance. . . . We were expecting a friend."

Giacomo noticed the younger one start laughing. "A fine

sort of friend," she said, "a friend we don't even know the name of. . . ."

"What d'you mean?" replied the other in an indignant voice, but without moving. "He's called . . ." she hesitated a moment, "he's called Meluschi."

The younger one laughed again. "But that's the name of our landlord . . . what's *he* got to do with it?"

"My sister *will* have her little joke," said the elder one, turning towards Giacomo.

"No, no, this isn't a joke," objected the other one, laughing. "The man has never been your friend, still less mine. We just picked him up in the street, so to speak—that was all." She seemed to infuse a kind of sensual cruelty into the sincerity with which she spoke. Her eyes were sparkling with malice, her nostrils quivering.

"Anyhow it was in a café," said the elder sister, turning to Giacomo as to someone more able to understand her; "and besides, he came up very politely and asked to accompany us . . . just like you this evening. If you talk like that," she concluded suddenly, turning towards her sister, "goodness knows what the gentleman will think of us."

But the girl did not stop laughing and twisting about in her seat, her pretty face flushed with unkind amusement. "He's already thought . . . he's already thought—don't worry. Otherwise he wouldn't have come over to us with that expression on his face . . . now isn't that so, Mr.—— By the way, what is your name? Yesterday we didn't ask the name and now you see what's happened."

"My name's Giacomo," said the young man, at the same time both amused and irritated by the girl's words; and then, with an effort, he went on: "Yes, it's quite true that I came over to your table for the reasons that you suppose. But it's possible I made a mistake. . . ."

"Oh no! you didn't make a mistake, you didn't make a mistake"; and she laughed heartily.

"My name is Rina," interposed the elder of the two with dignity, "and my sister's is Lori."

Her sister began laughing again. "But your name isn't Rina," she cried, "it's Teresa. And my name isn't Lori but Giovanna."

"I prefer Rina and Lori," said the elder sister; "they're shorter. . . . But do stop it, Lori. . . ."

"Mayn't I even laugh, now?"

"Laugh, yes. But you're so ill-mannered."

"I'm *not* ill-mannered," said Lori. But she became serious, as though her sister's last remark had stung her to the quick.

Giacomo asked: "And what is your surname?"

"Panigatti," replied Rina bashfully, lowering her eyes with a look of penitence.

"There's a town in Sicily called Canicattí," observed Giacomo, amused at her sheepishness.

"No . . . our surname is Panigatti. And anyhow we're not Sicilians."

"Where do you come from?"

"We belong to Verona," replied the elder sister. At which the younger one winked maliciously and remarked: "Actually we belong to Meolo—but she doesn't like it because she says it's like the noise a cat makes."

"Will you have something to drink?" enquired Giacomo.

"Yes—champagne, champagne!" cried the younger sister with a parody of enthusiasm.

"I should suggest going somewhere else. . . . What d'you think?" The elder sister picked up her gloves from the table and started putting them on.

"What about your friend Meluschi?" asked Giacomo.

"It doesn't look to me as if he was coming now," began Rina, turning to Giacomo. But Lori cried impetuously: "Oh him! We certainly shan't see *him* again! I expect he's broke, anyhow. . . ."

They all three rose and moved towards the door. Giacomo went over to the bar and asked for his bill.

"Are you paying for all three drinks?" enquired the barman.

"Yes. And a packet of Egyptian cigarettes."

"That'll be sixty lire, then—including the cigarettes."

Giacomo took the cigarettes and paid the bill; the barman, as he took up the money, bowed behind the counter and wished him good night.

They went out on to the broad pavement, under the thick foliage of the plane-trees. The moon was at the height of its splendour and, beyond the shadow of the trees, lit up the wide asphalt street and the beds of flowers. In that light the colours of the flowers—the greens and reds, the blues, the yellows—looked strange and unreal.

"Where shall we go?" asked Giacomo.

"Somewhere where we can get a drink," answered the younger sister. "I've been sitting quite long enough with a dry mouth. . . . I've got such a thirst. . . ."

"I should suggest going to the bar at the Splendid," said the elder one, moving away along the pavement and making a sort of parade of her own gestures in the moonlight.

"For goodness' sake, no! It's suffocating in there," protested the younger one.

"Let's go to the Caves of Ancus Marcius," proposed Giacomo.

This was a resort near by. It was an underground place full of sham Roman wine-jars, sham tomb-stones, sham ruins; but it had numbers of little recesses and tiny rooms and retired corners, hollowed out of the volcanic rock and hidden away behind pillars, where people could sit and talk at their ease. The elder of the two women did not appear satisfied; perhaps the place was not refined enough for her. But the younger one seized Giacomo's arm impetuously.

"Yes, let's go there," she said. "Let's go to the Caves. Who was Ancus Marcius?"

"A king of Rome."

They walked in a leisurely fashion along the wide, deserted

pavement to the entrance into the 'Caves', a staircase of red brick leading down to below ground level. At the entrance, a couple of enormous wine-jars proclaimed the style of the *décor*. At the bottom of the first flight of steps a blackened, mutilated stone slab bore a burlesque inscription in macaronic Latin. After they had passed this stone and ventured on down the second flight of steps, they ran into an atmosphere in which there was a mingled smell of tobacco smoke, wine and general mustiness, and were greeted by a remote, hollow clamour of voices and music. The caves were very large and full of twists and turns. From the bottom of the stairs could be seen, under the low, curving vaults, rows of large tables with small carafes of wine on them and people sitting round. With its arches and columns and pilasters and buttresses, the place sought to imitate the structure of a primitive underground basilica.

"Oh, how lovely!" cried Lori, clapping her hands together; "it's really old, isn't it! It looks like—what d'you call those underground places where the Christians used to meet?"

"Catacombs," suggested Giacomo.

"That's it—catacombs. You've never taken me there."

"To tell the truth, I've never cared for this place," said her elder sister.

The people at the tables looked at them without curiosity as they walked past. Most of them were unpretentious young men with their girl friends. There were a few larger groups of people drinking and making jokes in loud voices that echoed beneath the vaulted ceiling. At the far end, a long distance away, could be seen, moving up and down, the arms of three or four double bass and violin players seated on a small platform.

"Let's go over here," said Giacomo.

After walking round the tables in the first room, they entered a very narrow passage between two walls of red brick and came out into a small room in the Pompeian style. The

145

frescoes on the walls of this room were limited to a few incomplete fragments and represented, on a dark red background, cupids and satyrs and nude figures of women; they aimed at creating an impression of expert but careful restoration. But various customers had written their names in pencil right on top of these frescoes, together with exclamatory or facetious remarks. From the ceiling hung a wrought-iron lantern. A big table and a few stools occupied almost the whole of the floor space. Giacomo sat down at the head of the table with the elder sister on his right, the younger on his left.

"What would you like to drink?"

"Anything you like . . . so long as it's good," said Lori.

Her sister said she would like a liqueur. But it appeared that they had no liqueurs.

"We have red or white Chianti, Orvieto in flasks, and wines in bottle," said the waiter.

"What dessert wines have you?"

"Marsala . . . Passito . . . Aleatico."

"Let's have some Aleatico."

"So you come from Meolo," said Giacomo, resuming the previous conversation.

"Yes," answered the younger sister, "but I live in Milan and my sister lives here. Every now and then we visit each other; I come to see her here and stay with her . . . and then she comes to see me and stay with me."

"I don't like Milan," said Rina. "It's too cold in winter. I've been ill and I need the sun."

"What was wrong with you?" enquired Giacomo.

"I'm a little delicate," she explained, putting her hand to her chest.

Her chest was, in fact, thin and flat, Giacomo noticed. But her face, with its slightly puffy eyelids, had a vicious expression which aroused his curiosity.

"That isn't the real truth," said Lori; "the reason is that she has a boy friend here."

"What does he do?" asked Giacomo.

"He's in business," replied the elder sister with the same bashfulness with which, shortly before, she had said her surname was Panigatti.

"He sells cheeses," said the younger one; she laughed and pinched her nose with two fingers as though to indicate that her sister's lover smelt of his profession.

The waiter arrived with the wine. When he had uncorked the bottle, Giacomo poured out the Aleatico into the big green glasses.

"It's good," said Lori, looking at Giacomo. "It's nice and sweet."

"Aleatico," her sister corroborated.

Giacomo drank off his first glass at one draught and then poured himself out another. The two women, too, had soon emptied their glasses, which Giacomo promptly refilled. He then called the waiter and ordered a second bottle.

"Where is your friend at present?" he prudently enquired of Rina.

"He's travelling."

"Oh, there's no fear of his arriving unexpectedly," said the younger sister, laughing; "he always telegraphs, sometimes he even telephones; he behaves very well."

"Lori, don't talk about him like that," said the elder sister irritably; "you don't even know him."

"He's not so wonderful as all that, you know," said the younger one abruptly. "You're quite right to deceive him; I don't find any fault with you for that."

The elder sister said nothing. Giacomo felt he ought to win over Rina; or at least make some sort of an advance. And without giving any sign he put out his hand under the table and placed it on her knee. She gave him a hypocritical look and asked him: "And you—where do you come from?"

"From Ancona," replied Giacomo.

From her knee, thrusting her dress back roughly, Giacomo's

hand moved to her thigh. She was wearing very tight garters, and above these garters the bare flesh was swollen almost to bursting point. She was elaborately dressed underneath her skirt, with lace trimmings and silk and buttons and a complicated system of suspenders.

"Ancona is a beautiful town," she said, without moving or resisting Giacomo's hand.

By this time her skirt was pulled awkwardly to one side, in such a way that one white thigh was visible, the other not.

"D'you really think I can't see you?" the younger sister cried suddenly, but without any sign of jealousy. "But go on, go on—don't mind me!"

Giacomo withdrew his hand; then was sorry he had done so, reflecting that, after all, he had been doing just what she wanted; so he put his hand back again on her bare leg. However, so as to be quite fair, he put his other arm round the younger sister's waist. She laughed and looked at him sideways with her big, mischievous eyes, holding her wineglass close to her mouth. Giacomo leant forward and brushed her neck with his lips.

The elder sister pushed Giacomo's hand away and pulled down her skirt. She did not appear to be doing this out of jealousy of her sister, but merely for the sake of propriety, because just at that moment some people were passing at the far end of the room.

"What do you do in Milan?" Giacomo enquired of Lori.

"What do I do?" she repeated, laughing.

"She's a model," said the elder one promptly.

"I *was* a model," objected the girl, emphasizing the past tense with a laugh; "now I do what she does here. . . ."

"Why d'you say that?" asked the elder sister in annoyance; "you're trying to pass yourself off as something different from what you are."

"Now just listen to that!" said the girl slowly, with a pretence of great astonishment. She was tipsy now, and her fine eyes kept changing in a curious way, varying their expression and even their colour. "Just listen to that. . . . And what about you? According to your own account, what do *you* do?"

"I don't do anything," said Rina, with a disgusted shrug of the shoulders; "I'm a lady. . . . I live my own life."

"Just listen to that! Well then, that's what I do too. I'm a lady and I live my own life. . . . In the evening I put on a hat and go into a restaurant or a café and wait for an invitation. . . ."

Rina said nothing; but she stared at her sister with hatred. Finally she warned Giacomo: "If you go on making her drink like this, you'll soon find out what she's really like. . . ."

Lori suddenly flew into a temper. "In the first place I'm not drunk," she shouted. "Anyhow, with Signor Giacomo it's different. He doesn't give himself airs in the way you do."

"Now, now," said Giacomo conciliatingly, patting the girl's knee. She paid no attention to him; so he took a chance and placed his hand on her legs. She was sitting with them close together, and, however far Giacomo's hand ventured, it encountered no trace of stockings or drawers, or chemise or any other garment. From her thighs, which were cool and smooth and strong—very different from her sister's—he continued upwards along her hip and without hindrance reached her belly which, possibly owing to her position, sitting and leaning forward, projected and was folded over itself, and appeared to be rounded and plump. She was naked underneath her dress, in an innocent sort of way and without ulterior motives, simply because it was hot and it was pleasant not to feel one's clothes sticking to one's skin. The girl herself, meanwhile, took no notice of his explorations but went on shouting at her sister.

"Anyhow I'm quite frank about it. . . . I don't make a pretence of living with one particular man and then bring someone else home every evening."

149

Her sister remained silent, staring at her without blinking an eyelid, her little hat pulled well down over her narrow eyes.

"I'm quite frank about it," repeated the girl. But she seemed already less vehement and as though regretting her violence. "Keep still, you!" she suddenly commanded, turning her fury upon Giacomo.

"I told you you oughtn't to make her drink," said her sister.

Giacomo was now feeling tipsy himself; moreover the girl's frank, youthful nudity had excited him; and this combination of drunkenness and excitement produced in him, all at once, a kind of impatience.

"What about it?" he whispered to Lori at a moment when Rina was busy fitting a cigarette into her long cigarette-holder. "What about us two going off and leaving her . . . ?"

But, to his astonishment, the girl showed an unexpected loyalty towards her sister. "You must speak to *her*," she answered. "When I'm staying with her, it's she who decides everything."

Somewhat surprised, Giacomo turned to the elder sister and, lowering his voice, said: "I think it might perhaps be best if I went away. . . . Or one might go somewhere else—with just one of you, of course. . . ."

"With one of us, certainly not," said Rina promptly; "either both or nothing."

"Why?"

"Why? Because that's what we two have agreed."

What on earth am I going to do with *two* women? Giacomo asked himself in amazement. The idea of their being sisters appeared to him strange and novel. "And for the two of you— how much d'you want?"

"You can give us five hundred lire. Two hundred and fifty each."

It was a lot of money, Giacomo could not help saying to

himself; but Rina's tone seemed to exclude any sort of bargaining.

"All right," he said. "But where shall we go?"

"We'll go home with you," she replied.

She spoke calmly and in a normal voice. Her sister, more modest than she, took a drink and pretended not to hear.

"I haven't a home," said Giacomo. "I live in a boarding-house."

"Well then, I don't know," she said hesitatingly.

"But can't I come home with you?"

"Home," she answered slowly, with a kind of stolid haughtiness, "home is a sacred place."

"Considering she takes people back there all the time!" cried the younger sister languidly; her tipsiness now seemed to have got the better of her resentment.

"Which am I to believe?" asked Giacomo. Then, realizing that he had made a blunder: "Please," he begged, "just for once . . . only just this once," and as he spoke he took Rina's hand.

Rina smiled and shook her head. "No, no, not at home; that's impossible."

"But why?"

"It's impossible."

Giacomo saw that he would have to make some other suggestion. "Well then," he said, "let's go to an hotel."

"I shouldn't dream of it. They ask for your papers. . . ."

"What was the name of that hotel where we went a few days ago," cried the other sister, with a curious note of confusion in her voice, "with that man—you know . . . the Hotel Corona?"

"Very well, then," said Giacomo, bored, "there's nothing for it but to say good-bye, in a few minutes' time."

Silence followed. Rina sat smoking with a mysterious, insinuating, refined air, her puffy but benevolent eyes fixed on

Giacomo. "How much d'you think you would have paid at an hotel for the three of us?" she finally asked him.

"I don't know. . . . Fifty or sixty lire. . . ."

"More than that, because you would have had to take two rooms, one of them a double. . . . You would have paid at least a hundred."

"Why—what d'you mean?"

"If you promise me not to make any noise . . . Give us that extra hundred lire that you would have spent at the hotel— three hundred each. . . . Then you can come home with me."

The younger sister started laughing at the perplexity on Giacomo's face. "Isn't my sister clever?" she said. She reclined her head on the table, put her pretty, tipsy face between her arms and closed her eyes.

"Very well, then," said Giacomo. "But let's go at once."

"Come along."

They all three rose; the elder sister, who appeared to be in a hurry, walked on in front of the other two and disappeared down the narrow passage, between the tombstones and the brick arches. Giacomo went up to the younger one and drew her to him. The girl resisted with exaggerated, burlesque gestures as though to indicate that her sister might notice, then allowed herself to be kissed. They drew apart almost immediately and she said, with a smile: "A kiss does you good, once in a while, doesn't it?"

"Yes certainly, it does one good."

They all three went out past the tables and the many little rooms of the subterranean resort. The hubbub of voices, the clatter of glasses, the sound of music reverberated loudly and confusedly beneath the vaulted roof; the atmosphere seemed even thicker and smokier than when they came in. Giacomo reflected that he also had drunk too much. In the street it was almost hotter than in the Caves. The air beneath the plane-trees was perfectly still, the light from the lamp-posts shone only upon an endless mass of leaves hanging close and inert above them.

"We must take a taxi," said the elder sister, in the majestic, detached tone of a lady coming out after a reception or a public entertainment. So they walked down to the square near by; but of taxis there was no sign.

"Where is this home of yours?" enquired Giacomo gaily. He was now holding an arm of each of the two women and allowing them, more or less, to guide him.

"Home is a sacred place," said the younger one, laughing.

The elder one mentioned the name of the street, a street a very long way away, in a quarter on the outskirts of the town.

"The only thing we can do is to take the bus," said Giacomo, "and then, when we reach the terminus, the tram."

It was indeed the only thing to do. Luckily the bus arrived shortly afterwards. They climbed in. Giacomo took three tickets, and they went and sat down in the half-empty bus, the elder sister in front, Giacomo and the younger one behind, on the same seat.

"Certainly for you an hotel would have been better," said the younger sister loudly, as soon as the bus had started; "you'll have to walk all the way back. . . . But they make such a fuss in the hotels here. In Milan I know an hotel where they don't ask any questions and don't even make you pay in advance. . . ."

One or two people in the seats in front turned and cast a glance at Giacomo and his companion. But nobody smiled, for it was late and everyone seemed tired. The bus rushed with impetuous violence through narrow streets, past the tall façades of buildings. The elder sister turned and said, in an emphatic manner, to Giacomo: "Are you staying long this time? How delighted your wife will be! She certainly doesn't see much of you, with all this travelling!"

"His wife!" said the young one with a laugh. "D'you know his wife? Why, are you married?"

"Yes, to you," answered Giacomo, laughing and taking her hand. But she released herself and warned him, with pleasing severity: "Look out, my sister's watching us."

"Home is a sacred place," said Giacomo.

"Yes, home is a sacred place."

One or two people were again looking at them curiously. The elder sister turned round and asked: "Why can't you be quiet for a moment?"

"I'm going to talk as much as I like," replied the younger one.

On receiving this answer, the elder one drew herself up with dignity and turned her back decisively upon them. It was now obvious that she was seeking, in desperation, to convey to the other people in the bus the impression that she had nothing to do with the pair who were sitting behind her. She opened her bag and started powdering her face. In the tiny mirror of her powder-compact Giacomo could see her eyes, hard and full of ill-humour between her bulging eyelids.

The bus reached its final stopping-place and came to a standstill in a dark square. As they got out they could see, not far off, through the black, pointed palm-leaves of a public garden, the round yellow headlamp of a tram.

"That's ours!" cried the elder sister, quickening her pace.

The tram was almost full. However they found three places, in the same positions as they had been in the bus. The elder sister sat in front, and the younger, with Giacomo, behind. A few people got in at the second stop, including a man of about fifty with a conical head of greying hair topped by a black felt hat. He was dressed all in black, with a white collar and a white shirt and black tie. He had a long, prominent nose with a thick red tip to it, in the midst of a face that looked as if it was made of wood. This man sat down stiffly beside Rina and greeted her by raising his hat for an instant above his head, in the same way as you lift the lid of a cooking-pot.

"And when d'you go back to Milan?" asked Giacomo.

"Not just yet. . . . This time I want to enjoy myself," said the girl. "My sister takes me to all the smart places . . . and then we find people like that man yesterday who don't keep their appointments. Really I prefer restaurants where business men go. I've been told that the ——", and she named a well-known restaurant, "is the most suitable place."

Her sister stirred in her seat, but did not turn round.

"Yes," said Giacomo, "the food's very good at that restaurant."

"I want to enjoy myself," went on the girl. "What's the name of that place where there's dancing every night and variety turns too?"

"The Eden?" suggested Giacomo.

"I went there with a man some time ago. A Southerner, he was, but he knew how to spend money. . . . How about going there one evening?"

"Certainly, why not?"

"I do so love places like that," she concluded. Giacomo said nothing, and the girl went on: "If you turn up in Milan, you'll come and see me, won't you?"

"Where d'you live?"

"I'll give you my address," she replied, gazing at him with a kind of drunken satisfaction. "You can come whenever you like. *My* home isn't a sacred place."

The man in the black felt hat turned and took a lingering, searching look at the girl and Giacomo. The back of Rina's neck and shoulders was so still that even the jolts of the tram failed to shake it.

"That wine you gave us," resumed the girl a moment later, "has gone to my head, you know. But it certainly was good."

The tram stopped. Rina rose to her feet and walked off towards the door without saying a word. The man in the black hat also rose and, passing in front of Rina who had paused momentarily, again raised his hat in greeting. She responded

155

in a graceful and dignified manner, as though she were grateful
for such politeness after her sister's conversation.

"Where are you going?" cried Lori, rising in turn; "is this
our stop, already?"

Her sister said nothing, but got out of the tram. Giacomo
and Lori followed her. The tram started off again, and they
were all three reunited on a vast expanse of smooth, black
asphalt. On three sides this shapeless expanse was bordered by
high buildings with a few windows lit up here and there. But
in front of them, in desolate, glittering perspective, were two
rows of lamp-standards stretching away as far as the eye could
reach on each side of what appeared to be a perfectly paved and
levelled street entirely devoid of houses.

"Are we there?" asked the younger sister, looking round.
"I always get lost. . . ."

The elder sister waited until the gentleman in black who had
got out of the tram at the same time had disappeared; then she
spoke in a violent, intense tone of voice. "Yes, we're there. . . .
But get it clear now—this is the last time you're coming to
stay with me."

"Oh—but why? What's the matter?"

"I've told you again and again," went on the elder sister—
and as she spoke, she seemed to become more and more
furious; "at least in the quarter where I live, in the tram which
I take every day, I've told you not to talk like that. . . . But not
at all; you did nothing but make stupid remarks the whole
time . . . at the top of your voice, too."

"But what have I said?"

"In the tram everybody knows me. What will they think
of me?" continued Rina. "You saw the gentleman sitting next
to me—Picchio, the lawyer—he lives in the same building . . .
the door opposite mine. . . . What will he think of me now?—
that I have a strumpet for sister . . . that I bring men home with
me. . . ."

"But what does that matter to you?"

"It matters very much indeed to me. I don't want people saying things about me behind my back."

"Now just listen to me"—and the younger sister gave a jump and planted herself in the middle of the square with her hands on her hips—"listen to me. You bore me stiff with all this nonsense. After all, what is it that your co-tenants will get to know? The truth. . . . Oh, go to the devil!" And she gave another jump and went back to Giacomo's side.

"Very well, then," said the elder sister; "but this is the last time I ask you to stay with me."

They walked on in silence for a time. Then Rina went up to the entrance door of one of the buildings. "Now do please be quiet," she said in a low tone to Giacomo as she turned the key in the lock.

The vestibule which they entered had a dado of black marble, and a star-shaped, many-pointed glass lantern threw countless faceted reflections on the walls. From the vestibule they went on into the hall from which rose the staircase. Rina walked round the lift-shaft and stopped at a door on the ground floor, at the end of a corridor. "Quietly!" she urged them again, as she went in.

When they were inside, Rina switched on a lamp enclosed in a cube of white glass. It appeared that the flat was decorated in a very modern style. Everywhere there were pieces of furniture shaped like boxes, chromium-plated lamps, glass tables, tubular chairs. Rina led Giacomo down a narrow passage to a closed door, saying: "We can go straight through into the bedroom."

The room was small and the wide, very low double bed occupied it almost entirely. The bed was covered with a material the design of which consisted of numbers of squares set one within the other, each shading off in different tones of colour, from blue to violet and red and brown. This stuff was also to be seen on the small chairs and on an armchair. A cupboard composed of various boxes joined together, with a section of mirror in the centre, filled the whole of one wall. On the bedside tables were ball-shaped lamps. Everything was very clean and, in spite of the bright colours of the bed-cover, somewhat melancholy and bleak; it was like a room in an unassuming modern hotel. Rina took off her hat cautiously and put it away in the cupboard. Then she went into a corner and, slipping off her dress over her head, appeared in a black openwork undergarment. She had hardly any bosom, Giacomo noticed, but her figure was pleasing, with broad hips and big legs with fleshy calves. Giacomo did not know what to do: when Rina came within reach, he took hold of her round the waist. She allowed herself to be kissed with a good grace, but coldly. "Now I'll get the bed ready," she said. "If you like, you can go and undress over there, in the bathroom. . . ."

She stooped over the bed to pull off the coverlet, and in so doing raised her silk-clad leg, showing that the garter was too tight and caused her thigh to swell out above it. Having removed the coverlet, she carefully turned back the sheet. The sheet was clean and still showed the creases where it had been ironed; clearly, when she had affirmed that home was a sacred place, the remark had not been, for her, entirely devoid of meaning. Giacomo wondered whether he ought to undress; but he felt a certain shyness at the idea of lying down naked and all alone in that vast double bed. The elder sister was now sitting on the edge of the bed carefully pulling off her stockings, her back turned towards him. The younger one had vanished; she could be heard, through the half-closed door, rummaging about in the bathroom. Giacomo asked Rina whether it was possible to open the window: it was so very hot in there.

"When we've turned out the light," she answered; "at the moment, people might look into the room and see us."

All of a sudden Lori came back from the bathroom and went and stood in front of the wardrobe looking-glass. Giacomo saw her take a long look at herself with a kind of attentive curiosity; then, still gazing at herself and as though thinking of something else, she slowly unbuttoned her blouse, from the neck downwards. Having undone all the buttons, she stood hesitating a moment, then, still in the same slow way, took off the blouse and was naked to the waist. Her breasts were rather large and came down low as if flattened out and pulled down by their own weight, but their points were turned upwards, and from the firm, solid manner in which her whole bosom trembled at her every movement it was evident that this formation was a physical characteristic rather than the effect of a precocious maturity or fatigue. She passed close to Giacomo as she went over to put her blouse on the back of a chair. Then she went to a gramophone which was placed on a stool in a corner and said: "Let's have some music."

She bent down to wind it up and, as she did so, looked up with a cheerful expression at Giacomo through the hair that tumbled down over her eyes. As she made these movements her breasts trembled only very slightly; and this astonished Giacomo, for the effort required to turn the handle was considerable and shook her whole body. The first notes of a dance tune rang out; and she advanced towards him with her arms stretched out in front of her. "Let's dance," she said.

They started slowly rotating. The music became louder, and Rina, who had sat down at the dressing-table, called out, without turning round: "Turn off that gramophone!"

Instead of obeying her, Giacomo and Lori, still revolving, moved out into the passage. Giacomo felt now that he had lost all timidity; the adventure was now well under way, and all he had to do was to follow it through to the end. Soon Rina too would have undressed, Lori would finish undressing, he himself would take off his clothes, and they would all three lie down together in the big double bed.

This thought inspired him with an intense satisfaction and almost took away the impatience he felt for the act of love itself. He wanted, however, to clasp Lori in his arms while they were alone, for he felt shy of doing so in front of her sister. But just at the moment when he was quietly seeking to convert a dance-step into an embrace, the music suddenly ceased.

"It's that idiot Rina," said the girl; she broke away violently from Giacomo's arms and rushed into the bedroom. Giacomo followed her, intensely irritated.

"Why did you turn off the gramophone? We were dancing," she cried to her sister, who was standing beside the gramophone shutting down its lid.

"I told you before that I didn't want any noise," replied Rina. "I think you've made enough noise already, in the tram. You disgraced me in front of Picchio the lawyer so that I shall never have the courage to look him in the face again."

The two sisters were confronting each other now, with the gramophone between them, one of them half naked, the other in her underclothes.

"What do I care about Picchio the lawyer?" cried the younger one. "Besides, what he'll have understood is only the truth—that you go round looking for men. . . . What about it, then?"

"I care about it a great deal. . . . And anyhow it isn't true. It's you, in Milan, who go about looking for men."

"Oh indeed! And what do *you* do, I should like to know?"

"Never mind what I do. . . . But remember, as long as you're in *my* home you've got to behave yourself. This evening you've made me ashamed. . . . There are some things you can do in your own home if you like, but not here."

"Home is a sacred place, eh?" The younger sister started laughing, but with an effort; and all at once her face went red with anger. "I don't care a damn about your filthy home. . . . I'd rather go away at once—d'you see?"

"All right, go then, as far as I'm concerned. I shall be delighted," said the elder sister, in a voice that was less firm now and almost frightened.

But the younger one was in a fury. "Yes, I'm going, I'm

going." She picked up her blouse from the chair, slipped it on and began hastily buttoning it up.

"All right, go then," repeated the elder one; but it was clear that she was distressed by her sister's decision.

"Yes, I'm going . . . and you'll never see me again." Red in the face, the girl went behind the wardrobe and pulled out from a recess a cloth suitcase with leather corners and finishings. Then she opened a drawer and started pulling things out and bundling them higgledy-piggledy into the suitcase.

"Now, come along!" interposed Giacomo, going up to her. "Come along!"

But the girl thrust him away. "Leave me alone, you!"

"You can go, as far as I'm concerned," said her sister once again. She had remained standing beside the gramophone, a disconcerted look on her face.

"I'm going—don't worry—out of your filthy home."

"Go, then," said her sister sorrowfully, "go as quick as you can."

Lori this time made no reply. Resting the suitcase on her thigh and raising her knee, she closed it. She swept furiously across between Giacomo and her sister, went to the clothes-stand, took down a small, crumpled hat and left the room.

"Lori!" called her sister suddenly, as though giving way to a feeling that was too strong for her.

There was no answer. After a moment the whole flat shook as the front door was banged violently. Rina went and sat down on the edge of the bed and took her head between her hands.

Everything had happened so quickly that Giacomo had not had time to get over his first presumptuous conviction that his adventure was well under way and that there was nothing to do but follow the pleasant and easy path of events through to the end. He was still fully possessed by this intense and delightful feeling of certainty, even though the adventure had already evaporated.

Then there came over him an acute, grievous sense of boredom and disappointment and aimlessness. He looked at the woman sitting in her black, open-work undergarment on the edge of the bed which had been prepared to no purpose; her face was between her hands and he saw that she was weeping.

"When I think," she said in an unsteady voice that trembled with tears, "of all I have done for her . . . all the sacrifices I made. . . . When she was a little girl and I was barely sixteen, it was I who kept her alive, by my work. What would have become of her without me? Holidays and clothes and everything I gave her. When she was bigger I found her a job in a dressmaker's as a model. . . . For a long time I went without bread myself so as to send her money. And now you see how she treats me!"

She looked up at him between swollen and tearful eyelids that no longer had anything vicious about them, and shook her head.

"Now, now, come along," said Giacomo with an effort, sitting down beside her and taking her hand; "she'll come back."

"No, she won't . . . I know her. She won't come back so soon. In fact she won't come back at all," she stammered. She took a handkerchief from under the pillow and blew her nose loudly.

Giacomo was now wondering whether he ought to suggest to her that they should go on by themselves, just as though nothing had happened. But he decided that Rina, discomfited and in tears, might possibly accept, and that she would be altogether too melancholy as a partner in love.

"I think," he said, rising to his feet, "the only thing for me to do is to go away."

"I won't suggest your staying," she replied, also rising; "I feel so wretched. You saw how she treated me. . . . How unkind, how unkind. . . . What ingratitude!"

As she said this she went out into the hall. When they

reached the door, Giacomo took her in his arms and gave her a kiss. She returned his kiss with a kind of gratitude. "I'm sorry," she said.

"Never mind," said Giacomo.

When he was outside he looked round in the hope of encountering the infuriated Lori. But there was nothing to be seen but the wide, black lakes of asphalt, the far-off, glittering rows of lamp-standards and the tall, lightless buildings. "That's another day finished," he said to himself scornfully. And he walked away towards the lamp-standards.

CONTACT WITH THE
WORKING CLASS

THE car stopped and they got out. The road, at this point, passed in front of a narrow gorge formed by the junction of two rocky, uncultivated hills of moderate size. On the other side, the flooded plain stretched away as far as the eye could reach, the wide expanses of grey, icy water alternating with clumps of bushes and groups of green trees. Here and there the ruins of houses emerged above the level of the waters, in which their crumbling walls and sky-filled windows were bleakly reflected. The entrance to the gorge was also flooded; but farther back, where the two hills joined, blue smoke was rising, half-way up the slope, and hanging in the air. At a first glance this suggested the brazier of a charcoal-burner; but then, if you looked more carefully, you could distinguish a hut with a low, hood-like roof of blackened straw. The sun was setting, a cold, dark mass of clouds covered the sky, the air was still and as it were paralysed. Between the floods and the steep gorge the road, like a black ribbon of asphalt, made an S-shape which looked like the wriggle of a reptile trying with all its strength to escape.

"We shall have to go to that hut up there," said the young man, pointing to the blue smoke on the hillside; "they'll be able to give us a bucket and some water."

The girl made a grimace of displeasure. Round-faced, with a capricious mouth, a small aquiline nose and large, inexpressive, rather prominent eyes, she was tall, and her loose coat with big tartan checks softly moulded the outlines of her opulent hips and ample bosom. She was hatless, and her long brown hair fell in curls round her forehead and cheeks like an elegant mane. "Is there no other means of getting water without going up there?" she asked sulkily.

"What means?" enquired her companion. He was not more than twenty, but in the big features of his thin face, in his vigorous black moustache, in his nasal voice, he already displayed a kind of petulant virility. He too was wearing checked sports clothes, with a leather wind-jacket, baggy plus fours, thick stockings and a cap pulled down over his eyes.

"Well, you must manage it somehow," she answered, shrugging her shoulders.

"How? With my hands?" he asked ironically. She said nothing, but looked round and appeared disgruntled. "I know how it is," she said suddenly, "these stops are all the same . . . for one reason or another we go to a peasant's house and then, half-way, you always try and kiss me."

Her companion shook his head, but seemed flattered by the accusation. "Now come along, Ornella," he said with an affected, forced seriousness, "I swear to you that this time we're really going to fetch water. . . . In any case," he added, looking at the big gold watch that he wore on his wrist, "we haven't very much time to lose if we want to be in town for dinner. Now make up your mind; if you like, you can wait for me here."

"Yes, all alone here," she objected, in a quarrelsome tone of voice, "and then soldiers come past in lorries and annoy me, as they did this morning. . . . And in the meantime you're carrying out your researches into peasant life. You chatter away with them and forget my very existence."

"The truth of the matter is, then"—the young man's perplexity sounded false because he appeared exceedingly sure of himself—"you don't want to wait here because you're afraid the soldiers will annoy you, and you don't want to come with me because you're afraid that I'll kiss you. . . . May one be allowed to know what it is you *do* want?"

"I'll come," she suddenly made up her mind with a kind of peevish coquettishness that was characteristic of her, "if you'll promise me to be good."

"I swear I will."

"Let's go, then."

He closed the door of the car and started off up the path leading to the hut. The girl followed him, walking unsteadily over the stones.

"I wonder," said the young man as he led the way, "I wonder what the peasants live on who live in that hut. There's no cultivated land either here or for a long distance all around. The plain is flooded. Well, well, it's a mystery."

"No doubt they live on unearned income," replied the girl, grasping with her nails at the young man's sleeve to save herself from falling.

"How many times have I told you, Ornella," he said reprovingly, "that I don't at all like your lack of feeling about the sufferings of poor people. . . ? Good heavens! It looks as if you do it on purpose."

"All that matters to me," she said, pretending not to have heard, "is that you don't stand there for hours, as you usually do, asking the peasants all those endless questions. . . . I can't endure peasants."

"But one *must* talk to them," answered the young man. "If you talk to them you get to know all sorts of interesting things."

"Interesting to *you*."

"But don't you know," he said lightly, almost ironically, "don't you know that one *must* get into contact with the working class?"

By now they were half-way between the hut and the main road. The blue smoke could be distinctly seen issuing, not from a chimney, but from the bulging sides of the low thatched roof. The path ran along the side of the hill. Fifty yards or so below it, the water flooding the gorge did not reflect the sky, but it was possible to see, through its icy transparency, the meagre grass, of a dull green, that covered the ground. "What a dreary place!" said the girl, shuddering as she looked round.

From the top of one of the hills a great black bird rose into the air and started coming down in slow circles, its wings spread and motionless, towards the bottom of the gorge. "Never mind," said her companion awkwardly, "*we're* here." As he said this he turned round, put his arm about the girl's waist and drew her to him.

"There! . . . You swore to me that you wouldn't do that," she cried. The young man smiled and attempted to kiss her. She placed the open palm of her hand against his face, trying to push him away. As an accompaniment to this gesture, she twisted her pretty face into a grimace of ferocity and repugnance. But both gesture and grimace appeared to be dictated by coquettishness more than anything, to constitute a mere conventional repulse. The young man, in spite of the hand pressing against his face, still managed to bring his lips nearer and nearer to hers. Then she changed her gesture and began raining blows on his face with her small fists. But again these blows were feeble and without conviction. She seemed to be pretending to be stubborn and indignant rather than to be genuinely so. And indeed, after a moment she stopped hitting him and allowed herself to be kissed with a good grace, closing her eyes and throwing her arm round his neck. "Oh, that horrible moustache!" she said quickly, as they separated.

"Oh, that horrible lipstick!" he replied in a conceited tone, wiping his mouth and looking at the red stains left on his handkerchief.

They walked on towards the hut. By now they had gone three-quarters of the distance along the path and the main road looked almost remote, with the little dark motor-car standing beside the ditch, in the subdued light of the stormy sunset.

From up there they could see an even larger expanse of flooded plain. And more bushes, more groups of trees, more ruins of houses reflected sadly in the grey, still waters.

The young man was walking in front, swinging his hips in such an obviously conceited fashion that the girl suddenly felt violently irritated. "It would serve you right if I turned round and went back," she said, stopping and stamping her feet on the ground.

"You just try."

"That's what I'm going to do."

She turned and started stumbling back in the direction of the main road. The young man caught up with her, took her by the arm and, gazing at her with careful, ironical attention, said: "Ornella, do you really *always* have to be quite so capricious?"

"Why did you kiss me, then?" she asked. She had already come to a halt.

Soon they reached the hut, which consisted of a circular base of unmortared stones and a roof of dark straw, conical in shape and reaching almost to the ground. The small, low door, crushed down beneath an architrave formed by a single stone larger than the rest, put one in mind more of an animals' stable than of a human habitation. A completely dead, dry tree, its trunk denuded of bark, its branches reduced to big forked points, stood leaning towards the hut. Hanging by their handles on these points were two or three blackened cooking-pots, a few cups and a terracotta tureen. A woodman's hatchet was hanging by its blade in a fork of the tree. On the top of the highest branch, supported by a twig through its eye-socket, could be seen the large skull of some animal, its long white teeth pointing towards the dark sky. Other whitening bones—ribs, vertebrae, shinbones, skulls—lay scattered all over the open space in front of the hut. And in the middle of this space a black circle of dead embers and two or three stumps of trees arranged as chairs suggested the idea of people gathered round a fire.

"And now," asked the girl, turning and looking all round with repugnance, "and now what do we do?"

"We knock at the door and are received by the master of the house," answered her companion with satisfaction. He walked over to the door of the hut and knocked on it with his fist.

Almost immediately the door was unfastened, then it wavered and shook and opened completely. But no one appeared. "Hi!" shouted the young man petulantly, stooping down and peering into the inside of the hut. "Hi there, is there no one at home?"

"Come along in, Sir, come in, please come in," answered a shrill, cracked, but cheerful voice.

"Come on, let's go in," said the young man. "Go in there?" she asked, horrified. "What a fuss you make! Come along in," he repeated, taking her by the arm. The girl obeyed and, bending her head and shoulders, went into the hut. Behind her came her companion.

For a moment they stood upright, their backs to the door. A bright fire was burning on the floor, underneath an iron trivet surmounted by a big black pot. Filled with embarrassment and repugnance, the girl could see, all round this pot, a number of faces lit up unevenly by the fire. They were the faces of children, but they were swollen and rough, with small eyes and dishevelled, lank hair which looked as if it had been baked into a crust. Amongst her children who clung around her and stared silently at the visitors, their mother was leaning forward stirring the pot with a long ladle held in both hands; and when the girl turned her eyes towards her, she shuddered uneasily.

The woman's head put one in mind of one of those dolls made of cloth and sawdust, which through hard wear and ill-usage has become blackened and misshapen without being actually broken. In her flat, puffy face her little eyes, which were unusually sparkling, were lost in a sea of fine wrinkles.

From her big, laughing mouth a single tooth projected, long and yellow. Her hair stuck straight out all round her head, like pins from a pin-chushion. Her face had a certain good-natured quality about it; but this was counteracted by a look of disquieting and hilarious excitement. And the red gleam of the fire, shining fitfully upon her as the flames flickered, gave her the look of an apparition, of a witch busy at her cauldron. "Good evening, good evening," she repeated in her shrill voice.

"Are you the mistress of the house?" asked the young man. He too was disconcerted by the woman's appearance, but was unwilling to show it.

"The Germans destroyed our house, they flooded our farm, they took away our beasts and stole our belongings. . . . This was the shed where we kept the goats, Sir," cried the woman with boisterous gaiety.

"And how d'you manage now?" asked the young man. The girl, realizing that this was the beginning of one of his usual interminable interrogations, made a grimace of annoyance and nudged his arm with her elbow. But he shook his head, as much as to say: "Leave me alone." The girl raised her eyes to the heavens and sighed. "How do we manage?" went on the woman meanwhile. "We don't know how to manage. . . . My husband has malaria and can't work. The children haven't any clothes or any shoes, they go about half naked"—and she pointed to the rags and tatters and the bare, black feet of her children; "we finished the last of our flour only yesterday. . . . Look!" She rose, went to a corner of the hut and came back with an empty sack which she shook in the air, sending forth a cloud of white dust. "It's completely finished," she repeated with satisfaction, throwing away the sack. Then, thrusting forward her laughing face towards the girl, and with an even more violent burst of the same unjustified gaiety: "How shall we manage?" she cried. "We shall die of hunger."

"You'll die of hunger," repeated the young man, completely absorbed now in this conversation. "But look—can't you go to the nearest village and make them give you some rations on your food-card?"

"The nearest village was destroyed by the bombs," cried the woman excitedly, "it was destroyed by the bombs. . . . And there aren't any rations, there are only the cards. Anything there is, is for those who can pay . . . and we haven't any money, Sir."

These pieces of information, furnished with so much enthusiasm, appeared to arouse a painful uneasiness in the young man; it was obvious that he would have preferred them not to be true. "And yet your children don't look as if they were starving, no more do you," he remarked. And indeed the woman appeared quite plump, in the peculiar misshapen manner of a stuffed doll. And the children too, all four of them, looked well-fed, in their own queer forbidding way.

"We're not starving because my children find things to eat," cried the woman with renewed gaiety.

"How do they manage that?"

"They steal them, Sir," cried the woman, with the same enthusiasm with which, previously, she had screamed that they were dying of hunger.

"Come on, let's go," murmured the girl in alarm. But the young man paid no attention to her, although he himself was also perturbed. "What do they steal?" he asked, trying to give his voice a tone of normal curiosity.

"Oh well, Sir, anything they can . . . anything that's going. At present there are plenty of beasts up on the mountains. They steal kids and lambs . . . they go at night and steal kids and lambs."

"But the shepherds," enquired the young man, "don't they notice?"

"The shepherds—oh no, they don't notice . . . they only notice afterwards, Sir. They shut up their beasts, but my children go at night, they open the doors of the sheds and take away lambs and kids."

"You'll get arrested," said the young man with sudden severity.

"How can they arrest us? There are no carabinieri now"— her enthusiasm seemed to be at its utmost—"and anyhow the policemen are hungry too," she added, shouting as if the young man had been deaf; "everybody's hungry nowadays, Sir, everybody."

"But it's wicked to steal, it's a crime," he insisted stubbornly.

"It's wicked to steal," cried the woman, almost affectionately, "but it's even wickeder to starve to death, Sir."

"Now do stop, stop and be done with it, and let's go away," said the girl. She spoke almost loudly, and the woman heard her. "Don't you like our hut—eh, Signorina?" she cried. "But we're in the country here. . . . You must have pity on us and forgive us . . . have pity and forgive."

"The Signorina's in a hurry because we've got to get back home," said the young man.

"The Signorina is beautiful," cried the woman enthusiastically. "The Signorina is well-dressed. . . . You don't feel happy in here, do you, Signorina?"

At last the young man made up his mind to put an end to the conversation. "We came," he said, "to ask if you could lend us a bucket and show us a well where we could get some water."

"A bucket of water!" cried the woman; "certainly, at once. . . . Water doesn't cost anything." She rose, went to the back of the hut and came back with a bucket. "You'll have to go and get it outside," she went on, still shouting, "outside there, at the well. The well's a long way away . . . but my husband's at the well, my husband will help you." She went to the door and uttered a prolonged, plaintive call: "Hoy-ee, Alfredo!" A man's voice, no less plaintive, answered from a distance: "Hoy-ee, Leonia!" Then silence fell again.

"Go along now, Sir," said the woman, handing the bucket to the young man, "go along. . . . My husband will be waiting for you at the well. Take the path behind the hut. But it will be better for the young lady to wait here," she added hastily, "it's a very rough path. . . . The young lady can warm herself at the fire."

The young man, who had already put his head outside the door, straightened himself up again and looked at the girl. "I think it's really better for you to wait for me here," he said; "I'll be back in a moment." The girl wanted to protest but had no time to do so. "Sit down here," said the woman, zealously dusting a bench in front of the fire.

The young man had now gone out. The girl did not dare to run after him, so, with a fastidious movement, she sat down cautiously on the corner of the bench. The woman immediately went over and closed the door. The inside of the hut was suddenly plunged in darkness, except for a restricted glow round the trivet, beneath which the fire was now dying down.

"Warm yourself, Signorina," said the woman. She went to the back of the hut and started rummaging round. The four children, crowded one against the other in a single pile of rags, kept their eyes fixed intently, in silence, on the girl. She opened her bag, took out her cigarettes, lit one with a lighter, then put the cigarette-case and lighter back into the bag and crossed her legs.

The woman came back from the far end of the hut with an armful of sticks and a hatchet. She put down the hatchet on the bench and pushed the sticks in amongst the embers under the pot. Then she threw herself down on all fours on the floor, her cheek against the muddy earth, and started blowing. Flames ran about amongst the sticks, then flared up and wrapped their red tongues round the black sides of the pot. Red sparks rose crackling into the darkness of the hut.

"Now, there's a nice fire again," cried the woman merrily; "you like a fire, don't you, Signorina? It's nice and warm . . .

it keeps the cold out. . . . Give me your bag, Signorina." These last words were pronounced without any alteration in her usual gay, enthusiastic tone. The girl looked at her, and her face went pale and her lips trembled. "My bag? . . . Why?"

"But I've told you already, Signorina," cried the woman in a voice of grieved but affectionate reproof, almost imploringly, "I told you before. . . . We steal; otherwise how should we manage?" She leant forward, took the bag from the girl's knees, opened it and shook out everything it contained on to the floor. Down fell the cigarette-case, the lighter, a tube of lipstick, a powder compact and other things of the kind. One of the children, attracted perhaps by the glitter of the precious metal objects, put out his hand. His mother hit him on the head with a curious sort of blow, half punch and half slap: "Hands off!" Then, turning to the girl, she said: "Are they all made of gold, Signorina, all made of gold?"

"Mario, Mario," shouted the girl suddenly, jumping to her feet. But the woman was too quick for her; seizing the hatchet, she placed herself between her and the door. "Signorina, why do you call him? He's with my husband at the well." She looked at her obliquely, with her brilliant eyes, for a moment. "My husband has a gun," she added joyfully.

The girl said nothing. She looked at the woman, then raised her hand to her mouth and bit it.

"Sit down, Signorina," went on the woman, "but first take off your coat. . . . Your coat will be quite useful to me." And she made as though to place her hand on the girl's coat-sleeve.

"No, I'll take it off myself," said the girl in a loud, expressionless voice. She undid the big buttons from their button-holes, unbuckled the belt, and was about to slip her arms out of the sleeves. "Wait, Signorina," cried the woman, rushing forward, "wait, I'll help you." Notwithstanding the girl's desperately evasive movements, she helped her to remove her coat, took it and threw it over her arm. "And now take off your shoes, Signorina . . . yes, your shoes too."

"But . . . but . . ." began the girl, white in the face, her lips trembling, "but how am I going to walk?"

"You'll walk perfectly all right. . . . My children all walk barefoot. Then, when you get home, you can get some more shoes."

The girl, deprived of her coat, could now be seen to be wearing a light, snuff-coloured dress with white linen collar and cuffs. She sat down on the bench and, stooping down, was on the point of unlacing her shoes. They were light brown country shoes with rubber soles. "No, Signorina," cried the woman, "no, I'll take off your shoes for you!"

She threw herself down on her knees on the floor, took the girl's foot in her lap and, moving her short, thick fingers delicately amongst the laces, undid the shoe, slipped it off her foot and placed it on one side. Then she took off the other shoe in the same manner, but this time she could not help stopping to examine it by the light of the flames. "What a pretty foot you have," she began again, caressing the girl's small, curled-up foot, "what a pretty, tiny little foot! . . . and silk stockings," she added, lifting up her face in an attitude of prayer; "silk stockings, Signorina—won't you give them to me?"

"Take them, take everything," cried the girl, and burst into frightened, unnerved weeping, sobbing into the crook of her raised arm.

"That's right, Signorina, have a good cry. I cried too when the Germans went off with my valuables; I had a good cry and then I felt better."

"Take them, take them," the girl repeated. Without moving her arm from in front of her face, and still continuing to sob, she lowered her other hand to the edge of her dress, turned it back above her knee, stretched out her rounded, shapely, silk-clad leg and ran her fingers up her thigh in order to undo the bands of her garter. The woman, on her knees, gazed at her ecstatically, her hands raised and opened as though to signify that she did not mean to touch her, that she would allow her to do the job herself. Having unfastened the stocking on her left leg, the girl pulled it down as far as her knee, then leant over to her other side, stretched out her other leg, unfastened the second stocking and lowered it to her shin. Finally she covered her face with both hands and sat qtite still, in an attitude of desolation, her dress turned back over her knees, her legs extended as though she were offering them as a gift.

"Thank you, Signorina, thank you," the woman kept on saying with gratitude. Like an expert lady's maid she rolled down the stocking on the weeping girl's leg, collected it together on her foot and then, passing one hand under her heel, pulled it right off. She repeated the same procedure with the other stocking and rose to her feet. "I shall wear the stockings myself, and I shall wear the shoes too," she cried, as though she believed she would comfort the girl by revealing the destination of the things that had been stolen from her. "But the coat," she went on, sitting down and examining the material, "the coat I shall make into trousers for the boys. . . . It'll make into two pairs of trousers," she said with satisfaction. "And possibly a little jacket for Natalino too," she concluded.

The girl said nothing. She was sobbing, her long white legs stretched out towards the fire. The woman, having finished her examination of the coat, folded it up carefully and laid it on the bench. Then she rolled up the stockings and put them inside the shoes, which she placed on the floor underneath the coat. Finally she turned towards the girl again and cheerfully asked her: "Haven't you anything else, Signorina? Haven't you any rings, or any necklaces or bracelets? When I was married I had rings and necklaces and bracelets . . . and the Germans took everything. The Germans took everything, Signorina."

"I've nothing more," answered the girl in the midst of her sobs.

"You're wearing a very pretty dress," the woman said, as if she were talking to herself; "a very pretty dress . . . but I won't take that from you. It's not nice for us women to let ourselves be seen half naked, is it, Signorina? . . . No, I'll leave you your dress, Signorina." Leaning forward, she took the lid off the pot and started vigorously moving the ladle round and round amongst the steam rising from the food. The children, who so far had stayed quite still, stretched their faces forward towards the steam. "D'you want something to eat?" cried the woman. "D'you want some of our supper? Stewed kid—just plain country fare, of course. . . ."

"No, I don't want anything to eat," said the girl. She took away her arm from in front of her face, pulled down her dress and twisted herself to one side, almost turning her back on the woman. She tried not to put her bare feet down on the floor; but her heels were already black with mud.

The woman remarked, in a jubilant tone of voice, to her children: "The young lady doesn't want anything to eat"; then, with a large tin fork, she fished up a piece of meat from the pot and held it out to one of the children, who seized it and fixed his teeth in it. She distributed three other pieces, one to each child, then took one for herself and began furiously devouring it, smearing the gravy all over her face. "You don't want anything to eat? You really don't?" she insisted, her mouth full, turning towards the girl.

The latter did not move, nor did she speak. The door opened and the young man, without his cap and with a white, frightened face, thrust his head inside the hut. "Ornella," he said.

The girl jumped up hurriedly and ran out of the hut. It was almost dark now; but in the shadows behind the young man she could just distinguish the erect figure of a man with a long, unshaven face and watchful eyes, his hand on the strap of his gun. She looked at her companion: he also was barefooted, wearing nothing but his drawers and shirt.

"It's dark," cried the woman, "but Alfredo will go with you. . . . Here you are, Alfredo." She came suddenly out of the hut, holding out towards her husband a bunch of burning reeds. The red light leapt to their faces and all around was complete darkness.

Silently the man moved away, walking in front of the two victims with the improvised torch in his hand.

"Good-bye, Signorina, good-bye"; the woman's voice followed them in the darkness.

The girl kept silence, pressing close to her companion's side. He too was silent. Carrying the bucket of water, he walked with his head bowed, placing his feet with difficulty amongst the stones and the mud. Alongside his feet, the small, reluctant feet of the girl seemed to be performing some kind of a dance. The light in front of them left the man who was carrying it in darkness, appearing thus to be moving forward all by itself into the night.

Shivering with cold, their whole attention directed towards avoiding the sharp pebbles and thick mud, they did not notice that they had reached the end of the path until the stony surface of the ground was succeeded by smooth asphalt. The young man went over to the car, unscrewed the radiator-cap and started pouring in the water. The girl opened the door and threw herself down on the seat.

The young man emptied the bucket and handed it back to the other man. The latter said, calmly: "Good night", and disappeared into the darkness.

The young man got into the car, closed the door and started the engine. "They robbed me of everything, everything, everything," said the girl, huddling up against him, in a voice which, owing to her fear, sounded at the same time both vacuous and thoughtful.

"And how about me?" he replied, pointing to the bare foot with which he was pressing on the pedal. The car moved off, entered on a long, straight stretch of road and ran swiftly on through the night, preceded by a white halo thrown by the headlights on to the black ribbon of asphalt.

THE WOMAN FROM MEXICO

I T was a warm, rainy day, and the moment he was out of the house Sergio was aware of his mistake. He had put on a heavy winter suit, whereas, in this almost tropical weather, he ought to have been wearing a light spring suit. Moreover, he had also burdened himself with a winter overcoat, a double-breasted one, which meant that he had not one, but the equivalent of two, overcoats on his chest and belly. In addition he was wearing a woollen vest under his shirt, next to his skin, woollen socks on his feet and a woollen scarf round his neck. In one hand he held his umbrella, in the other his gloves. He had moved only a few steps when he began to feel he was accoutred like a medieval knight. It was the fault, he realized, of those detestable black clouds that formed a confused mass in the sky; and also of his mother, who had come while he was dressing to implore him, for goodness' sake, to wrap himself up well. For a moment he thought of going back and reducing his burden of clothes, but he at once gave up the idea: he lived on the top floor, the lift was not working, and climbing up the stairs with all those clothes on him would be too disagreeable an effort. Nevertheless, the further he walked along the crowded streets, the more did the discomfort and heat and weight of his clothes increase, and with them his ill-humour. It was raining, into the bargain—a fine rain, not enough to justify the use of an umbrella but enough to cover the pavements with a dew-like moisture slippery to the feet. This rain seemed to make the air even more stifling; when he reached the top of the street he became conscious that he was dripping with sweat.

He had come out in order to go for a walk, but he saw that,

with all this mass of clothes on him, his walk was not producing its usual diverting, restful effect; on the contrary, with the unhealthy heat in which he was imprisoned from head to foot, his eye concentrated angrily upon all the meanest and ugliest. aspects of the city. As though seeing them for the first time, he became alive to the vulgarity of the shop windows filled with objects which all seemed to him quite useless; to the damp, murky wretchedness of narrow lanes strewn with rubbish and frequented by shadowy, prowling cats; to the awkwardness of the women's clothes; to the poorness of the men's clothes; and to the sweaty, greasy, worn-out look of the faces that came ceaselessly towards him out of the dimness of the street, rushed forward to meet him and then disappeared. The whole city, which usually he loved so much, now appeared to him like an enormous heap of dirt in which, thrown confusedly together, men and things that in another place and in different conditions would have kept their freshness and integrity became corrupted and rotten.

Meanwhile, darkness was rapidly falling. Not knowing what to do, he stopped in front of the window of a tobacconist's shop, observing, almost without seeing them, the pipes and the packs of cards displayed there. The thing that troubled him most, at that moment, was his woollen socks: he tried to move his toes inside his shoe and felt them all stuck together, as though they were on the point of melting, like candles. Then someone coming out of the shop knocked against him; he looked up and recognized Luciano, who at one time had been a friend of his.

He had never been very fond of Luciano, who had been one of his old school companions; and during the last ten years he had seen him perhaps once or twice a year. But, though he did not like him, and in fact had no desire to see him, he had never succeeded in breaking off this absurd and desultory relationship. In reality he perceived in Luciano the personification of a part of himself which he hated and which he would willingly have got rid of if he had been able to. In person, they were very much alike: both of them small and dark, with fine features, both of them careful in their dress. But Luciano's face bore the signs of vulgar dissipation, whereas Sergio's had a gentle, rather melancholy expression. Luciano was pale, almost grey in the face, with a bald forehead that stretched back beneath thin hair, and dull, lifeless eyes. Sergio had a fresh face, thick, glossy hair, and a lively look in his eye. They were both, as they say, of good family. But, while Sergio lived with his parents and worked as a lawyer in the office of his father, also a lawyer, Luciano had left home and lived in furnished rooms; he did no work, but spent his time with people he picked up all over the place—variety actresses, professional gamblers, idle young men. This world was quite as distasteful to Sergio as was his old school friend in person. But, by some kind of incomprehensible fascination, both Luciano's world and Luciano himself, though repugnant to him, also attracted him, and he was never able to cold-shoulder his friend when, at rare intervals, he fell in with him. On these occasions they would remain in each other's company for an evening, or a night, for dinner or in some other place. Next day Sergio would feel humiliated at the memory of the evening spent with his despicable friend and would swear to himself that he would never allow such a thing to happen again.

On seeing Luciano, Sergio's first instinct was to avoid him. But his friend had already seen him, and came up to him. They shook hands and walked off together down the street. Luciano had been buying cigarettes, and he offered one to Sergio. The latter would have liked to refuse, but he accepted. "How are you?" asked Luciano after a moment.

"I'm all right," said Sergio tartly.

"Everyone well at home?"

"Yes, everyone."

"And you're still working in your lawyer's office?"

"Yes, still there."

His friend appeared to be in a bad humour; and Sergio suspected that he had noticed his first instinctive movement to avoid him. He wanted to be polite and thought of asking, in turn, for news of someone closely connected with him. But, since he did not know his family, he could think of nothing better than enquiring after Luciano's mistress—that is to say, after his last mistress, with whom he had seen him about six months before. She had been, as far as he could remember, a quite young woman and by no means ugly, though, like all Luciano's women, extremely common. But, apart from this confused impression of youth, attractiveness and vulgarity, he could not manage to remember at all what she was like nor who she was. Even the name Albina, which he dug up out of the back of his mind, seemed to him uncertain. Nevertheless he asked: "And how is Albina?"

Luciano stopped to re-light his cigarette which had gone out. By the gleam from the little flame of his lighter, Sergio observed that his question had produced an effect which was obvious but not easy to define. Luciano's coolness was too ostentatious to be genuine. "Ah, Albina—you remember her, do you?" he said in a sarcastic tone. "Perhaps it'll please you to hear that this very day we've parted for good and all."

"Why *please* me?" asked Sergio in surprise.

The other man went on: "Albina is a . . .", and here he uttered an ugly word that startled Sergio, who could not bear such language, especially in relation to women. "I was completely fed up with her . . . and so I told her to get out. That pleases you, doesn't it?"

"It doesn't please me in the least," said Sergio, embarrassed; "on the contrary, I'm sorry . . ."

Luciano stopped and looked him up and down with a sardonic expression. "You're a nice kind of person," he said. "So you're sorry, are you? Say it again, won't you?"

"Yes, I'm sorry."

"You're shameless, into the bargain."

"But I . . ."

"You like Albina—quite a lot, don't you? And now you're pleased that she isn't living with me any longer. . . ." Luciano paused for a moment, relishing, apparently, the bitterness contained in these words. Then he added contemptuously: "A fine sort of friend, certainly . . . but of course all friends are the same. They all aim at making a cuckold of you."

Sergio was astonished. He did not remember ever having paid any particular attention to Albina on the two or three occasions on which he had seen her in Luciano's company; nor did he remember observing that Albina had taken any interest in him. Somewhat nervously, he said: "But I assure you that I . . ."

His friend interrupted him. "D'you really think I didn't notice you that day when we went to the races and then had dinner together? I'm not blind, you know. . . . Anyhow, it's human . . ."

"But that day—really . . ."

"Now," said Luciano, stopping in front of a small entrance-door in a side street, "this is where Albina lives. I had to come here to give her back these gloves . . . but it would be much better if you would go and do so. Go on then—go and give her the gloves", and he thrust a pair of crumpled gloves into his hand. "Go on; and tell her that as far as I am concerned it's all over. And of course the succession is open, the coast is clear. Go on, and make the most of it. She'll be very pleased . . . it's just what she wants."

"But, my dear chap, I . . ."

"What are you waiting for? Get along, go on!" Luciano gave him an ill-mannered push which forced him into the door-way. "Go on. . . . You'll be delighted, you know you will. And I've spared you the trouble of finding out the address, I've brought you right to the door. . . . Or d'you want me to come and undress her for you, eh?"

"But Luciano . . ."

The other man was paying no further attention, by this time, to anything he said. "Well, that's agreed, then. Be nice to her, ask her out to dinner, don't be stingy. . . . Good luck to you." He saluted him with a wave of the hand and disappeared.

.   .   .   .   .

Now that he was alone again, Sergio felt more sweat-drenched than ever. To the heat there was now added the disagreeable sensation of a false position. What was happening to him seemed to be a thing of the highest improbability; yet it was not its improbability that troubled him, so much as Luciano's attitude and his own. The improbability might be explained in this way: either Luciano was jealous of him without any reason, or Albina had made use of him to make her lover jealous. But what gave him food for thought was, on the one hand, the quiet contempt of his friend, as though it were obvious that he was aiming to supplant him in Albina's favours; and, on the other, his own sudden inclination to accept this role of traitor that was being fastened upon him. Sergio had a dignified, if somewhat rigid, idea of himself. And now the temptation which Luciano's mistake aroused in his mind made him doubtful of himself. "It's quite clear," he thought; "all I need to do is to give up the idea of going up to Albina's flat and go home, and then Luciano will be convinced that he was wrong." But he noticed that—in spite of himself, so to speak— he had in the meantime advanced a step or two along the passage into the house. It was an old, dirty house, the passage was dark, and a damp, musty smell filled the air; and yet, inexplicably, the decrepitude, the dirtiness, the smell, the gloom attracted and excited him. His heart had started to beat faster and his breath almost failed him. "I'll hand over the gloves to her and then I'll go," he said to himself finally, as he walked on towards the end of the passage.

He ran up three flights of stairs, his mind in a state of

combined oppression and eagerness, and, in a dim, uncertain light, rang the bell at a small door that appeared to be coated with pitch. It was opened by a bony woman with untidy hair, wearing an apron, with a baby on her arm and a charcoal-fan in her hand. At the mention of Albina she pointed with the fan, without saying a word, to a door at the end of a passage. Sergio, his hat in one hand and his umbrella in the other and feeling more ill at ease than ever, crossed a small, bare hall, went to the end of the passage and knocked at the door.

A woman's voice called to him to come in. He pushed open the door and found himself in a narrow little room which appeared to be a mere prolongation of the passage. In a row, on one side, were a small wardrobe, a sofa covered with worn red material, and a little table and chair; on the other side there was just enough room left for a person to move. At the far end, in front of the closed window, stood an old dressing-table with faded draperies and dirty ribbons; and at the dressing-table sat Albina. Her rounded hips, firm and youthful, bulged out from the little stool on which she was perched; she was in a greenish undergarment, and was finishing the brushing of her hair, her head held to one side and her bare arm raised as she wielded the hairbrush. She said, in a quiet voice: "Is that you, Luciano?"

Sergio said to himself: "I'll give her the gloves and then go away." Then he answered, embarrassed: "No, it's Sergio."

Albina turned round abruptly, with an almost convulsive movement of her whole body, the whites of her eyes showing and her swelling brown bosom tightly stretched beneath the lace trimmings of her chemise. Sergio walked towards her. "Perhaps you don't remember me," he began, seeking to adopt a polite, detached tone, "and you will be surprised to see me dropping in here in place of Luciano. . . . I'm sorry, but I am the bearer of bad news. Luciano, a few minutes ago, requested me to tell you that he is not coming and that he does not intend seeing you again . . . and he asked me to give you these gloves." He leant forward and put the gloves on the dressing-table.

It was to be expected that she would make some sort of comment on Luciano's behaviour. But Albina remained silent, gazing at him with curiosity. He, too, looked at her and noted, almost with regret, that she was indeed a very pretty girl and that he was attracted by her: her small head, with its round, black eyes, its aquiline nose and fine mouth, had the grace of a bird's head; but her neck was thick, her shoulders ample and her bosom opulent, with a warm, brown colour of skin. Albina, with her faded old green undergarment and her un-shaven armpits, soft and black and bushy, gave an impression of great slovenliness if not of actual dirtiness. But even this, he realized, was not unattractive to him. Confused, and almost against his will, he added: "If you like, and if you have nothing better to do, we might have dinner together."

He immediately regretted having given this invitation and hoped that she would refuse it. Albina, at last, said slowly: "Luciano is a liar. . . . It's I who don't want to have anything more to do with *him*. . . . But that's no reason for *you* to crow over anybody. D'you really think I didn't see what was going on?"

So Albina too, as well as Luciano, was convinced that he had been trying to make advances to her. Irritated, he replied: "Whether I think it or not, I simply came to bring you back your gloves."

"And to ask me out to dinner," Albina prompted him. "Well, where shall we go?"

So she *was* accepting his invitation. Sergio could not help feeling pleased. "Wherever you like," he said.

"Let's go to Paolone's," she answered; "the food's good there." She took up the hairbrush again and resumed her energetic toilet. "Why don't you sit down?" she said. "What are you doing, standing there stiff as a poker?"

Sergio sat down awkwardly on the sofa, encumbered by his

heavy clothes. The adventure with Albina was now mixed up in his mind with the frantic desire to rid himself of these garments. He thought of the moment when he would undress in that little room, which did not appear to be heated in any way, and it seemed to him that undressing would give him even greater pleasure than possessing Albina. But alas, it would be a long time before that blessed moment arrived. "And so you're pleased," said Albina without looking at him, "that Luciano and I have parted."

"Really," stammered Sergio, "really, I . . ."

"You couldn't believe it was true," went on Albina, "but I seem to see the whole thing. . . . The moment Luciano told you that everything was over between us, you chuckled with joy and came rushing up here . . . thinking that this was the best possible moment. Isn't that so?"

"I swear you're mistaken," said Sergio with some energy. But he was no longer so sure. Was it really true that she was mistaken?

"What d'you think, then? That I hadn't noticed?"

"Noticed what?"

"Last time we saw each other, with Luciano . . . in that restaurant . . . you never for one moment stopped pressing my foot under the table. You practically ruined one of my shoes. You're a nice sort of chap, you are."

Sergio, at this, remained silent for some little time. Now at last it was a question of a precise fact: he had pressed her foot with amorous intentions. He remembered indeed having gone to a restaurant with Luciano and Albina; he remembered also that Luciano and Albina had sat opposite to him, on a seat against the wall. But he was absolutely sure he had not intentionally pressed Albina's foot. Perhaps, without meaning to, he might have kicked against it under the table. It was more likely—as had already occurred to him—that Albina had invented the whole story in order to make Luciano jealous. Reassured by this examination of the situation, he said slowly:

"I'm pretty certain you're making a mistake. . . . It's impossible that I could have thought of pressing your foot under the table; it's a thing I would never do in any circumstances. . . . Perhaps you're confusing me with someone else."

"Isn't he a darling!" she exclaimed scornfully. "No, I'm not confusing you with anyone. In things like this I never make mistakes."

"She really *is* common," thought Sergio, affronted. But he was conscious that this vulgarity, so thoroughly in tune with the place and the person, was not unattractive to him. He tried to take a frivolous, rakish line. "Oh well, then, since you're so positive about it, let's admit that I pressed your foot under the table. . . . What comes next?"

Albina put down her brush; her hair was now all smoothed out and unravelled and lay in a fan shape over her shoulders. Then she turned towards him: "Come here," she said.

She had used the familiar "tu", and this troubled Sergio. He rose and took a step forward. "I said 'Come here,'" she insisted.

Sergio took another step. "And now," said the woman playfully, in the way one speaks to a dog, "lie down!"

"Whatever d'you mean?"

"Lie down!"

Sergio bent his knees inside the heavy folds of his overcoat and knelt down, finding himself face to face with Albina sitting on her stool. She lifted her strong, rounded arm and, placing her hand on the back of his neck, began: "It's not true that I don't like you. . . . In fact I certainly *do* like you. . . ."

"What am I doing?" thought Sergio. But he brought his face close to Albina's, as if to kiss her. She immediately pushed him away. "No, no. . . . Be good, now. I said I liked you, but that's not quite reason enough. . . . Oh, he's an artful one, isn't he?" She laughed in a rather awkward way, showing her small, white teeth, and dealt him a blow in the chest, a real peasant woman's blow, strong and hard. Sergio lost his balance and fell back on the floor in a sitting position.

Furious with himself, he struggled to his feet again. He realized that, what with admitting to having pressed Albina's foot and having then tried to kiss her, he had given a decisive acknowledgment that Luciano was right. And without any result, into the bargain. He asked irritably: "Once and for all, do you like me or do you not?"

"You wouldn't let me finish," replied Albina. "Yes, I do like you, but it's no good, I'm not for you . . . I belong to Luciano." She uttered these last words in a tone of challenging, purblind loyalty—just exactly, thought Sergio, like a woman of the slums who never discusses her lover even if he betrays or disgraces her. "But Luciano," he could not refrain from saying, "doesn't want to have anything more to do with you."

"That doesn't matter: I belong to Luciano. And, what's more, you're a friend of Luciano's and you ought not to try and get his girl friend away from him. . . . It's not at all nice, what you're trying to do."

She shook her head with an air of disapproval and got up from the dressing-table. Standing there, in her slippers, she looked too broad in the hips for her height. She went over to a clothes-hanger, took down two stockings that were hanging there and looked at them with a dubious air. The stockings that she had on at present were heavily darned and had highly visible seams that looked like scars. She put back the other stockings on the clothes-hanger and went to the wardrobe. Sergio, still sweating freely, heedlessly went up to her and put his arm round her waist. She took no notice of him, but opened the wardrobe and took from it the only garment it contained, a shabby brown coat. "Help me on with it, will you?"

Sergio took the coat and, when Albina bent back between his arms in order to slip into the sleeves, kissed her on the neck. He noticed that her skin felt greasy and that her hair had a coarse smell. She made a movement as if chasing away a fly. "Ugh, how obstinate you are!" she exclaimed.

She buttoned up the coat, with its exaggeratedly tight waist that made her hips and bosom look as if they were bursting out of it. Then she went into a corner of the room, took off her slippers and, hopping from one foot to the other, put on a pair of decrepit shoes. "Come on, let's go," she said.

Sergio took his umbrella and hat and followed her with an acute sense of boredom and irritation. The bony, dishevelled woman with the baby in her arms appeared in the doorway of the kitchen. "If Signor Luciano comes," said Albina, "ask him to wait in my room."

They went out and started side by side down the narrow stairs. As they went, their hips touched and Albina said, with a laugh that to Sergio seemed offensive: "Rubbing up against me, eh?"

"Go to the devil," he said to himself. But his arm, as if moved by an independent will, raised itself and encircled Albina's waist. Without saying a word she gave him, almost in the dark as they were, a violent blow with her hip which nearly knocked him down. Sergio understood and let go of her waist.

Outside it was raining, and it was warmer than ever. "Put up your umbrella," Albina said to him. He obeyed, and Albina clung to his arm, with a movement that was almost affectionate. They walked off together.

"What d'you think of Luciano?" she suddenly asked him.

Without reflecting, Sergio answered: "I think he's an idler and that he'll come to a bad end."

She remarked, in a judicious tone of voice: "You're not going about it in at all a good way. I've told you already. . . . You won't succeed in making me fall in love with you by speaking ill of Luciano."

Sergio replied irritably: "I think far worse of him than that . . . I only told you the least important part of what I feel."

"And yet you try to pass as his friend."

"But I'm *not* a friend of Luciano's," said Sergio vehemently. "Will you, or won't you, understand? I scarcely know him."

"Well, it may be so. But *he* says you're such great friends."

"We were at school together, that's all. . . . I could never be a friend of a type like Luciano."

"Why not?"

All of a sudden Sergio's nostrils curled in anger. "Because Luciano is a person of unreliable character and I am not."

"Well, it may be so," she repeated obstinately. "It may even be, as you say, that Luciano is an unreliable person. But he trusts you, and you, on the other hand, are trying to take his girl friend away from him. Those are the facts."

"But what's that got to do with it? Anybody might try and make love to you."

"Yes, but for you it's different. . . . You and Luciano are friends."

There was nothing to be done, then. Sweat-soaked and furious, Sergio remained silent. "I ought to leave her and drop the whole thing," he thought. But the pressure of Albina's arm, the light contact of her rounded hip, sufficed to make him change his mind. They came to a dark square which was in process of demolition. Violet neon signs cast reflections upon heaps of trampled mud, and here and there red lamps gave warning of the presence of deep holes full of water. "Wait for me here," said Albina; "I'm going into the post office for a moment."

She went into the post office building and Sergio stayed in the doorway. It was still raining, and the light from the lamp-posts showed a thick drizzle that looked almost like a cloud of dust. People were going in and out of the post office, many of them humble, working-class women like Albina. "Surely this is the moment to vanish," he said to himself; and he walked slowly away along the side of a high fence. But as he went he remembered that he had a letter to post, and he turned back again. Just as he was putting his letter into the box he felt someone touch him on the arm. "Come along," said Albina.

She was turning a letter round and round in her hands. Then, without opening it, she put it in her pocket. "Aren't you going to read it?" asked Sergio.

"It's from my husband. All in good time. . . ."

"From your husband?"

"Yes," she replied, "I'm married, you know . . . or didn't you know? He's in the Goretti Variety Company . . . poor devil. . . . He's travelling, travelling all the time, and he's always writing to me. I worked with him for a bit. . . . I sang and he accompanied me on the guitar. . . . Then I got fed up. We had to go to all sorts of funny places in the provinces . . . and I preferred to stay in Rome." They had come out of the square by this time and were walking along a wide, muddy street without any pavements and encumbered by a double row of pedlars' handcarts.

Albina was in no hurry to get to her dinner. One by one, she examined each of the handcarts, even the ones which held second-hand books, even the ones which sold razor-blades. Really and truly, Sergio could not help thinking, she was a typical little vagabond, the kind of person that creeps out at twilight from some miserable lodging to enjoy the spectacle of the streets. But not even the devouring light of the acetylene lamps seemed to impair her characteristic, rather brutal attractiveness; at most, it showed up the pallor of her cheeks and the yellowish halo of fatigue round her black eyes. At a men's outfitter's shop, above which a long band of rain-soaked cloth proclaimed in large letters: "Sensational Fall in Prices", she turned resolutely and went in, saying: "Come on in, I want to buy a tie for Luciano."

Sergio followed her, piqued by this stubborn faithfulness. The shop was small and in a state of great disorder; it looked as though it were not only the prices that had fallen, but also the entire stock of merchandise, all over the counter. The shopkeeper displayed under the eyes of Albina a tangled mass of cheap ties, and Albina carefully selected the ugliest of them all; she then asked Sergio: "That really is a pretty one, isn't it?"

"Very pretty indeed."

"Is it for this gentleman?" asked the shopkeeper. "It's just the right thing for the gentleman." Albina fumbled in her purse in an embarrassed way. "Let me pay for it," said Sergio, urged on by a kind of vindictive punctilio.

When they were outside again, Albina said to Sergio: "Thank you. . . . But don't go and tell Luciano it was you who paid for it."

"What d'you take me for?"

They started looking into the shop windows again. Albina paused for a long time in front of a shoe shop and then said: "As you spoilt a pair of shoes of mine by kicking my foot under the table, you ought to buy me a new pair." Her tone was playful, but not entirely so: Albina, sponger as she was, really hoped to extort a present of a pair of shoes. Sergio hesitated a moment, then decided that he would buy Albina the shoes. Having bought the shoes, he would still have enough money left for the dinner, but not for the customary present after the act of love. He thought, however, that Albina would be content with the shoes. She was looking at him hopefully. He said slowly: "How on earth is it that Luciano, who is so very fond of you, lets you go about in such terrible shoes?"

"I don't want anything out of Luciano."

"I suppose it's *you* who pay for *his* shoes?"

Albina did not choose to answer and Sergio concluded that, as he had always suspected, Luciano did not scruple to take money from his mistresses. "Come along then," he said after a moment; "let's go and buy these shoes."

Albina, by this time, had evidently given up hope of the shoes, for she gave a brisk, joyful start of surprise. "Are you talking seriously?"

"Yes, perfectly seriously."

They went into the shop. Albina was beside herself with delight, as could be seen from the way in which she strutted along like a peacock, her hips swaying, past all the mirrors and piles of boxes. She sat down and extended her small, well-formed foot to a fair-haired, talkative assistant. Sergio was surprised to see that, of all the many shoes that the assistant diligently suggested to her, she ended by choosing a pair of sports shoes, massive, light-coloured, and with thick, lemon-yellow crêpe rubber soles. "Wouldn't a pair of black town shoes be better?" he hazarded.

"No," replied Albina; "these are better, because they won't spoil when you press my foot under the table." This was a joke in which her gratitude found a way of expressing itself. But Sergio blushed, partly because the assistant looked at him and smiled.

Outside the shop, Albina rushed at him and kissed him impetuously on the cheek, saying: "Thanks, I'm very grateful, you know." Sergio replied discontentedly: "You kissed me on the cheek just as if I'd been your father."

"Luciano's the only person I kiss on the mouth."

In her new shoes that were too bright in colour and too heavy, in her brown coat stretched tight over her ample hips, and carrying the old shoes in a parcel under her arm, Albina, filled with joy and pride and poverty, was almost touching; and Sergio, at her reply, comforted himself with the thought that he had at any rate done a good deed.

On leaving the shop where she had bought her new shoes, Albina went straight to a little cubby-hole of a shop near by which specialized in the repair of old shoes. Standing amongst piles of misshapen, dust-covered boots and shoes smelling mustily of damp leather and feet, she explained her requirements, at some length, to the cobbler. Then she bought some polish for her new shoes and went out again.

They walked on through the same dark, sordid quarter, from street to street, from one alley to another. Suddenly Sergio, on looking round, saw on one side the coloured glass door of a brothel, on the other side a urinal, and, a little further on, the entrance to a restaurant. Underfoot were the usual muddy, glistening paving-stones, with cabbage-stalks scattered here and there and hungry cats prowling. Three men came out of the brothel laughing and talking in loud voices, and made for the urinal. "This is a nice sort of place," Sergio was on the point of remarking. But he had no time to do so, for Albina stopped in front of the restaurant and announced: "Here we are."

On the glass panes of the entrance door, in fact, was painted in a maroon colour, in running script: *Paolone. Specialità romane. Vino dei Castelli.* Albina pushed the door open and, followed by Sergio who looked round disgustedly as he closed his umbrella, went into the hot, smoky atmosphere of the restaurant. This consisted of a row of minute little rooms. In the first room, larger than the rest, there was a central table upon which were pyramids of oranges and a few bunches of fennel and a large ice-box of rough wood, surmounted by a lordly pair of horns. It was a restaurant with no pretensions at all, as could be gathered from the frequent call of "half-portion" echoing from one room to another. Sergio noticed that the customers all resembled, in some way, either Albina or Luciano: the women were young, very much made up and badly dressed, the men dissipated-looking, jaded, and showily dressed with dubious elegance. Albina made her way slowly from room to room, constantly greeted by one or other of these unlovely customers; and she appeared to be looking for something or somebody. When she reached the far end of the restaurant, she beckoned to Sergio, as much as to say: "I've found what I wanted."

Sergio went forward in his turn and saw a tiny room, like a cell, containing only two small tables. One of them was free, and Albina had already sat down at it; at the other were sitting Luciano and a woman.

"Ah, so that's what it was," he thought. Luciano did not appear surprised: "Hullo, Sergio," he said in a quiet voice. Sergio went to Albina's table and said in a low voice, stooping forward: "Let's go away. . . . I see Luciano's here."

"A pleasant discovery," she answered. She was pretending to examine the menu, her head lowered.

"Let's go to the Splendid," suggested Sergio, thinking that the idea of an expensive restaurant might induce her to follow him.

She lifted her head and stared at him with feigned astonishment. "Why?" she said. "It's perfectly all right here."

So there was nothing for him to do but sit down. Sergio took off his overcoat and placed it, with his umbrella and hat, on a chair. The two tables were right opposite one another, and it was impossible for the four people occupying them not to look at each other. Albina and he were sitting on a seat with its back to one wall, and, on a seat with its back to the other wall, sat Luciano and his companion. Over the doorway hung a curtain, which increased the feeling of intimacy and seclusion.

Sergio was by this time fully conscious of being nothing but a pawn in the game of Albina's jealousy, and there was no knowing how long it was since this game had begun. And yet, glancing at Albina, he admitted the hope that he himself would play the part, in this game, of the proverbial onlooker who derives more advantage from it than the contestants—in other words, that he would succeed, whatever the reason for that success might be, in gaining possession of Albina. "I'm an idiot," he said scornfully to himself. Although he had taken off his overcoat, he was hotter than ever; the air inside the restaurant, thick with smoke and smells of cooking, was stifling. Once again, in this heat, his adventure with Albina attracted him as a speedy and pleasant means of ridding himself of his woollen socks, of tearing the clothes off his back and remaining naked in the cool air of some squalid rented room. Albina, in the meantime, had called the waiter and was ordering what seemed to Sergio, always very sober in these respects, a Gargantuan dinner—*hors d'œuvres*, spaghetti, roast lamb with potatoes. As for a sweet, she added, she would decide about that later. He could not refrain from admiring this valiant appetite that not even jealousy was able to extinguish. "You're hungry?" he asked, turning towards her.

"Yes, certainly I'm hungry," she answered aggressively.

It was remarkably difficult for the two couples to sit opposite and not look at each other. Sergio, after trying in vain to avoid turning his eyes towards the other two, decided that he might as well take a frank look at them. Luciano was sitting sideways, so that he saw him in profile. But the woman sat directly facing him. She was a woman of singular aspect, and for a moment she aroused Sergio's curiosity. Black-haired, she had a sharp-featured, long face of a coppery yellow colour. Her eyes were large, black and unmoving, wide open but unseeing, glittering and inexpressive as a couple of stones. Her long nose, aquiline but broad at the nostrils, her mouth with its scornful expression and corners turned downwards, gave her face an air of virility. She seemed to be tall, with ample shoulders and a very well-formed bosom tightly swathed in the black silk of her low-necked dress. What struck him most in her face was the reddish colour of her complexion and the savage, unmoving expression. Beside this woman, Luciano looked fragile and wan, and even Albina appeared femininely slender. He was startled out of these thoughts by a blow in the ribs from Albina's elbow. "D'you know who that woman is?" she said in her normal voice, so that Luciano could hear her. "She's a Mexican who sings at the Teatro Nuovo . . . d'you think she's attractive?"

"No," answered Sergio, lowering his voice.

"She *is* ugly, isn't she? She's a Redskin. . . . Sitting down like that she looks tall, but when she gets up—you'll see—she looks as if she'd sunk into the floor . . . as if she'd had a piece taken off her legs."

"Why d'you talk so loud?"

"*She* can't understand, anyhow," replied Albina, shrugging her shoulders. "She only understands Spanish. . . . She calls herself by a man's name—Consuelo."

"It's not a man's name, it's a woman's. It means Consolation."

"Luciano's consoling himself with her because I've chucked him," said Albina maliciously.

Sergio looked again at the couple opposite and noticed that they scarcely spoke to each other. The Mexican woman was eating composedly and Luciano addressed brief remarks to her from time to time, illustrating his meaning with gestures of his hand. But it was a question of simple things: "Would you like something to drink? . . . D'you like that? . . . Some bread?" The waiter brought the *pasta asciutta* and Albina who, notwithstanding her jealousy, had already swallowed a plateful of *salame*, immediately rolled a huge tangled heap of spaghetti round her fork and raised it to her mouth without ever taking her eyes off the Mexican woman. The latter made Luciano pour out some wine for her and then drank, sending to her companion, over the top of her glass, a signal of sentimental understanding, serious and almost ritual. Luciano, in turn, took the glass from her hand and also drank, placing his lips where she had placed hers. "Just look what a fool the man must be," muttered Albina furiously, her mouth full of spaghetti. She did not, however, fail to empty her plate and, to finish up with, mopped up what was left of the gravy with a hunk of bread. "And then we'll go home," she said loudly, pushing away the empty plate.

Sergio knew quite well that she was talking merely in order to be overheard and possibly did not even know what she was saying. However he could not resist answering: "But you said, before, that you didn't want me."

"I've changed my mind now," said Albina loudly; "besides, I always liked you . . . more than Luciano."

"Don't shout so loud!"

"You're not a scoundrel like him. You're a gentleman—anyone can see that."

Luciano took the Mexican woman's hand, which she permitted him, quite willingly, to hold. He raised her hand to his lips, eyeing her slily as he did so, and then gave it a bite. The

Mexican woman smiled, showing her white, sharp, wolf-like teeth. Luciano kissed her hand where he had bitten it. Albina said to Sergio, with unexpected affection: "I bought a tie for you. Now I'm going to put it on for you."

Sergio, faced with this sudden improvisation, was flabbergasted. "But . . . but I . . ." he began.

"Come on, don't be silly. . . . No need to be ashamed."

Albina took the parcel containing the tie from her bag and undid it with vengeful pride. Sergio reflected that he was being punished for having taken pleasure in the ugliness of the tie that Luciano was to receive from Albina. Not merely was it he, instead of Luciano, who now had to wear the horrible band of silk, but he had even paid for it. Albina, chuckling ironically, turned back his collar, untied the old tie and put the new one on him, with a knot that was much too slack. "It suits you very well," she said, drawing back and admiring it. Sergio tightened the knot and said: "At least give me my old one."

Luciano put his arm round the Mexican woman's waist, laughing and whispering some joke or other. The Mexican woman defended herself feebly, making a sententious remark in a warm, hoarse voice. Then Luciano, with a quick movement, threw himself upon her and gave her a lingering kiss on the neck. The Mexican woman sat quite still, her eyes wide open, while Luciano sucked at her neck just below the ear. Afterwards, when Luciano had drawn away his head again, she shook herself and tidied her hair, exactly like a hen tidying its feathers after an assault by a cock. The waiter arrived with Albina's roast lamb and also with another dish for Luciano's table. "Is that for Signor Luciano?" Albina asked him.

"Yes."

"Wait a moment." Albina took the pepper-pot, a terracotta chicken with holes in its head, unscrewed it and quickly upset the whole of the pepper into Luciano's dish. The dish contained a meat hash with sauce. The waiter was alarmed. "Whatever are you doing?" he asked.

"Don't you worry. I'll take the responsibility." Sergio, too, was puzzled. Albina started eating her roast lamb, her eyes fixed on Luciano. The latter had not seen her exploit with the pepper-pot and with great composure cut up a piece of meat and raised it to his mouth. Albina, stifling her laughter, gave Sergio another blow in the ribs with her elbow. "Now you'll see what a scene he'll make. . . . He's so fussy about his food anyhow."

But Luciano did not make a scene. After the first mouthful, he calmly put down his knife and fork, drank half a glass of wine and lit a cigarette. Albina, repressing another burst of laughter, observed: "Just think how his mouth must be burning! But he's so proud he'd die rather than show it."

A fair-haired young man, in a ragged jacket and without a hat, came in carrying a small fibre suitcase. He opened the suitcase and proceeded, without a word, to set out a number of coloured plaster statuettes on Luciano's table. The Mexican woman, to tell the truth, did not seem very eager to possess any of these statuettes; but Luciano insisted on her accepting a black and white poodle. Sergio, all of a sudden, felt Albina's hand seeking his own under the table. She took hold of his hand and then, in a loud voice, cried: "Ugh, how impatient you are! Can't you at least wait until we get home?" Sergio was confused and tried instinctively to release his hand. But Albina clung to it firmly. "Leave me alone, will you?" she said; and as she said it, she threw herself against Sergio and, still holding his hand tightly, pretended to be struggling with him. Sergio felt that this time he ought at least to derive some advantage from the pretence, so he tried to put his arm round Albina's waist. But she pushed him away. Luciano loudly asked the Mexican woman: "Fruit? Sweet?"

"Sweet."

"I want a sweet too," said Albina in a furious voice. A moment later the waiter brought the sweet for the two women. Luciano and Sergio, on the other hand, ate fruit. The sweet was a creamy one; the Mexican woman ate part of it and then stubbed out her cigarette in what was left. Albina, her head down, devoured the whole of her portion with her customary animal-like impetuosity and then, putting her hand to her stomach, said with a sigh of satisfaction: "Whew! I've eaten too much. . . . This dress is too tight." She threw herself back on the seat and tried to undo the zip fastening of her skirt along her hip. But the skirt was so tight that she could not manage it. "Look," she said to Sergio, "pull down the zip fastening for me, will you?" He bent down, took hold of the little hook of the fastener and drew it downwards. At once Albina's round, youthful belly burst forth from the skirt, the navel clearly visible through the transparent green veil of her undergarment. "Coffee?" asked Luciano of the Mexican woman.

"Yes, coffee."

Albina was now sitting with half her belly out of her skirt; on one side, through a split in her chemise, could be seen her bare hip, brown and warm-looking, with the plump crease of her groin. A couple of strolling musicians came in, a man and a woman. He was an old man, small and thin, with a long face. His black overcoat came right down to his feet and he had a big cap pulled down over his ears. The woman was about fifty; she was tall and handsome, dressed in black, and with a cold, sad face. They took their instruments out of their cases and began strumming an old song. "That Mexican woman over there," remarked Albina loudly, "she oughtn't to be singing in a theatre. She ought to be going round like these two musicians, holding out a plate. . . . If you only knew how out of tune she sings."

Sergio asked casually: "Does she sing in Spanish?"

"Yes, of course. I told you she doesn't know anything but Spanish."

The two musicians finished their song and Luciano beckoned to them. They went across to his table; the old man took off his cap; Luciano spoke to them and then to the Mexican. The latter tried to protest, but in the end she agreed. The two musicians, standing beside Luciano's table, settled their instruments in position and struck up a well-known Spanish song. The Mexican woman remained seated and, gazing into the void with her strange, wide-open black eyes, waited for a moment, motionless. Then she began to sing. Her voice was harsh, warm, rich in inflexions that were at the same time melancholy, disdainful and sensual. In its higher ranges it acquired a tone of wildness, of greater profundity, of a sadness that seemed to be rendered discordant and angry by the abrupt falls in the refrain. Sergio, at first, was surprised, then admiring, and finally, in spite of himself, moved. This was due, perhaps, to the disasters of the evening, he thought, or perhaps to the momentary inclination of a mind which for too long had been drawn into trivial habits that afforded little place for affection. The Mexican, as she sang, held the musicians with her eye and every now and then gave them a sign with her hand, approving or asking them to heighten their tone. A few customers of the restaurant had appeared in the doorway and were listening in silence. Luciano did not appear to be conscious of the beauty of the singing; he was smoking with an air of combined uneasiness and scepticism, and it was obvious that his purpose in asking the Mexican to sing was simply to make Albina jealous. The singer came to an end of her song and sat quite still, her eyes unseeing, her hands clasped in her lap. At once there was hearty applause from the audience in the doorway. Luciano, too, applauded, but in a condescending sort of manner, without taking the cigarette out of his mouth. Sergio clapped vigorously. Albina, like a street urchin, put two fingers in her mouth and whistled.

The prolonged, shrill whistle was followed by silence. The Mexican woman looked at Albina as though she had just seen her for the first time, then rose and came towards Sergio's table. The latter was forced to recognize that Albina had been right: when the Mexican stood up, she was short, extremely short, in fact, though broad in the shoulders and with an ample, well-formed bosom. She planted herself in front of Albina and vomited forth a torrent of incomprehensible Spanish words. Yet even as she spoke thus vehemently, she kept her eyes and her face motionless. "I don't understand a word," cried Albina, "and it doesn't matter to me anyhow. . . . People whistle at the theatre, don't they? I have a right to whistle as much as I like." The Mexican woman seized Sergio's full glass and flung the wine in Albina's face.

There followed a scene of confusion. Albina, wine trickling down her face and neck, had jumped to her feet and was trying to fling herself upon the Mexican. But she was prevented not only by Sergio, who held her back by the arm, but also by her unfastened skirt which was falling off her. "Redskin!" she shouted. "Let me go! I want to tear the eyes out of that Redskin!" Luciano sat motionless, smoking with an air of ostentatious, sceptical indifference. The Mexican woman had moved gradually back to her own table, and stood there, still and silent, looking at Albina. A few customers had come into the little room, others were looking in at the door, and all were asking what had happened. Finally Luciano called the waiter, paid the bill and, beckoning to the Mexican, left the restaurant with her.

The waiters and the musicians went away. Albina, breathless, sat down again and started wiping off the wine with her table-napkin. Some of the wine had fallen on her belly, and her undergarment, sticking to it, revealed its plump, childish rotundity. "I told you," said Sergio, "I told you it would be better not to stay here."

To his surprise he saw that Albina's rage had completely subsided. She asked him: "Do you like me?"

"Yes," said Sergio, disturbed.

"D'you want to go to bed with me?"

"Of course I do."

"Well then, just think about that and don't bother with anything else."

Sergio was sure now that Albina would give herself to him that night, even if only in order to avenge herself on Luciano. Their little room was empty now, and from the adjoining room they could not be seen. He put his arm round Albina's waist and drew her towards him to kiss her. This time she allowed herself to be kissed, and in the end, as if with a sudden kindling of her senses, she returned his kiss with rapture. She smelt strongly of wine, in a way, however, that was not repugnant but rather naïve and helpless. When they drew apart again, Albina, pulling up the fastening of her skirt, said: "Well then, shall we go?"

Sergio paid and they went out. It had stopped raining now, and the black paving-stones in the streets were gleaming under the light of the lamp-posts; the air was exhausted and flat. But it was warm, warmer than before; and again Sergio looked forward with relief to the moment when he would undress in Albina's room. The latter was walking at some distance from him, as though on her own, her hands in the pockets of her coat, her face bent forward and thoughtful. Her new shoes with their thick soles made her look small and thickset. "Shall we have some coffee first?" enquired Sergio.

She came close to him and placed her arm about his waist in a somewhat constrained manner. "No," she said; "let's go home. . . . But you'll stay all night with me, won't you?"

She spoke in a sad voice, almost as if she were weeping. Sergio in turn put his arm round her waist and answered: "Yes, of course."

"We'll sleep together, and tomorrow morning," she concluded in a tone of entreaty, "you can go away just when you like. . . . You can stay in bed until midday if you want to."

They walked through many streets and lanes and then, still with their arms round one another's waists, came to the house where Albina lived, and began climbing the stairs. At the first floor Sergio kissed her on the neck. Albina said nothing.

They reached the little black door of the flat. Albina opened it with her own key and went forward into the passage. Sergio followed her, encumbered, as before, by his overcoat and umbrella. Albina opened the door of her room and exclaimed: "Why, look at that! What are *you* doing here?"

Her voice was full of joy. Sergio looked into the room and saw, first, the Mexican woman, sitting with an air of ill-humour on the sofa; and then Luciano, seated at the dressing-table, his face turned towards the door. Luciano's pose was conventional and at the same time ill-bred as he sat there with a sceptical, impudent smile on his face, his cigarette held between two fingers. Sergio felt he could even recollect a similar scene in some film or other. Irritated, he said to himself: "That's done it!"—and entered the room.

Albina went straight over to Luciano and took up her position beside him with her hand on his shoulder, in an attitude of defiance, as it were, towards Sergio and the Mexican. Luciano, just like a bad film actor, took a long pull at his cigarette, let forth a cloud of smoke and then said, with an affected drawl: "Splendid, splendid, that's really splendid. . . . So I was quite right, wasn't I, eh? . . . You were just longing for it. A fine sort of friend, I must say. . . ."

Sergio felt himself blushing. It was not so much that he had been caught in the act, as that he now found himself in a position of inferiority in relation to a man he despised. He reflected, however, that it's an ill wind that blows no one any good: this, surely, was the moment to break with his friend. And so, forcing himself to a tone of resentment, he said: "In any case I'm not your friend."

"Well, what then?" said Luciano dramatically.

"Furthermore," went on Sergio, "Albina is not your wife. She's free to go with anyone she likes. She asked me to come up here and I came."

"Is that true?" demanded Luciano, turning to Albina.

It was all turning out exactly like a scene in a film. Albina burst out with a vehement contradiction. "No, it's not true, he's a liar. It was he who kept on insisting. I didn't in the least want him to come . . . he forced his way in." She had taken Luciano's hand and was kissing it, frantically, on the palm and on the back.

"So you're a liar too," said Luciano with a mocking laugh.

"Oh, go to hell," cried Sergio fervently.

The Mexican woman got up from the sofa, went over to Sergio and, placing a hand on his shoulder, said something that Sergio did not understand but which he interpreted as: "Let it be. . . . You'd better go away." He thrust her from him and went on angrily: "Let it be understood that from now onwards everything's finished between us. If you happen to meet me, I forbid you absolutely to greet me or speak to me. . . ."

"Vamos," said the Mexican woman, trying to draw him towards the door. With unexpected mildness Luciano answered: "Don't be angry; there's no harm done. We'll go on being friends just the same. . . . After all, it's only human, you were attracted by Albina. . . . But now you can go with Consuelo. I've talked to her about you, and she likes the look of you. . . . Consuelo, you go off together, you two; go off and make love together." He made an expressive gesture with his hand. But the Mexican woman shrugged her shoulders and answered him with a remark that was contemptuous and cutting in its tone, as though to make him understand that she was accepting no advice from him and would act on her own initiative. Luciano started laughing and Albina, sure now of getting what she wanted, let go of his hand, went round behind the dressing-table and proceeded to take off her coat. The Mexican succeeded in pulling Sergio by the arm out of the room and then shut the door.

She spoke a few words in Spanish, as if to say good-bye, and held out her hand. Sergio shook it automatically. She turned her back on him and went to a door half-way along the passage. So she lived, evidently, in the same house as Albina. All at once Sergio felt his face and ears burning and was seized again with the same fierce desire to undress that had pursued him all the evening. He ran after the Mexican, who was just entering her room, and, pulling a packet of cigarettes from his pocket, offered her one. She took a cigarette and, without saying a word, ushered him into the room, closing the door behind them.

It was a square room, small and very low, furnished with the same sort of poor, shabby furniture as Albina's. The only difference was that here, in place of the sofa, there was a real double bed, with a white coverlet and a curly black iron bedstead. The long, low window seemed to look out under a projecting cornice, and through the glass could be seen the vibrating reflection of a neon sign. This reflection cast stripes of red and purple on the wall opposite the window and on the ceiling. The Mexican woman moved hither and thither about the room, talking ceaselessly now, in a harsh, sensible tone, giving him, it seemed, a kind of motherly lecture. With her warm, rapid, sententious way of speaking, she appeared to be saying to him: "Really you are a silly, heedless boy. Didn't you realize that Albina was not thinking of anyone but Luciano the whole time? But now you're here with me, and I'll do all I can to console you." He felt comforted by her voice although he did not understand a word she said, and he remembered how she had sung and had a great wish to hear her sing again. In the meantime the Mexican had disappeared behind a screen which evidently concealed the wash-stand.

With infinite relief he began to undress. He took off his overcoat and then he took off his shoes and socks. From his feet, which were red and swollen, there rose a coolness right up to his brain, and for a moment he sat looking at them with pleasure and moving his toes. Then he took off his suit, his shirt and his underclothes, and felt that his body, like his feet, was able to breathe again. When he was naked, he crossed his legs, lit a cigarette and, for the first time during the whole course of the evening, felt comfortable.

But he had no desire to make love. He wished he knew Spanish and could tell the Mexican woman that he wanted to hear her sing. He looked at the corner of the wash-stand and saw that her clothes were piled up, all anyhow, on top of the screen. Then she came out.

Now that she was quite naked, her squat, exotic appearance was even more clearly revealed. Watching her coming towards him across the red and black lozenges of the floor, he felt he was being approached by a statue of an Aztec divinity which he had happened to see some time before in a museum. Like that statue, the Mexican woman had short, thick legs, so short and thick, indeed, that they made you think her feet were attached to her knees. On top of these legs her torso, disproportionately long, stood bolt upright in a manner that seemed unnatural. Her buttocks were flat, her belly large and protuberant, with the navel sunk deeply in the flesh. Her breasts were oblong, like two gourds with their ends cut off, and they stood out stiff and firm, one pointing this way and one that. At the top of her long neck, round which coiled a thin black tress of hair, her face was motionless, without expression; and her feet rested with their entire soles flat on the floor, like those of her native land's divinities. She passed in front of the window, and the neon lights threw a reflection across her face and her breast, a red and purple reflection exactly like a piece of barbaric tattooing. From her hand hung a towel, and she held it out to him, nodding in the direction of the screen, as if inviting him to wash. But Sergio refused the towel and said: "No, no, not love. . . . Sing, sing"; and he opened his mouth and placed his hand on his chest.

She understood at once and smiled with professional satisfaction. She threw the towel on the bed, bent down towards Sergio and, taking his chin in the palm of her hand, as one does with a child, said something to him in a lively, caressing voice, in a tone of flattering commendation; then she gave him a little slap on the cheek. Sergio smiled gratefully at her. She sat down on the bed at a little distance from him, and took hold of his hand as it rested on the coverlet. Her own hand was large, rough and cool. She clasped his hand, crossed her short legs, gazed for a moment straight in front of her with black, shining eyes and then, swelling out her chest as though with a sudden inspiration, began to sing.

THE NEGRO AND THE OLD
MAN WITH THE BILL-HOOK

A S they came into the pine-wood, they were struck, for a
moment, with astonishment: beneath the lofty dome of
trees, as though beneath the arcades and vaults of some
huge public building—barracks or workhouse—an entire en-
campment, swarming with men, met their eyes. Everywhere,
backed against pine-trunks or bushes, were military vehicles,
green with a white star on them, belonging to the American
Army; everywhere were groups of soldiers, eating meals spread
out on newspapers or listening to gramophones; everywhere
lay gutted food-tins, empty beer-bottles, bits of paper, rubbish.
Other soldiers were roaming about or sleeping; two of them,
in sun-hats, bare-armed, were hitting a ball back and forth, in
a clear space among the trees, with leather-gloved hands.
"What a lot of soldiers! . . . It's quite impossible to go to the
bathing-place," said Cosimo untruthfully. "We must go somewhere else." He was glad about the camp, because it gave him
an excuse for taking Cora to some sequestered spot, well away
from the public bathing-huts. She answered: "I don't mind the
soldiers." "But I do," retorted Cosimo; and he turned the car
towards a track that led away to one side. "All right, let's go
then . . . but," she warned him after a moment, "you must
promise me to be good." Cosimo said nothing.

They followed the vague, winding track through the thick
scrub of undergrowth, as far as they could. When they came
to a clearing from which a sort of path appeared to go straight
towards the sea, they stopped. Cosimo got out of the car, took

the leather bag that contained their lunch and their bathing-costumes and then helped Cora out. She thrust her legs out of the car with an almost convulsive movement, and her yellow linen skirt stretched open almost up to her groin, displaying her magnificent thighs, straight, heavy, pressed tightly together. Cosimo could not help thinking that she was naked underneath, and he felt suddenly happy, as though in anticipation of an adventure both easy and intense. In silence he started off with her towards the sea.

The path was grass-covered and the pine-trees leant over them on either side. Soon the pines thinned out and were replaced by scrub. The first tongues of sand appeared amongst the long grass. Then at last they saw the sea, sparkling, blue, motionless in the sun. "I can't wait to plunge into it," she said in an eager voice. She was sweating freely through her dress under the armpits, and at every step her skirt opened and her legs thrust forward impatiently, as though seeking to free her hips. They were advancing with some difficulty now amongst the dunes, across the stinging, thistle-grown sand and shingle. Then they crossed the beach and started walking along by the sea, just above the black edgings left by the waves on the gleaming sands.

Cosimo was aiming to take Cora as far away as possible from the public bathing-place. And, in point of fact, this part of the shore was deserted, though a few boats pulled up high and dry, and some conical roofs of blackened straw, like African huts, rising behind the sand-dunes, revealed the presence of a fishing-village. "Let's go over there," he said, pointing to a fragment of wreckage sticking up from the beach beyond the last of the boats. Cora said nothing: she was walking in front of him, carrying her shoes in her hand, enjoying the sensation of pressing her bare feet into the moist sand.

He lagged behind so as to admire her at his ease. Cora, at nineteen, was already handsome, and gave promise of a matronly appearance by the time she was twenty-five. Her figure, he reflected, seeking to sidetrack his desire by means of images and comparisons, her figure was just like a certain kind of bottle that is wide in the middle but narrow at the neck and base. Those rounded, massive hips, whose projecting curves made her skirt look as though it were hanging in a void and caused it to swing gently at every step like a crinoline, were caught sharply in at the slim waist and at the small knees. Above the waist, her back was delicately, even slenderly, formed, and her arms were thin; below the knees her legs were long and fine, with hardly any calf to them, and her feet were tiny. But the true beauty of her body, as he knew, lay not in her back but in her belly. Cora was like certain classical statues, slim in the upper part of the body but with a prominent, plump belly that had an innocent look like a child's and yet, also, an appearance of power and energy—a circle of brown flesh in which the navel was swallowed up and disappeared. It was a belly that seemed to give promise of a strong, though healthy, sensuality; but, on the contrary, to Cosimo's sorrow, Cora was cold, if not actually frigid. A typist by profession, she seemed— modest, ignorant girl that she was, gentle but not sentimental —to be fast asleep, wrapped in her own good sense. Sometimes, to rouse her, Cosimo would tell her that her fate was to rear ten children and to become enormous. Cora did not protest.

When they came to the wreckage they went up the beach again as far as the dunes. Cosimo dropped the bag, sat down and started to take off his shoes, which were full of sand. Cora knelt down, opened the bag, took out of it two small, brightly-coloured rags and said, in her drawling, good-natured voice: "Now I'm going to undress . . . you must look the other way. But if you can't be sure that you won't turn round, tell me so at once and I'll go and undress behind those bushes."

Cosimo could not help feeling affronted by this remark. It was not so much the modesty of her precautions that offended him as her tone, utterly lacking in coquettishness and so good-natured that it was almost harsh. He answered drily: "Don't worry . . . I won't turn round."

She said nothing, and Cosimo, looking away, stared at the sea as he waited for her to be finished. He felt a strong desire to turn round and cry: "Let me look at you, you're so lovely"; but he resisted the temptation and did not move until that gentle, indifferent voice informed him: "I've done now; you can turn round." He turned then and saw her standing in front of him, a band of flowered material swathing her breasts and a triangle of the same stuff her loins. At the top of the hip the costume consisted merely of a button and a button-hole by which the front part was attached to the back. Standing there with her legs together and her belly drawn in, she raised her arms, gathered her hair into a bunch and twisted it so as to push it inside her bathing-cap; there was a simple, serious look on her face, with its round, black, slightly protruding eyes, its long, straight nose and its full-lipped, diffident mouth. "Now I'm going to have a swim," she announced; and she walked away, hips swaying, stomach well out, shoulders and arms drawn back. Cosimo hastily put on his bathing-costume and ran down across the beach to join her. "Let's go in together," he said, taking her hand. She did not refuse him her hand, and quickened her pace. But when they reached the edge of the sea she broke away and flung herself head first into the water, her splendid legs the last of her to vanish beneath the surface. She reappeared some distance away and started swimming vigorously. "Good-bye then," thought Cosimo, disappointed. He himself, not being fond of swimming, remained floundering near the shore.

Cora went for a long swim, consciously enjoying the sea and entirely forgetful, it seemed, of her companion. She returned at last to the shore, wading slowly through the water, her feet on the sandy bottom. When the water was up to her groin, she stopped to take off her india-rubber cap. The water cut across her hips at their widest point, forming a liquid, glistening base for her brown belly. Innumerable drops still clung round her navel and it looked as though her belly were sweating in a warm, desirous sort of way, like a terracotta vessel full of water exposed to the sun. Again he felt a great longing for her, and he walked away along the shore so as to look at her better. She shook out her hair which had been crushed flat by the cap, and then said: "How about something to eat? I'm absolutely dying of hunger." Cosimo bit his lip: every time Cora spoke, his desire faded away, giving place to contempt.

They went back across the beach to the place where, in the shelter of the dunes, they had left the bag and their clothes. Cora knelt down and opened the packet that contained their lunch. She appeared to be starving and at once started devouring a sandwich without even sitting down comfortably, kneeling there on the sand, her round, bare belly jutting over her massive, closely joined thighs, her hair thrown all to one side on to her delicate shoulder. Cosimo, on the other hand, ate with difficulty, the urge of his senses taking away his appetite. As she ate, Cora chattered away in a confidential tone, while Cosimo longed for her to be silent, since this good-natured talkativeness of hers destroyed all his feeling for her beauty and reminded him only too well of how cold she was, how lacking in imagination. She was telling him of an incident such as was very ordinary at that time, when the Allies had only just arrived and every girl in Rome had been swept off her feet by the soldiers. "I liked this officer but that was all. . . . Some days ago, he told me to come and see him in his office and he would find me a job. . . . So I went; you never know . . . but as soon as I got there I could see what it was all about . . . you can tell at once with Americans. . . . Well, he sat on the desk and then started making certain remarks to me—you know the sort of thing I mean . . . and then in the end he took my hands . . . and so I said to him: in the first place, keep your hands to yourself . . . if you want me as a typist, that's all right . . . but if it's something else you're after, there are plenty of girls in Via Veneto that ask nothing better . . . go and get one of them. . . .

He pretended not to understand me, but of course he understood perfectly well . . . in fact, after a little, with the excuse that I didn't know shorthand, he sent me away."

"Oh well," said Cosimo, trying to make a joke of it, "after all, that officer hadn't got bad taste."

"Yes, I know, but what difference does that make to me?" she answered, biting into another sandwich. "In the first place I want to be respected. . . . I should like to see how they behave in their own country, with their own women . . . they wouldn't act like that."

She was all dried up with common sense, thought Cosimo; but this common sense of hers was so intense as to seem positively mysterious. "I should have done the same," he said.

"You men are all alike," she declared. Cosimo put down his sandwich on the greaseproof paper and slithered over the sand till he was close beside her. "Give me a kiss," he said.

"No, no kissing."

"Give me a kiss."

She leant forward and kissed Cosimo on the forehead. "There!" Cosimo laughed and, flinging his arms round her hips, violently kissed her belly, plunging his face into the warm, moist flesh, just below the waist. She jumped to her feet immediately, shaking sand all over him. "Whatever's come over you?"

"Nothing, nothing. I'm sorry," said Cosimo sadly.

They finished their meal in silence. Cosimo was offended, but Cora seemed to be merely hungry. She was quick to forget an affront, and this was yet another proof of her complete lack of coquettishness. As they were gathering up the remains and the pieces of paper, a shadow fell on the sand between them and a voice asked: "Any mussels?"

They raised their eyes: in front of them stood a fisherman who had come up noiselessly over the sand. Small, thin, dark-skinned as a gipsy, he had the face of an old man, with a fallen-in mouth between a hooked nose and a protruding chin.

But the hair, glossy and vigorous as seaweed, which hung untidily over his bright eyes, was black. Smiling, he held out an apron full of bluish-white mussels. All he wore was a pair of drawers of coarse greyish cloth, and through a tear at one side could be seen the whole of his lean, brown leg which looked as though made of bronze, with all the muscles and sinews showing in relief, as in an anatomical model. He was naked to the waist and on his chest the hair was grey. Stuck sideways through his belt he carried a woodman's bill-hook, and over his shoulder was his fishing-gear.

"No, thank you," said Cosimo.

Cora, without looking at the fisherman, said: "There's a risk of catching typhoid."

The old man laughed, displaying a black and almost completely toothless mouth. "Good gracious no!" he said. "Why, we eat them all the time, ourselves," and he pointed towards the straw roofs of the huts beyond the sand-dunes.

"Have some wine," Cosimo suggested. The old man thanked him, took the glass, raised it in a silent toast and swallowed the wine at a gulp, afterwards wiping his mouth with the back of his hand. He repeated again, as a matter of form: "No mussels, then?" and without waiting for an answer went off towards the huts, his lean, powerful legs moving in a leisurely fashion. "Did you notice how fine-looking he was?" Cosimo asked, forgetting, for a moment, the ignorance and insensibility of his companion.

"Why, he's an old man," she said, with a twist of her lip.

They had finished eating now, and Cora threw away the remains behind the dunes. Then she stretched herself on the sand, face downwards, and said: "Now I'm going to take a sun-bath." She put her hands behind her back and unbuttoned the band of material that went round her chest; then, burrowing her small white breasts into the sand, she contrived to roll back her costume over her buttocks until it was reduced to nothing more than a meagre triangle. As she lay thus, face downwards, her hips seemed to spread out; and below the hollow of her back could be seen her belly half-buried in the sand. "Why don't you take the whole thing off, altogether?" Cosimo teased her.

She answered, quite seriously: "Some days ago, at Castel Fusano, I was lying naked in the sun. . . . It was a place where there wasn't anybody . . . well, you wouldn't believe it—an aeroplane that was going past saw me and began going up and down the beach, getting lower and lower. . . . I had to get up and go away."

The sun was blazing hot now, and Cosimo, dazed, could find nothing more to say. In any case he was aware that the heat, the bathe and the food had put the finishing touch to Cora's dullness, making her even colder and more insensible than usual. However, he stretched himself out beside her as she lay there motionless, her face resting on her arms, and called her name. She started—perhaps she was already asleep—and with one hand brushed away the hair from her face, uncovering one eye. "Give me a kiss," said Cosimo foolishly.

"Ugh, you and your kisses," she said; "and you promised me you'd be good."

"One promises all sorts of things."

"If I'd known, I should have gone to the public bathing-place."

"All among the soldiers?"

"Well, what harm is there in that? . . . At any rate *there* you'd have left me in peace."

These were harsh words, even though spoken in a good-natured tone of voice. Cosimo, in order to hide his disappointment, pretended that he too wanted to go to sleep. He lay still for some time, irritated and bored, his head on his arms, his mouth resting on the sand. He was on the point of falling really asleep when he heard her voice saying roughly: "Once and for all, will you or will you not leave me alone?"

"Whatever's wrong with her now?" he asked himself in

astonishment. He thought of answering her back in the same tone, but when he raised his eyes he saw, lying on Cora's shoulder, a large black hand with purple nails. His heart gave a sudden plunge. Then a gentle, sing-song voice, urgent with desire, said imploringly, with a foreign accent: "Signorina . . . signorina."

This time Cora realized her mistake, and, almost simultaneously with Cosimo, jumped up into a sitting position. And then they saw, squatting beside them, a Negro in military uniform. He was evidently very tall, judging by the breadth of his shoulders and the length of his doubled-up legs. He was extremely black, and his face, shiny with sweat, caught the light in a line that ran from his forehead down across his wide nose to his purplish lips, which were twisted into an awkward, almost sickly smile. His scalp was shaven, and his neck, which issued forth, muscular and insolent, from his open shirt, gave a sense of animal robustness.

Cora, still in a sitting position, drew herself back over the sand. Cosimo asked, with an effort: "What do you want?"

The Negro turned to Cora, inviting her in a yearning, almost mournful, voice: "Signorina . . . come with me." And he waved his hand towards the distant beach.

Cosimo was conscious of a tightness in his chest as though he was suffocating, and he knew he had turned very pale. He managed, however, to utter the words: "Are you crazy?"; at which the Negro, without looking at him, still turning towards Cora and taking hold, now, of her arm, repeated, in an even more urgent tone: "Come, signorina . . . come . . . come with me."

"Go away," shouted Cosimo loudly. The Negro raised astonished eyes towards him and then rose to his feet. He was in truth a giant, and, as he stood erect, his head, almost without forehead and flat at the back, looked minute. Cosimo thought he meant to go away and was surprised at having got off so lightly. But the Negro did not go away: he cast his eyes round, bent down, picked up from the sand a worn stump of wood and brandished it threateningly in Cosimo's face, saying, "*You* go away . . . go on, quick." Before he knew what he was doing, Cosimo realized that he was running away. He ran a short distance, then turned and saw that the Negro was standing beside Cora, who had also risen to her feet, and that he was holding her by the arm. Then, panting, his heart beating wildly, he automatically threw himself flat on the ground behind a sand-dune.

The Negro spoke, then he and Cora walked off in a leisurely fashion across the beach towards the sea. The Negro was holding Cora by the arm and, his shaven neck politely bent, was talking to her. Beside him Cora looked small, and even those hips which, shortly before, had appeared to Cosimo so massive now seemed quite slim. When they reached the sea they started walking along it side by side, towards the distant mountains. Cora walked in a docile manner, swaying her hips as usual; the Negro let go of her arm, and Cora continued to walk beside the Negro. She was not in the least like a woman carried off forcibly by a brute, thought Cosimo despondently; they were like two friends, two sweethearts, two lovers going for a walk together. All at once it flashed into his mind that perhaps the girl was not altogether displeased with her adventure. He remembered having heard of the attraction that Negroes held for some white women, and he thought that Cora must be one of these. In the meantime the two of them were going further and further away, and now the Negro had taken Cora's arm again—but no longer, it seemed, in order to keep a hold of her; rather it was to show her plainly, by physical contact, how much he desired her. Frightened, indignant, Cosimo began, in a low voice, to abuse her: "The bitch . . . she won't do it with me, but she will with the Negro." They were still walking and he was afraid, every moment, that he would see them go up across the beach again and disappear behind the dunes.

As he was looking at them he noticed, in the sea and at no

great distance from them, the man who was fishing for mussels. All alone, up to his hips in the sparkling blue water, he was moving backwards, sweeping the sandy bottom with his little wicker dredge. They were far away, all three of them, lapped in the shimmer of the scorching air, against the dazzling background of the sea. "Bitch, bitch," he kept repeating, his eyes full of tears. And then, all of a sudden, something happened that he did not expect. Cora, with one bound, broke away from the Negro's side, ran into the water and went and took refuge behind the fisherman, placing her hands on his shoulders.

The Negro had stopped; the fisherman, without hurrying, freed himself from the straps of his fishing-gear and came slowly out of the sea. Now the fisherman was standing on the beach in front of the Negro, looking very small. Then something flashed in the sun and Cosimo knew it was the bill-hook. The old man held out the bill-hook in front of him while he spoke, and the gesture he made with it was oratorical rather than threatening, and it looked as though the Negro was listening attentively. Then the Negro moved away, resuming his slow walk along the edge of the sea. The old man stood still on the shore, holding the bill-hook which glittered brightly in the sunshine. The Negro walked away slowly into the distance; then cut diagonally across the beach and soon disappeared behind the dunes.

The old man then turned towards Cora who had remained in the sea, beside the fishing-gear, and made a signal to her with the bill-hook, as if to say: "All clear now." Cora came out of the water and walked along the shore. The old man shouted something, in a loud voice, in the direction of the dunes, waving his bill-hook; then he went back into the sea again. Cora started running to meet Cosimo who in the meantime had come out from his hiding-place.

He was nervous at having to explain himself and justify his own cowardice. As they met, he said to her at once: "I'm sorry ... I behaved disgracefully."

But she answered, quite simply: "Why, what could you do?... He was a giant, that man.... Oh, I *was* frightened.... Luckily there was that old man with his knife." She had many more things to say of the danger of Negroes, and of soldiers in general, while, in a great hurry, they put on their clothes again.

They started on their way home. The fisherman was still there, far away in the sea, dredging the sand; he was black and small in the dazzling glare of the sun. Cosimo said: "I want to go back and give him a present."

"I think you ought to," she said, without a shadow of scorn.

But in the car, before they started, she suddenly threw her arms round his neck and kissed him long and hard on the mouth. And then, in the warmth and sweetness of that kiss, the first that he had received, he was aware of something that had nothing at all to do with him, something that had been awakened by the yearning, sing-song voice of the Negro and by the fisherman's bill-hook. And he felt, at the same time, both remorse and jealousy.